THE
CLAIMING
OF
SLEEPING
BEAUTY

an

erotic novel of

tenderness and cruelty

for the enjoyment

of men and

women

THE CLAIMING OF SLEEPING BEAUTY

A. N. Roquelaure

E. P. DUTTON, INC.   NEW YORK

Published in the United States by
E. P. Dutton, Inc.,
2 Park Avenue, New York, N.Y. 10016

Library of Congress Cataloging in Publication Data
Roquelaure, A. N.
The claiming of Sleeping Beauty.
I. Title.
PS3568.696C5   1983   811'.54   82–14715

ISBN: 0–525–48054–4

Published simultaneously in Canada by
Clarke, Irwin & Company Limited, Toronto and Vancouver

Designed by Nancy Etheredge

10 9 8 7 6 5 4 3 2

For

S. T. Roquelaure

with love

CONTENTS

(vii)

THE CLAIMING OF SLEEPING BEAUTY

The Prince had all his young life known the story of Sleeping Beauty, cursed to sleep for a hundred years, with her parents, the King and Queen, and all of the Court, after pricking her finger on a spindle.

But he did not believe it until he was inside the castle.

Even the bodies of those other Princes caught in the thorns of the rose vines that covered the walls had not made him believe it. They had come believing it, true enough, but he must see for himself inside the castle.

Careless with grief for the death of his father, and

too powerful under his mother's rule for his own good, he cut these awesome vines at their roots, and immediately prevented them from ensnaring him. It was not his desire to die so much as to conquer.

And picking his way through the bones of those who had failed to solve the mystery, he stepped alone into the great banquet hall.

The sun was high in the sky and those vines had fallen away, so the light fell in dusty shafts from the lofty windows.

And all along the banquet table, the Prince saw the men and women of the old Court, sleeping under layers of dust, their ruddy and slack faces spun over with spider webs.

He gasped to see the servants dozing against the walls, their clothing rotted to tatters.

But it was true, this old tale. And, fearless as before, he went in search of the Sleeping Beauty who must be at the core of it.

In the topmost bedchamber of the house he found her. He had stepped over sleeping chambermaids and valets, and, breathing the dust and damp of the place, he finally stood in the door of her sanctuary.

Her flaxen hair lay long and straight over the deep green velvet of her bed, and her dress in loose folds revealed the rounded breasts and limbs of a young woman.

He opened the shuttered windows. The sunlight flooded down on her. And approaching her, he gave a soft gasp as he touched her cheek, and her teeth through her parted lips, and then her tender rounded eyelids.

Her face was perfect to him, and her embroidered gown had fallen deep into the crease between her legs so that he could see the shape of her sex beneath it.

He drew out his sword, with which he had cut back all the vines outside, and gently slipping the blade between her breasts, let it rip easily through the old fabric.

Her dress was laid open to the hem, and he folded it back and looked at her. Her nipples were a rosy pink as were her lips, and the hair between her legs was darkly yellow and curlier than the long straight hair of her head which covered her arms almost down to her hips on either side of her.

He cut the sleeves away, lifting her ever so gently to free the cloth, and the weight of her hair seemed to pull her head down over his arms, and her mouth opened just a little bit wider.

He put his sword to one side. He removed his heavy armor. And then he lifted her again, his left arm under her shoulders, his right hand between her legs, his thumb on top of her pubis.

She made no sound; but if a person could moan silently, then she made such a moan with her whole attitude. Her head fell towards him, and he felt the hot moisture against his right hand, and laying her down again, he cupped both of her breasts, and sucked gently on one and then the other.

They were plump and firm, these breasts. She'd been fifteen when the curse struck her. And he bit at her nipples, moving the breasts almost roughly so as to feel their weight, and then lightly he slapped them back and forth, delighting in this.

His desire had been hard and almost painful to him when he had come into the room, and now it was urging him almost mercilessly.

He mounted her, parting her legs, giving the white inner flesh of her thighs a soft, deep pinch, and, clasping her right breast in his left hand, he thrust his sex into her.

He was holding her up as he did this, to gather her mouth to him, and as he broke through her innocence, he opened her mouth with his tongue and pinched her breast sharply.

He sucked on her lips, he drew the life out of her into himself, and feeling his seed explode within her, heard her cry out.

And then her blue eyes opened.

"Beauty!" he whispered to her.

She closed her eyes, her golden eyebrows brought together in a little frown and the sun gleaming on her broad white forehead.

He lifted her chin, kissed her throat, and drawing his organ out of her tight sex, heard her moan beneath him.

She was stunned. He lifted her until she sat naked, one knee crooked on the ruin of her velvet gown on the bed which was as flat and hard as a table.

"I've awakened you, my dear," he said to her. "For a hundred years you've slept and so have all those who loved you. Listen. Listen! You'll hear this castle come alive as no one before you has ever heard it."

Already a shriek had come from the passage outside. The serving girl was standing there with her hands to her lips.

And the Prince went to the door to speak to her.

"Go to your master, the King. Tell him the Prince has come who was foretold to remove the curse on this household. Tell him I shall be closeted now with his daughter."

He shut the door, bolting it, and turned to look at Beauty.

Beauty was covering her breasts with her hands, and her long straight golden hair, heavy and full of a great silky density, flared down to the bed around her.

She bowed her head so that the hair covered her.

But she looked at the Prince and her eyes struck him as devoid of fear or cunning. She was like those tender animals of the wood just before he slew them in the hunt: eyes wide, expressionless.

Her bosom heaved with anxious breath. And now he laughed, drawing near, and lifting her hair back from her right shoulder. She looked up at him steadily, her cheeks suffused with a raw blush, and again he kissed her.

He opened her mouth with his lips, and taking her hands in his left hand he laid them down on her naked lap so that he might lift her breasts now and better examine them.

"Innocent beauty," he whispered.

He knew what she was seeing as she looked at him. He was only three years older than she had been. Eighteen, newly a man, but afraid of nothing and no one. He was tall, black haired; he had a lean build which made him agile. He liked to think of himself as a sword—light, straight, and very deft, and utterly dangerous.

And he had left behind him many who would concur with this.

He had not so much pride in himself now as immense satisfaction. He had gotten to the core of the accursed castle.

There were knocks at the door, cries.

He didn't bother to answer them. He laid Beauty down again.

"I'm your Prince," he said, "and that is how you will address me, and that is why you will obey me."

He parted her legs again. He saw the blood of her innocence on the cloth and this made him laugh softly to himself as again he gently entered her.

She gave a soft series of moans that were like kisses to his ear.

"Answer me properly," he whispered.

"My Prince," she said.

"Ah," he sighed, "that is lovely."

When he opened the door, the room was almost dark. He told the servants he would have his supper now, and he would receive the King immediately.

Beauty he ordered to dine with him, and to remain with him, and he told her firmly that she was to wear no clothing.

"It's my wish to have you naked and always ready for me," he said.

He might have told her she was incomparably lovely,

with only her golden hair to clothe her, and the blushes on her cheeks to cover her, and her hands trying so vainly to shield her sex and her breasts, but he didn't say this aloud.

Rather he took her little wrists and held them behind her back as the table was brought in, and then he ordered her to sit opposite.

The table was not so wide that he couldn't reach her easily, touch her, caress her breasts if he liked. And reaching out he lifted her chin so that he could inspect her by the light of the servants' candles.

The table was laid with roast pork and fowl, fruit in big glistening silver bowls, and immediately the King stood in the door, dressed in his heavy ceremonial robes, a gold crown atop his head as he bowed to the Prince and waited for the command to enter.

"Your Kingdom has been neglected for a hundred years," said the Prince as he lifted his wine goblet. "Your vassals have many of them fled to other lords; good land lies fallow. But you have your wealth, your Court, your soldiers. So much lies ahead of you."

"I am in your debt, Prince," the King answered. "But will you tell me your name, the name of your family?"

"My mother, Queen Eleanor, lives on the other side of the forest," said the Prince. "In your time, it was my great-grandfather's kingdom; he was King Heinrick, your powerful ally."

The Prince saw the King's immediate surprise and then his look of confusion. The Prince understood it perfectly. And when a blush came to the King's face, the Prince said:

"And in those times you served your time in my great-grandfather's castle, did you not, and perhaps your queen also?"

The King pressed his lips together in resignation and slowly nodded. "You are the son of a powerful monarch," he whispered. And the Prince could see that the

King would not raise his eyes to see his naked daughter, Beauty.

"I will take Beauty to serve," said the Prince. "She is mine now." He took out his long silver knife and, cutting the hot, succulent pork, he laid several pieces on his own plate. The servants all about him vied with one another to place other dishes near him.

Beauty sat with her hands over her breasts again; her cheeks were moist with tears, and she was trembling slightly.

"As you wish," said the King. "I am in your debt."

"You have your life and your Kingdom now," said the Prince. "And I have your daughter. I will spend the night here. And tomorrow set out to make her my Princess across the mountains."

He had placed some fruit on his plate, and other hot morsels of cooked food, and now he snapped his fingers gently and in a whisper told Beauty to come around the table to him.

He could see her shame before the servants.

But he brushed her hand away from her sex.

"Never cover yourself like that again," he said. He spoke these words almost tenderly, as he lifted her hair back from her face.

"Yes, my Prince," she whispered. She had a lovely little voice. "But it's so difficult."

"Of course it is," he smiled. "But for me you'll do it."

And now he took her and placed her on his lap, cradling her in his left arm. "Kiss me," he said, and feeling her warm mouth on his again, he felt his desire rising too soon for his taste, but he decided he could savor this slight torment.

"You may go," he said to the King. "Tell your servants to have my horse ready in the morning. I won't need a horse for Beauty. My soldiers you've found, no doubt, at your gates," and the Prince laughed. "They were afraid to come in with me. Tell them to be ready at dawn, and then you can say goodbye to your daughter, Beauty."

The King glanced up very quickly to accept the Prince's commands and with unfailing courtesy he backed out of the doorway.

The Prince turned his full attention to Beauty.

Lifting a napkin he wiped at her tears. She kept her hands obediently on her thighs, exposing her sex, and he observed that she did not try to hide her stiff little pink nipples with her arms and he approved of this.

"Now don't be frightened," he said to her softly, feeding a little on her trembling mouth again, and then slapping her breasts so they shivered lightly. "I could be old and ugly."

"Ah, but then I could feel sorry for you," she said in a sweet, tremulous voice.

He laughed. "I'm going to punish you for that," he said to her tenderly. "But now and then just a little very ladylike impertinence is amusing."

She blushed darkly, biting her lip.

"Are you hungry, beautiful one?" he asked.

He could see she was afraid to answer.

"When I ask you will say, 'Only if it pleases you, my Prince,' and I shall know the answer is yes. Or, 'Not unless it should please you, my Prince,' and I shall know the answer is no. Do you understand me?"

"Yes, my Prince," she answered. "I'm hungry only if it pleases you."

"Very good, very good," he said to her with genuine feeling. He lifted a small cluster of glistening purple grapes and fed them to her one by one, taking the seeds out of her mouth and casting them aside.

And he watched with obvious pleasure as she drank deeply from the wine cup he held to her lips. Then he wiped her mouth and kissed her.

Her eyes were glistening. But she had stopped crying. He felt the smooth flesh of her back, and her breasts again.

"Superb," he whispered. "And were you terribly spoilt before and given everything that you wished?"

She was confused, blushing again, and then full of shame she nodded.

"Yes, my Prince, I think perhaps . . ."

"Don't be afraid to answer me with many words," he coaxed, "as long as they are respectful. And never speak unless I speak to you first, and in all these things, be careful to note what pleases me. You were very spoilt, given everything, but were you willful?"

"No, my Prince, I don't think I was that," she said. "I tried to be a joy to my parents."

"And you'll be a joy to me, my dear," he said lovingly.

Still holding her firmly in his left arm, he turned to his supper.

He ate heartily, pork, roast fowl, some fruit, and several cups of wine. Then he told the servants to take it all away and leave them.

New sheets and coverlets had been laid on the bed; there were fresh down pillows, and roses in a vase nearby, and several candelabra.

"Now," he said as he rose and set her before him. "We must get to bed as we have a long journey before us tomorrow. And I have still to punish you for your earlier impertinence."

Immediately the tears stood in her eyes; she looked up at him imploring. She almost reached to cover her breasts and her sex, and then remembering herself she made her hands into two little helpless fists at her sides.

"I won't punish you very much," he said gently, lifting her chin. "It was just a little offense, and your first after all. But Beauty, to confess the truth, I shall love punishing you."

She was biting her lip, and he could see she wanted to speak, and the effort to control her tongue and her hands was almost too much for her.

"All right, lovely one, what do you want to say?" he asked.

"Please, my Prince," she begged. "I'm so afraid of you."

"You'll find me more reasonable than you expect," he said.

He removed his long cloak, tossing it over a chair, and bolted the door. Then he snuffed all but a few candles.

He would sleep in his clothes as he did most nights, in the forest, or in the country inns, or in the houses of those humble peasants at which he sometimes stopped, and that was no great inconvenience to him.

And as he drew near her now, he thought he must be merciful and make her punishment quick. And seating himself on the side of the bed, he reached out for her, and pulling her wrists into his left hand he brought her naked body down over his lap so that her legs dangled over the floor helplessly.

"Very, very lovely," he said, his right hand moving languidly over her rounded buttocks, forcing them ever so slightly apart.

Beauty was crying aloud, but muffling her cries into the bed, her hands held out in front of her by his long left arm.

And now with his right hand he spanked her buttocks hard and heard her cries grow louder. It wasn't really much of a slap.

But it left a red mark on her. And he spanked her hard again, and he felt her writhing against him, the heat and moisture of her sex against his leg, and again he spanked her.

"I think you are sobbing more from the humiliation than the pain," he scolded her in a soft voice.

She was struggling not to make her cries too loud.

He flattened out his right hand, and feeling the heat of her reddened buttocks drew it up and delivered another series of hard, loud slaps, smiling as he watched her struggle.

He could have spanked her much harder, for his own pleasure, and without really hurting her. But he thought the better of it. He had so many nights ahead of him for these delights.

He lifted her up now so that she was standing in front of him.

"Toss your hair back," he commanded. Her tear-stained face was unspeakably beautiful, her lips trembling, her blue eyes gleaming with the dampness of the tears. She obeyed immediately.

"I don't think you were so very spoilt," he said. "I find you very obedient and eager to please, and this makes me very happy."

He could see her relief.

"Clasp your hands behind your neck," he said, "under your hair. That's it. Very good." He lifted her chin again. "And you have a lovely modest habit of looking down. But now I want you to look directly at me."

She obeyed shyly, miserably. It seemed she felt her nakedness and her helplessness more fully now as she looked at him. Her lashes were matted and dark, and her blue eyes larger than he had thought.

"Do you find me handsome?" he asked her. "Ah, but before you answer, I should like to know the truth from you, not what you think I should like to hear, or what would be best for you to say, you understand me?"

"Yes, my Prince," she whispered. She seemed calmer.

He reached out, massaged her right breast lightly, and then stroked her downy underarms, feeling the little curve of the muscle there beneath the tiny wisp of golden hair, and then he stroked that full, moist hair between her legs so that she sighed and trembled.

"Now," he said, "answer my question, and describe what you see. Describe me as if you had only just met me and were confiding in your chambermaid."

Again she bit her lip, which he dearly loved, and then, her voice a little diminished by uncertainty, she said:

"You are very handsome, my Prince, no one could deny that. And for one . . . for one . . ."

"Go on," he said. He drew her just a little closer so that her sex was against his knee, and putting his right arm about her, he cradled her breast in his left hand and let his lips touch her cheek.

"And for one so young to be so commanding," she said, "it's not what one might expect."

"And tell me how does that show itself in me, other than my actions?"

"Your manner, my Prince," she said, her voice gaining a little strength. "The look of your eyes, such dark eyes . . . your face. There are none of the doubts of youth in it."

He smiled and kissed her ear. He wondered why the wet little cleft between her legs was so very hot. His fingers could not keep from touching it. Twice already he'd had her today, and he would have her again, but he was thinking he should go about it more slowly.

"Would you like it if I were older?" he whispered.

"I had thought," she said, "that it would be easier. To be commanded by one so very young," she said, "is to feel one's helplessness."

It seemed the tears had welled up and were spilling out of her eyes, so he pushed her gently back so he might see them.

"My darling, I have awakened you from a century's sleep, and restored you father's Kingdom. You're mine. And you won't find me such a hard master. Only a very thorough master. When you think night and day and every moment only of pleasing me, things will be very easy for you."

And as she struggled not to look away, he could see again the relief in her face, and that she was in complete awe of him.

"Now," he said, pushing his left fingers between her legs, and drawing her close again so that she let out a little gasp before she could stop herself, "I want more of you than I've had before. Do you know what I mean, my Sleeping Beauty?"

She shook her head; for this moment she was in terror.

He lifted her up onto the bed and laid her down.

The candles threw a warm, almost rosy light over her. Her hair fell down on either side of the bed, and she seemed on the verge of crying out, her hands struggling to keep still at her sides.

"My darling, you have a dignity about you that shields you from me, much like your lovely golden hair shrouds you and shields you. Now I want you to surrender to me. You'll see, and you'll be very surprised that you wept when I first suggested it."

The Prince bent over her. He parted her legs. He could see the battle she fought not to cover herself or turn away from him. He stroked her thighs. Then with his finger and thumb, he reached into the silky damp hair itself and felt those tender little lips and forced them very wide open.

Beauty gave a terrible shudder. With his left hand he covered her mouth, and behind his hand she cried softly. It seemed easier for her with him covering her mouth and that was all right for now, he thought. She shall be taught everything in time.

And with his right fingers, he found that tiny nodule of flesh between her tender nether lips and he worked it back and forth until she raised her hips, arching her back, in spite of herself. Her little face under his hand was the picture of distress. He smiled to himself.

But even as he smiled, he felt the hot fluid between her legs for the first time, the real fluid which had not come before with her innocent blood. "That's it, that's it, my darling," he said. "And you mustn't resist your Lord and master, hmmmm?"

Now he opened his clothing and took out his hard, eager sex, and mounting her he let it rest against her thigh as he continued to stroke her and work her.

She was twisting from one side to the other, her hands gathering up the soft sheets at her sides into knots, and it seemed her whole body grew pink, and the nipples of her breasts looked as hard as if they were tiny stones. He could not resist them.

He bit at them with his teeth, playfully, not hurting her. He licked them with his tongue, and then he licked her sex, too, and as she struggled, and blushed and moaned beneath him, he mounted her, slowly.

Again she arched her back. Her breasts were suffused with red. And as he drove his organ into her, he felt her shudder violently with unwilling pleasure.

An awful cry was muffled by the hand over her mouth; she was shuddering so violently it seemed she all but lifted him on top of her.

And then she lay still, moist, pink, with her eyes closed, breathing deeply as the tears flowed silently.

"That was lovely, my darling," he said. "Open your eyes."

She did it timidly.

But then she lay looking up at him.

"This has been so hard for you," he whispered. "You could not even imagine these things happening to you. And you are red with shame, and shaking with fear, and you believe perhaps it's one of the dreams you dreamed in your hundred years. But it's real, Beauty," he said. "And it is only the beginning! You think I've made you my Princess. But I've only started. The day will come when you can see nothing but me as if I were the sun and the moon, when I mean all to you, food, drink, the air you breathe. Then you will truly be mine, and these first lessons . . . and pleasures . . ." he smiled, "will seem like nothing."

He bent over her. She lay so very still, gazing up at him.

"Now kiss me," he commanded. "And I mean, really . . . kiss me."

THE JOURNEY AND THE PUNISHMENT AT THE INN

The NEXT morning all the Court was gathered in the Great Hall to see the Prince off, and all of the Court, including the grateful King and Queen, stood with their eyes down, bowing from the waist as the Prince came down the steps with the naked Beauty walking behind him. He had commanded her to clasp her hands on the back of her neck beneath her hair, and to walk just a little to his right so that he might see her in the corner of his eye. And she obeyed, her bare feet making not the slightest sound on the worn stone steps as she followed him.

"Dear Prince," said the Queen, when he reached the

great front door and saw that his soldiers stood mounted on the drawbridge, "we are in your eternal debt, but she is our only daughter."

The Prince turned to look at her. She was yet beautiful, though more than twice Beauty's age, and he wondered if she too had served his great-grandfather.

"How can you question me?" the Prince asked patiently. "I have restored your Kingdom, and you know full well if you remember anything of the ways of my land, that Beauty will be much enhanced by her service there."

Then the telltale blush came to the Queen as it had to the King before, and she bowed her head in acceptance.

"But surely you will allow Beauty some clothing," she whispered, "at least until she reaches the border of your Kingdom."

"All those towns between here and my Kingdom have owed their allegiance to us for a century. And in each I will proclaim your restoration and new dominion. Can you ask for more than that? The spring is warm already; Beauty shall suffer no ill effects from serving me immediately."

"Forgive us, your Highness," the King hastened to say. "But is it the same in this age? Beauty's servitude will not be forever?"

"It is the same now as it was always. Beauty will be returned in time. And she shall be greatly enhanced in wisdom and beauty. Now, tell her to obey as your parents commanded you to obey when you were sent to us."

"The Prince speaks the truth, Beauty," the King said in a low voice, still unwilling to look at his daughter. "Obey him. Obey the Queen. And though you find your servitude surprising and difficult at times, be confident you will return, as he says, greatly changed for the better."

The Prince smiled.

The horses were restless on the drawbridge. The Prince's charger, a black stallion, was particularly hard to restrain, so the Prince, bidding them all farewell again, turned and picked up Beauty.

He heaved her easily over his right shoulder, clasping her ankles to his waist, and heard her cry out softly as she fell over his back. He could see her long hair sweep the ground just before he mounted the stallion.

All the soldiers fell into place behind him.

He rode into the forest.

The sun spilled down in glorious rays through the heavy green leaves, the sky now brilliant and blue overhead only to vanish in a shifting green-tinted light as the Prince rode on at the head of his soldiers, humming to himself, and now and then singing.

Beauty's lithe, warm body swayed slightly over his shoulder. He could feel her trembling, and he understood her agitation. Her naked buttocks were still red from the spanking he had given her, and he could well imagine the succulent vision she was to the men who rode after him.

As he walked his horse through a dense glade where the fallen leaves were thick and red and brown beneath him, the Prince tied the rein on his saddle, and with his left hand felt the soft hairy little pelt between Beauty's legs, and leaned his face against her warm hip, kissing it gently.

After a while, he pulled her down into his lap, turning her as before so she rested against his left arm, and he kissed her red face and brushed the long golden strands of her hair away from it, and then he suckled her breasts almost idly as though taking little drinks from them.

"Put your head on my shoulder," he said. And she inclined to him obediently at once.

But when he went to sling her over his shoulder again, she gave a little desperate whimper. He did not allow this to stop him. And having her firmly in place, her ankles clasped to his hip, he scolded her lovingly, and gave her several hard spanks with his left hand until he heard her crying.

"You must never protest," he repeated. "Not with sound, not with gesture. Only your tears may show your Prince what you feel, and never think that he does not wish to know what you feel. Now, respectfully, answer me."

"Yes, my Prince," Beauty whimpered softly.

He thrilled at the sound of it.

When they came to the small town in the middle of the forest, there was great excitement, as everyone had already heard of the enchantment being broken.

And as the Prince rode into the crooked little street with its high half-timbered houses blocking out the sky, people ran to the narrow windows and doorways. They crowded into the cobblestone alleyways.

Behind him, the Prince could hear his men in hushed voices telling the townspeople who he was, that it was their Lord who had broken the enchantment. The girl he carried with him was the Sleeping Beauty.

Beauty was sobbing softly, her body struggling with these sobs, but the Prince held her firmly.

Finally with a great crowd following him, he arrived at the Inn, and his horse, with loud clops, entered the courtyard.

His page quickly helped him down.

"We'll stop only for food and drink," said the Prince. "We can go miles before sundown."

He stood Beauty on her feet and watched with admiration as her hair fell down around her. And he turned her around twice, pleased to see she kept her hands clasped behind her neck and her eyes down as he looked at her.

He kissed her devotedly.

"Do you see how they all look at you?" he said. "Do you feel how they admire your beauty? They are adoring you," he said. And opening her lips again, he sucked another kiss out of her, his hand squeezing her sore buttocks.

The Journey and the Punishment at the Inn

It seemed her lips clung to his as if she were afraid to let him go, and then he kissed her eyelids.

"Now everyone is going to want to have a look at Beauty," the Prince said to the Captain of his Guard. "Bind her hands over her head by a rope from the sign over the Inn gate, and let the people have their fill of her. But no one is to touch her. They can look all they like, but you stand guard and see that no one touches her. I'll have your food sent out to you."

"Yes, my Lord," said the Captain of the Guard.

But as the Prince gently gave Beauty over to him, she leaned forward, her lips out to the Prince, and he received her kiss gratefully. "You're very sweet, my darling," he said. "Now be modest and very very good. I should be very disappointed if all this adulation made my Beauty vain." He kissed her again, and let the Captain have her.

Then going inside and ordering his meat and ale, the Prince watched through the diamond-paned windows.

The Captain of the Guard did not dare touch Beauty, except to put the rope about her wrists. He led her by this to the open gate of the courtyard, and throwing the rope up over the iron rod that held the sign of the Inn, he quickly secured her hands above her head, so that she was almost on tiptoe.

Then he motioned for the people to move back, and he stood against the wall with his arms folded as they pressed to look at her.

There were buxom women with stained aprons, and coarse men in breeches and heavy leather shoes, and the young well-to-do men of the town in their velvet cloaks with their hands on their hips as they eyed Beauty from a distance, unwilling to elbow in the crowd. And several young women, their elaborate white headdresses freshly done up, who had come out lifting their hems fastidiously as they looked at her.

At first everyone was whispering, but now people began to speak more freely.

Beauty had turned her face into her arm and let her hair shield her face, but then a soldier came out from the Prince and said:

"His Majesty said to turn her and lift her chin so they might have a better look at her."

An approving murmur went up from the crowd. "Very very lovely," said one of the young men.

"And this is what so many died for," said an old Cobbler.

The Captain of the Guard lifted Beauty's chin, and holding the rope above her, said gently:

"You must turn around, Princess."

"O, please, Captain," she whispered.

"Don't make a sound, Princess, I beg you. Our Lord is very strict," he said. "And it's his wish that everyone admire you."

Beauty, her cheeks flaming, obeyed, turning so the crowd could see her reddened buttocks and then again to show her breasts and her sex as the Captain kept his finger under her chin lightly.

It seemed she breathed deeply as though trying to remain very calm. The young men were calling her beautiful and saying her breasts were magnificent.

"But such buttocks," whispered an old woman nearby. "You can see that she's been spanked. I doubt the poor Princess did anything much to deserve it."

"Not much," said a young man near her. "Except have the most beautiful and pertly shaped buttocks imaginable."

Beauty was trembling.

Finally the Prince himself came out, ready to leave, and seeing the crowd as attentive as before, he himself took the rope down, and holding it like a short leash above Beauty's head, he turned her. He seemed amused by the crowd's grateful nods, and thanks, and bows to him; and very gracious in his generosity.

"Lift your chin, Beauty, I shouldn't have to lift it,"

he reproved her with a little deliberate frown of disappointment.

Beauty obeyed, her face so red that her eyebrows and eyelashes gleamed golden in the sun, and the Prince kissed her.

"Come here, old man," the Prince said to the old Cobbler. "Have you ever seen such loveliness?"

"No, your Majesty," said the old man. His sleeves were rolled to the elbows, and his legs were slightly bowed. His hair was gray but his green eyes gleamed with a special almost wistful pleasure. "She is truly a magnificent Princess, your Majesty, worth all the deaths of those who tried to claim her."

"Yes, I suppose so, and worth all the bravery of the Prince who *did* claim her," smiled the Prince.

Everyone laughed politely. But they couldn't conceal their awe of him. They were staring at his armor, at his sword, and above all at his young face and dark black hair that fell to his shoulders.

The Prince drew the Cobbler closer. "Here," he said, "I give you permission if you like just to feel her treasures."

The old man smiled at the Prince gratefully and almost innocently. He reached out, and hesitating a moment, felt Beauty's breasts. Beauty shivered, and tried obviously to repress a little cry.

The old man touched her sex.

Then the Prince drew up her little leash so she was standing on tiptoe; her body stiffened and seemed to grow more tense and at the same time more lovely, breasts and buttocks high, her calf muscles lifted, her chin and throat a perfect line down to her swaying bosom.

"That's all. You must all go now," said the Prince.

Obediently they backed away, but they continued to watch, as the Prince mounted his horse, and instructing Beauty to clasp her hands behind her neck, he ordered her to walk before him.

Beauty led the way out of the Inn yard, the Prince walking his horse behind her.

The people made way for her. They couldn't take their eyes off her lovely vulnerable body, and they squeezed against the narrow walls of the town to follow the spectacle to the edge of the forest.

When they had left the town behind, the Prince told Beauty to come to him. He gathered her up and seated her before him again, and kissed her again, and scolded her:

"You found that so hard," he crooned. "Why were you so proud? Did you think yourself too good to be shown to the people?"

"I'm sorry, my Prince," she whispered.

"Don't you see, if you think only of pleasing me, and pleasing those to whom I show you, it will be simple for you." He kissed her ear, holding her tight to his chest. "You should have been proud of your breasts and your shapely hips. You should have asked yourself, 'Am I pleasing my Prince? Do the people find me pleasing?'"

"Yes, my Prince," Beauty said meekly.

"You are mine, Beauty," the Prince said a little more sternly. "And there is no command that you must shrink from obeying ever. If I tell you to please the lowliest vassal in the field, you will strain to obey me perfectly. He is your Lord then because I have said so. All those to whom I offer you are your Lords."

"Yes, my Prince," she said, but she was in great distress. He stroked her breasts, pinching them firmly now and then, and kissed her until he could feel her body struggling against him, and feel her nipples growing hard. It seemed she wanted to speak.

"What is it, Beauty?"

"Pleasing you, my Prince, pleasing you . . ." she whispered, as though her thoughts had spread into a delirium.

"Yes, pleasing me, that is your life now. How many of those in the world know such clarity, such simplicity? You please me and I shall always tell you exactly how to please me."

"Yes, my Prince," she sighed. But she was crying again.

"I will treasure you all the more for it. The girl I found in the castle room was nothing to me such as you are now, my devoted Princess."

But the Prince was not entirely satisfied with the way in which he was instructing Beauty. He told her when they reached another town at nightfall that he was going to strip a little more dignity away from her to make it easier for her.

And while the townspeople pressed their faces to the leaded glass windows of the Inn, the Prince had Beauty wait on his table.

On her hands and knees she hurried across the rough boards of the Inn floor to fetch his plate from the kitchen. And though she was allowed to walk back with it, she was again on all fours to fetch his flagon. The soldiers devoured their supper, throwing silent glances at her by the light of the fire.

She wiped the table for the Prince and when a morsel of food spilled from his plate to the floor, he commanded Beauty to eat it. With tears spilling from her eyes, Beauty obeyed, and then he gathered her, still on her knees, into his arms and rewarded her with dozens of wet and loving kisses. Obediently she put her arms around his neck.

But this little morsel spilling had given him an idea. He ordered her to quickly fetch a plate from the kitchen again, and then told her to lay it on the floor at his feet.

He put food for her there from his plate, and told

her to lift her heavy hair behind her shoulders and eat it only with her mouth.

"You are my kitten," he laughed gaily. "And I would forbid you all those tears if they weren't so beautiful. Do you want to please me?"

"Yes, my Prince," she said.

With his foot he pushed her plate several paces away and told her to turn her buttocks to him as she continued her meal. He admired it, realizing the red marks from her spanking had almost healed. With the toe of his leather boot, he nudged at the silken hair he could see between her legs, felt the moist plump lips beneath the hair, and sighed, thinking her so very beautiful.

When she had finished her meal, with her lips she pushed the plate back to his chair as he ordered her to do it, and then he wiped her lips himself and fed her some wine from his cup.

He watched her long beautiful throat as she swallowed, and kissed her eyelids.

"Now listen to me, I want you to learn from this," he said. "Everyone here can see you, all your charms, you're aware of it. But I want you to be very aware of it. Behind you, the townspeople at the windows are admiring you as they did when I brought you through the town. This should make you proud of yourself, not vain, but proud, proud that you have pleased me, and caught their admiration."

"Yes, my Prince," she said when he paused.

"Now think, you are very naked and very helpless, and you are mine completely."

"Yes, my Prince," she cried softly.

"That is your life now, and you are to think of nothing else, and regret nothing else. I want that dignity peeled away from you as if it were so many skins of the onion. I don't mean that you should ever be graceless. I mean that you should surrender to me."

"Yes, my Prince," she said.

The Prince looked up at the Innkeeper who stood

at the kitchen door with his wife and his daughter. They came to attention at once. But the Prince looked only at the daughter. She was a young woman, very pretty in her own way, though nothing compared to Beauty. She had black hair and round cheeks, and a very tiny waist, and she dressed as many peasant women did, in a low-cut ruffled shirtwaist, and a short broad skirt that revealed her smart little ankles. She had an innocent face. She was watching Beauty in wonder, her big brown eyes moving anxiously to the Prince and then shyly back to Beauty who knelt at the Prince's feet in the firelight.

"Now, as I told you," the Prince said softly to Beauty, "all here admire you, and they enjoy you, the sight of you, your plump little rear, your lovely legs, those breasts which I cannot stop myself from kissing. But there is no one here, not the lowliest, who is not better than you, my Princess, if I command you to serve him."

Beauty was frightened. She nodded quickly as she answered "Yes, my Prince," and then very impulsively she bent and kissed the Prince's boot, but then she appeared terrified.

"No, that is very good, my darling," the Prince, stroking her neck, reassured her. "That is very good. If I allow you one gesture to speak your heart unbidden it is that one. You may always show me respect of your own accord in that manner."

Again Beauty pressed her lips to the leather. But she was trembling.

"These townspeople hunger for you, hunger for more of your loveliness," the Prince continued. "And I think they deserve a little taste of it that will delight them."

Beauty kissed the Prince's boot again, and let her lips rest there.

"O, don't think I should really let them have their fill of your charms. O, no," the Prince said thoughtfully.

"But I should use this opportunity, both to reward their devoted attention and teach you that punishment will come whenever I desire to give it. You need not be disobedient to merit it. I will punish when it pleases me. Sometimes that will be the only reason for it."

Beauty couldn't keep herself from whimpering.

The Prince smiled and beckoned to the Innkeeper's daughter. But she was so frightened of him that she didn't come forward until her father pushed her.

"My dear," said the Prince gently. "In the kitchen, have you a flat wooden instrument, for shoveling the hot pans into the oven?"

There was a faint movement throughout the room as the soldiers glanced at one another. The people outside were pressing closer to the windows. The young girl nodded and quickly returned with a wooden paddle, very flat and smooth from years of use, with a good handle.

"Excellent," said the Prince.

But Beauty was crying helplessly.

The Prince quickly ordered the Innkeeper's daughter to seat herself on the edge of the high hearth which was the height of a chair, and told Beauty, on her hands and knees, to go to her.

"My dear," he said to the Innkeeper's daughter, "these good people deserve a little spectacle. Their life is hard and barren. My men deserve it as well. And my Princess can well use the chastisement."

Beauty knelt crying before the girl who, seeing what she was to do, was fascinated.

"Up over her lap, Beauty," said the Prince, "hands behind your neck, and lift your lovely hair out of the way. At once!" he said, almost sharply.

Pricked by his voice, Beauty almost scurried to obey, and all those around her saw her tear-stained face.

"Keep your chin up like that, yes, lovely. Now, my dear," said the Prince looking at the girl who held Beauty over her lap and the wooden paddle in her other hand. "I want to see if you can wield that as hard as a man might wield it. Do you think you can do that?"

He could not keep from smiling at the girl's delight and desire to please. She nodded murmuring a respectful reply, and when he gave her the command, she brought the paddle down hard on Beauty's naked buttocks. Beauty couldn't keep still. She struggled to keep quiet, but she couldn't keep still, and finally even the whimpers and moans escaped her.

The tavern girl spanked her harder and harder, and the Prince enjoyed this, savoring it far more than the spanking he had given Beauty himself.

It was because he could see it much better, see Beauty's breasts heaving, and the tears spilling down her face, and her little buttocks straining, as if, without moving, Beauty might somehow escape or deflect the girl's hard blows.

Finally, when the buttocks were very red but not welted, he told the girl to stop.

He could see his soldiers enthralled and all the townspeople as well, and then he snapped his fingers and told Beauty to come to him.

"Now eat your suppers, all of you, talk amongst yourselves, do as you like," he said quickly.

For a moment no one obeyed him. Then the soldiers turned to one another, and those outside, seeing that Beauty was retired down to kneeling at the Prince's feet, her hair veiling her red face, her raw and stinging buttocks pressed to her ankles, were murmuring and talking at the windows.

The Prince gave Beauty another drink of wine. He was not sure he was entirely satisfied with her. He was thinking of many things.

He called the Innkeeper's daughter to him and told her she had been very good, gave her a gold coin, and took the paddle from her.

Finally it was time to go up. And driving Beauty before him, he gave her a few gentle but brisk spanks to hurry her up the stairs to the bedchamber.

BEAUTY

BEAUTY STOOD at the foot
of the bed, her hands clasped to her neck, her buttocks
throbbing with a warm pain that felt so much better now
than the spanking she had lately received that it was almost pleasure.

She had for the moment stopped crying. She had
only just pulled down the covers for the Prince, with her
teeth, her hands clasped behind her back, and then with
her teeth taken his boots to the edge of the room.

And now she waited for further commands, trying
to watch him, though her eyes were cast down, without
his realizing it.

He had bolted the door, and he was sitting on the side of the bed.

And his black hair, loose and curling at his shoulders gleamed in the light of the tallow candle. His face was very beautiful to her, perhaps because in spite of the size of the features, they were all rather delicately molded. She did not know for certain.

Even his hands enthralled her. The fingers were so long, so white, so delicate.

She was terribly relieved to be alone with him. The moments below in the Inn had been such an agony to her, and even though he had brought the wooden paddle with him and might spank her much harder with it than that dreadful girl, she was so glad to be alone with him that she could not be afraid of it. She was afraid, however, that she hadn't pleased him.

She searched her mind for faults. She had obeyed all his commands, and he understood how difficult it was for her. He knew completely what it meant for her to be stripped naked and revealed to everyone, to be helpless and made public and that this surrender of which he spoke could come in acts and gestures long before it could come from her mind. But no matter how hard she tried to excuse herself, she could not help but wondering if she could have tried harder.

Did he want her to cry out more when she was spanked? She was uncertain. Just thinking of that girl spanking her in front of everyone made her cry again, and she knew that the Prince would see her tears, and he might wonder why now, when she'd been told to stand still at the foot of the bed, she was crying.

But the Prince seemed deep in thought.

This is my life, she told herself, trying to calm herself. He has awakened me and claimed me. My parents are restored, their Kingdom is theirs again, and more significantly, life is theirs again, and I belong to him. She felt a great relaxation when she thought these things and a stirring in herself that seemed to make her sore and throbbing buttocks feel suddenly warmer. The pain made her so shamefully aware of that part of her body! But then as she squeezed her eyes against these soft and slow tears, she looked down at her swelling breasts and the tiny hard nipples and felt that same awareness of herself there too, just as if he'd slapped her breasts which he hadn't done in a great while, and she felt softly bewildered.

My life, she struggled to understand. And she remembered that in the afternoon in the warm forest when she had been walking before his horse, she had felt her own long hair on her buttocks, brushing them as she walked ahead of him, and she had wondered if she looked beautiful to him, and she had wished that he would pick her up then, and kiss her and caress her. Of course she had not dared to look back. She couldn't imagine what he would have done had she been so foolish as to do that, but the sun had thrown their shadows ahead of them and she had seen the shadow of his profile, and felt such a pleasure that she was ashamed of it, and her legs had felt weak and there had been the oddest feeling in her, something she had never known in her earlier life, though perhaps in her dreams.

She was awakened now, at the foot of his bed, by his low but firm command.

"Come here, my darling." He motioned for her to kneel before him.

"This shirt is to be opened down the front, and you will learn to do so with your lips and teeth, and I will be patient with you," he said.

She had thought it would be the paddle. And, very relieved, she went almost too quickly to obey, pulling the thick tie that closed the shirt at his throat. His flesh felt warm and smooth to her. Men's flesh. So different, she thought. And she quickly pulled loose the second tie and the third. She had a struggle with the fourth which was at his waist, but he didn't move, and then when she was finished, she bowed her head, her hands as before on the back of her neck and waited.

"Open my breeches," he said to her.

Her cheeks flamed; she could feel it. But again she didn't hesitate. She pulled the fabric forward over the hook until the hook slipped out and let it go. And now she could see his sex, bulging there, painfully twisted. She wanted suddenly to kiss it, but she didn't dare and was shocked at her impulse.

He had lifted it free. It was hard. She thought of it between her legs, filling her, rough and too big for her virginal opening, and of that terrible pleasure which had suffused her and wasted her the night before, and she knew she was blushing furiously.

"Now go to the stand in the corner," he said, "and bring back the basin with water in it."

She almost scurried across the floor. Several times in the Inn he had told her to move fast, and though she had hated it at first, she now did it instinctively. She brought the basin in both hands and set it down. There was a cloth in the water.

"Wring out the cloth tightly," he said, "and bathe me quickly."

She did as she was told at once, staring in amazement at his sex, its length, its hardness, and the tip of it with its tiny opening. She had been so sore from it yesterday, yet that pleasure had paralyzed her. Never had she guessed at such a secret.

"Now, do you know what I want of you?" the Prince said gently. His hand lovingly stroked her cheek, lifting her hair back. She ached to look at him. She wished so much he would command her to look into his eyes. It terrified her, but after the first instant it was so wondrous to her, his expression, that handsome and almost delicate face, and those black eyes that seemed to accept no compromise.

"No, my Prince, but whatever it is . . ." she started.

"Yes, darling . . . you are being very good. I want you to take it in your mouth, stroke it with your tongue and your lips."

She was shocked. She had never thought of this. She thought suddenly, cruelly of who she had been, a Princess, and she thought of all her young life before she had fallen asleep, and she almost gave a little whimper. But this was her Prince who was commanding her, not some dreadful person she was being given to as a wife who might have demanded this of her. She closed her eyes and took it into her mouth, feeling its huge size, its hardness.

It nudged at the back of her throat, and she pushed up and down on it as the Prince guided her.

The taste of it was almost delicious; and it seemed a salty liquid in tiny droplets came out into her mouth, and then she stopped because he had said it was enough.

She opened her eyes.

"Very good, Beauty, very good," said the Prince.

And she could tell he was in pain with his need suddenly. It made her feel proud, and there was in her, even in her helplessness, a sense of power.

But he had risen and was guiding her to her feet. And she realized as she straightened her legs that that debilitating pleasure had caught hold of her. She felt for a moment that she couldn't stand, but to disobey him was unthinkable. Quickly she stood straight, hands behind her neck, and she struggled to keep her hips from going into some slight humiliating movement. Could he see it? She bit her lip again and felt its soreness.

"You've done marvelously well today, you've learned so very much," he said tenderly. His voice could be so soft and yet so firm at the same time. It made her feel almost drowsy; that pleasure was melting inside of her.

But then she saw that he was reaching for the paddle behind him. She let out a little gasp before she could stop herself, and she felt his hand on her arm, taking her hands away from the back of her neck, and turning her around. She wanted to cry out, "What have I done?"

But his voice came low, crooning in her ear.

"And I've learned a very important lesson myself, that pain softens you, makes it easier for you. You are infinitely more malleable from the spanking given you in the Inn than you were before it."

She wanted to shake her head, but she didn't dare. The thought of all those who had seen her spanked tormented her. She had been turned so those at the windows could see her buttocks and between her legs, and the soldiers could see her face, and it had been excruciating. Well, it would only be her Prince now. If only she could tell him, for him anything, but those others were such punishment . . .

She knew this was wrong. It was not what he wanted her to think, what he was trying to teach her. But now she couldn't think.

He was at her side. He held her chin in his left hand, and he had told her to fold her arms behind her back which was difficult for her. It was worse than clasping her hands behind her neck. This position arched her body, forced her breasts out, and made her breasts and face feel painfully naked. She moaned slightly as he lifted her hair and folded the great mane of it over her right shoulder, away from him.

It covered her arm, but he pushed it away from her nipples and pinched both of them hard between his finger and thumb, lifting her breasts and letting them fall naturally as he did so.

Her face was positively smarting. But she knew what was to come would be worse.

"Spread your legs ever so slightly. You must be firmly planted on the ground," he said, "so that you can withstand the blows of the paddle."

She wanted to cry out, and through her tightly pressed lips her sobs sounded very loud to her.

"Beauty, Beauty," he crooned. "Do you want to please me?"

"Yes, my Prince," she cried, her lip trembling uncontrollably.

"Then why are you crying so when you haven't even felt the paddle yet? And your buttocks are only a little sore. Why, the Innkeeper's daughter had little strength."

She cried almost bitterly, as if to say in her soft wordless way that it was all true but it was so difficult.

He held her chin firmly now, bracing her whole body. And then she felt the first crack of the paddle.

It was an explosion of stinging pain on the hot surface of her flesh, and the second spank came much more swiftly than she had thought possible and then there was the third and the fourth, and in spite of herself she was crying aloud.

He stopped and gently kissed her all over her face. "Beauty, Beauty," he said. "Now, I give you permission to speak . . . tell what it is you would have me know . . ."

"I want to please you, my Prince," she struggled, "but it hurts so, and I've tried so hard to please you."

"But, my darling, you please me by bearing this pain. I explained to you earlier that punishment would not always be for a transgression. Sometimes it would be for my pleasure only."

"Yes, my Prince," she cried.

"I shall tell you a little secret about the pain. You are as a tight bowstring. And the pain loosens you, makes you soft as I want you to be. It is worth a thousand little orders and scoldings, and you must not think of resisting it. Do you know what I am saying? You must give yourself over to it. With each crack of the paddle you must think of the next and the next and that it is your Prince doing it to you, giving you this pain."

"Yes, my Prince," she said softly.

He lifted her chin again without further ado and spanked her hard again and again on the buttocks. She felt her buttocks growing hotter and hotter with pain, and the cracks of the paddle sounded loud and somehow shattering to her, as if the sound itself were as dreadful as the pain. She could not understand it.

When he stopped again, she was breathless and almost frantic in her tears, as if the torrent of blows had so humiliated her it was far worse than even a greater pain would have been.

But the Prince folded her in his arms. And feeling his rough clothing against her, and his hard naked chest, and the strength of his shoulders, she felt such a soothing pleasure that her sobs grew soft and open mouthed and languid against him.

His rough breeches were against her sex, and she found herself pressing against him only to have him guide her gently back as if silently reproving her.

"Kiss me," he said, and such a shock of pleasure went through her at the closing of his open mouth over hers that she was almost unable to stand, letting her weight fall against him.

He turned her toward the bed.

"That's enough for tonight," he said softly. "We have a hard journey tomorrow."

And he told her to lie down.

It occurred to her suddenly that he was not going to take her. She heard him moving to the door, and this pleasure between her legs became suddenly an agony. But all she could do was cry softly into the pillow. She tried to keep her sex from touching the sheets because she feared that if it did she could not resist some undulating movement. And she felt sure he was watching her. Of course he'd meant her to feel pleasure. But without his permission?

She lay rigid, afraid, crying.

A moment later she heard voices behind her.

"Bathe her and put a soothing ointment on her buttocks," the Prince was saying, "and you may talk to the Princess if you like, and she to you. You are to treat her with the utmost respect," said the Prince and then she heard his steps dying away.

She lay too afraid to look behind her. The door was closed again. She heard steps. She heard the cloth in the basin of water.

"It's me, dearest Princess," said a woman's voice, and she realized it was a young woman, a woman her own age, and could only be the Innkeeper's daughter.

She buried her face in the pillow. "This is unbearable," she thought, and suddenly with all her heart she hated the Prince, but she was far too humiliated to think of it. She felt the girl's weight on the bed beside her, and just the rough cloth of her apron brushing against Beauty's buttocks caused the sore and stinging flesh to ache more keenly.

She felt as if her buttocks must be enormous, though she knew they were not, or giving off some terrible light with their redness. The girl would feel their heat; this girl, of all girls, who had tried so hard to please the Prince by spanking her far harder than the Prince had realized.

The wet cloth stroked her shoulders, her arms, her neck. It stroked her back and then her thighs and legs and feet, the girl carefully avoiding her sex and the soreness.

But then after the girl had wrung out the cloth, she touched the buttocks lightly.

"O, I know it hurts, dearest Princess," she confided. "I'm so sorry, but what could I do when the Prince commanded me?" The rag was rough on the soreness, and Beauty realized this time that the Prince had left her with a score of welts. She moaned, and though she loathed this girl with a violent feeling she'd never had for anyone else in her brief life, the cloth nevertheless felt good to her.

The moist cloth was cooling her; it was like the gentle massaging of an itch. And Beauty grew quiet as the girl continued to bathe her in a gentle circular motion.

"Dearest Princess," the girl said, "I know how you

suffer but he is so very handsome, and he will have his way, there's nothing to be done about it. Please talk to me, please tell me that you don't despise me."

"I don't despise you," Beauty said in a small spiritless voice. "How could I blame you or despise you?"

"I had to do it. And what a spectacle it was. Princess, I must tell you something. You may be angry with me, but maybe it will be a consolation to you."

Beauty closed her eyes and pressed her cheek into the pillow. She did not want to hear it. But she liked the girl's voice, its respect and gentleness. The girl did not mean to hurt her. She could feel that awe in the girl, that humility Beauty had known in all her servants all her life. It was no different, not even with this one who had held her over her knee in a tavern and spanked her in the presence of crude men and villagers. Beauty pictured her as she remembered her from the kitchen door: her dark curly hair in ringlets about her little round face, and those big eyes full of apprehension. How fierce the Prince must have seemed to her! Why she must have been terrified that at any moment, the Prince would order her stripped and humiliated! Beauty smiled to herself, thinking of it. She felt a tenderness for the girl, and for her gentle hands which were now bathing the hot, aching flesh so carefully.

"All right," Beauty said, "what is it you want to tell me?"

"Only that you were so lovely, dearest Princess, that you have such beauty. Even as you were there, why, how many who seem beautiful could have kept their beauty in such a trial, and you were so beautiful, Princess." Over and over she said this word, beautiful, clearly reaching for other words, better words she did not know. "You were so . . . so graceful, Princess," she said. "You bore it so well, with such obedience to his Highness, the Prince."

Beauty said nothing. She was thinking of it again, of how it must have seemed to the girl. But it gave Beauty such a frightful sense of herself that she stopped thinking of it. This girl had seen her so closely, had seen the redness of her flesh as it was punished, and had felt her writhing uncontrollably.

Beauty would have cried again, but she didn't want to.

For the first time, through a film of ointment, she felt the girl's naked fingers on her. They massaged the welts.

"Oooh!" the Princess gasped.

"I'm sorry," said the girl. "I am trying so to be gentle."

"No, you must go on. Rub it in well," sighed Beauty, "it feels good, actually. Maybe it's that moment when you take your fingers away." How try to explain it, her buttocks flooded with this pain, itching with it, the welts little hard pebblelike bits of pain, and those fingers pinching them and then releasing them.

"Everyone adores you, Princess," the girl whispered. "Everyone has seen your beauty, with nothing to disguise it or hide your defects, and you have no defects. And they are swooning over you, Princess."

"Is that really so? Or do you say it to console me?" asked Beauty.

"O, it is so," said the girl. "O, you should have heard the rich women out in the Inn yard tonight, all of them pretending they weren't envious, but all of them knew that stripped they couldn't hold a candle to you, Princess. And of course the Prince was so beautiful, so handsome and so . . ."

"Ah, yes," sighed Beauty.

The girl had coated the buttocks now and was putting even more ointment into the flesh. And she worked some of it into Beauty's thighs, her fingers stopping just before the hair between Beauty's legs, and again, with fierce annoyance and shame, Beauty felt that pleasure coming back. And with this girl!

"O, if the Prince were to know it," she thought suddenly. She couldn't imagine him being pleased, and it suddenly occurred to her that he might punish her any time she felt this pleasure without his giving it to her.

She tried to put it out of her mind. She wished she knew where he was now.

"Tomorrow," the girl said, "when you go on to the Prince's castle, the road all along the way will be lined with those who want to see you. Word is spreading all through the Kingdom . . ."

Beauty gave a little start at these words. "Are you sure of it?" she said fearfully. It was too much to think of suddenly. She remembered that peaceful moment in the afternoon forest. She had been alone ahead of the Prince and had some how managed to forget the soldiers following him. And suddenly to think of people all along the road waiting to see her! She remembered the crowded village streets, those inevitable moments when her naked thighs or breasts even had been brushed by an arm or the fabric of a skirt—she felt her breath halt.

"But he wants this of me," she thought. "Not just that he see me but that all see me."

"It gives the people such pleasure to see you," he had said tonight as they entered this little town. He had prodded her on up ahead of him, and she had been crying so fiercely as she saw all about her those shoes and boots from which she dared not look up.

"But you are so lovely, Princess, and they will be telling their grandchildren about it," said the tavern girl. "They cannot wait to feast their eyes upon you, and you will not disappoint them, no matter what they have heard. Imagine that, never disappointing anyone . . ." The girl's voice trailed off as though she were in thought. "O, I wish I could follow you to see it."

"But you don't understand," Beauty whispered, unable suddenly to contain herself. "You don't realize . . ."

"Yes, I do," said the girl. "Of course I do . . . I've seen the Princesses when they come through in their magnificent gowns covered with jewels, and I know how it must feel to be opened to the world as if you were a flower, all of their eyes like fingers prying at you, but you are so . . . so splendid finally, Princess, and so rare. And you are his Princess, and he has claimed you and all know you are in his power and must do as he commands you. It is no shame to you, Princess. How could it be, with such a great Prince to command you? O, do you think that there aren't women who would give up everything to take your place, if only they had your beauty?"

Beauty was startled by this. She thought about it. Women giving up everything, taking her place. It had not occurred to her. She remembered that moment in the forest.

But then she remembered being spanked in the Inn, and all of those others watching. She remembered sobbing helplessly, and hating her buttocks propped up in the air, and her legs open, and that paddle coming down again and again. Finally the pain was the least of it.

She thought of the crowds on the road. She tried to picture it. It would happen to her tomorrow.

She would feel this drenching humiliation, this pain, but all those people would be there to witness her humiliation, to amplify it.

The door had opened.

The Prince had come into the room. And the little tavern girl jumped up and was bowing to him.

"Your Highness," the girl said breathlessly.

"You've done your work very well," said the Prince.

"It was a great honor, your Highness," said the girl.

The Prince came to the bed, and clasping Beauty's right wrist, he drew her up out of the bed and stood her beside it. Obediently, Beauty looked down, and not knowing what to do with her hands, quickly brought them to the back of the neck.

She could almost feel the Prince's satisfaction.

"Excellent, my darling," he said. "Isn't she lovely, your Princess?" he said to the tavern girl.

"O, yes, your Highness."

"Did you talk to her and console her as you were bathing her?"

"O, yes, your Highness, I told her how much everyone admired her and how much they wanted to . . ."

"Yes, to see her," the Prince said.

There was a pause. Beauty wondered if they were both looking at her, and suddenly she felt herself naked in the sight of both of them. It seemed one or the other she could bear, but both of them staring at her breasts and sex was too much for her.

But the Prince embraced her as if seeing that she needed embracing, and gently squeezing her sore flesh, sent another soft shock of shameful pleasure through her. She knew her face was red again. She had always blushed so easily. And were there other ways in which he could tell what his hands did to her? She would cry again if she could not conceal this mounting pleasure.

"Down on your knees, my darling," said the Prince with a little snap of his fingers.

In a shock Beauty obeyed, seeing the rough floorboards before her. She could see the Prince's black boots, and then the crude leather shoes of the serving girl.

"Now, approach your servant and kiss her shoes. Show her how grateful you are for her devotion to you."

Beauty didn't stop to think of it. But she felt her tears come again as she obeyed, depositing each kiss on the worn leather of the girl's shoes as gracefully as she could. Above she heard the girl's murmured thanks to the Prince.

"Your Highness," the girl said, "it is I who want to kiss my Princess, I beg you."

The Prince must have nodded, because the girl fell to her knees, and, stroking Beauty's hair, kissed her upturned face with great reverence.

"Now, you see there the posts of the foot of the bed," the Prince said to the girl. Beauty of course knew that the bed had high posts which held a coffered ceiling over it.

"Tie your mistress to those posts with her hands and legs quite wide apart so that as I lie down I can look up at her," said the Prince. "Tie her with these satin bands so her skin won't be injured, but tie her very firmly for she must sleep in this position and her weight must not pull her loose."

Beauty was stunned.

She was in a delirium as she was lifted to stand at the foot of the bed. She obeyed pliantly as the girl told her to spread her legs. She felt the satin go tight around her right ankle and then it firmly bound her left ankle, and then the girl, standing before her on the bed, bound the Princess's hands high on either side of her.

She was spread-eagled, looking down at the bed, and with terror, she realized that the Prince must see how she suffered; he must see the shame of the dampness between her legs, those fluids she could neither check or conceal, and, turning her face into her arm, she whimpered softly.

But the worst of it was that he did not mean to take her. He had tied her here out of reach of himself so that as he slept she must look down on him.

Now the girl was dismissed, secretly depositing a little kiss on Beauty's thigh before she left. And Beauty, crying softly, realized she was alone with the Prince. She did not dare to look at him.

"My beautiful obedient one," he sighed.

And to her horror she felt, as he drew near, the hard handle of that dreadful wooden paddle nudging her moist and secret place, so cruelly exposed by her open legs.

She struggled to pretend this was not happening. But she could feel that revealing fluid, and she knew the Prince knew of her tormenting pleasure.

"I have taught you much, and I am so very pleased with you," he said, "and so now you know a new suffering, a new sacrifice for your Lord and master. I could soothe the burning craving between your legs but I shall let you suffer it and know the meaning of it, and that only your Prince can give you that relief you long for."

She couldn't control her moan, even though she muffled it against her arm. She feared that any moment she might move her hips in helpless, humiliating entreaty.

He had snuffed the candles.

The room was dark.

Beneath her feet she felt the mattress give with his weight.

She leaned her head against her arm and felt secure in the satin bonds as she let herself hang there. But this torment, this torment . . . and there was nothing she could do to alleviate it.

She prayed the swelling between her legs would die away, as the throbbing in her buttocks was cooling and dying away. And then falling to sleep, she thought calmly, dreamily almost, of the crowds awaiting her on the roads to the Prince's castle.

THE CASTLE AND THE GREAT HALL

Beauty was breathless and flushed as they left the Inn; but it was not so much on account of the crowds that lined the village streets, nor those she would see ahead following the ribbon of road as it ran through the wheat fields.

The Prince had sent couriers ahead, and as Beauty's hair was dressed with white flowers, he told her they would reach his castle by afternoon if they were to hurry.

"We shall be in my Kingdom," he announced proudly, "as soon as we are on the other side of the mountains."

Beauty could not quite anatomize the feeling this aroused in her.

But the Prince, as if sensing her strange confusion, kissed her full on the mouth before mounting his horse, and said in a soft voice so that only those around them could hear:

"When you enter my Kingdom, you shall be mine more completely than ever. You will be mine beyond reprieve, and it will be easier for you to forget all that went before that time, and devote your life to me only."

And now they left the village, the Prince walking his magnificent horse just behind Beauty as she made her way quickly over the warm cobblestones.

The sun was hotter than before, and the crowds were very great, the farmers having all come to the road, and people were pointing and staring, and standing on tiptoe all the better to see, as Beauty felt the soft gravel under her feet and now and then tufts of silken grass or wildflower.

She walked with her head up as the Prince commanded her, but her eyes were half closed, and she felt the cool air soothing her naked limbs, and she could not stop thinking of the Prince's castle.

Now and then a low voice from the crowd would make her suddenly and painfully aware of her nakedness, and even once or twice a hand shot out to touch her thigh before the Prince behind her cracked his whip immediately.

Finally they entered the dark wooded pass that led through the mountains, and there were only occasional clusters of peasants here and there peeping out from the thick-limbed oaks, and a mist lay upon the ground, and Beauty felt herself drowsy and soft even as she walked. Her breasts felt heavy and soft to her, and her nakedness felt oddly natural.

But her heart became a tiny hammer when the sunlight streamed ahead to reveal an ever-widening green valley.

A great cry rose from the soldiers behind her, and she realized that indeed the Prince was home, and up ahead, across the sloping green, she saw upon a great precipice overhanging the valley the Prince's castle.

It was far greater in size than Beauty's home, a wilderness of dark towers. It might enclose a whole world, it seemed, and its open gates yawned like a mouth before the drawbridge.

Now from everywhere the subjects of the Prince, mere specks in the distance growing ever and ever larger, ran toward the road that wound down and then up again before them.

Riders came over the drawbridge and rode toward them with a blast of trumpets, their banners streaming behind them.

The air was warmer here, as if this place were protected from the sea breeze. It was nothing as dark as the narrow villages and forests through which they had passed. And Beauty could see everywhere the peasants dressed in lighter and brighter colors.

But they were drawing ever nearer to the castle, and in the distance Beauty could see not the peasants whose admiration she had received all along the road, but a great crowd of magnificently dressed Lords and Ladies.

She must have uttered a little cry and bowed her head, because the Prince came up alongside of her. She felt his arm gather her close to the horse, and he whispered:

"Now, Beauty, you know what I expect of you."

But they had already reached the steep approach to the bridge, and Beauty could see it was just as she feared, men and women of her own rank and all clad in white velvet trimmed in gold, or gay and festive colors. She dared not look, and felt the blush in her cheeks again and for the first time was tempted to throw herself on the mercy of the Prince and beg him to conceal her.

It was one thing to be shown to the rustics who praised her and would make a legend of her, but she could already hear the babble of haughty speech and laughter. This was unendurable to her.

But when the Prince dismounted, he ordered her down on her hands and knees and told her softly that this was how she must enter his castle.

She was petrified, her face burning, but she fell quickly to obey, glimpsing the Prince's boots to her left as she struggled to keep up with him in crossing the drawbridge.

Through a great dim corridor she was led, not daring to raise her eyes, though she could see rich gowns and shining boots all around her. Lords and Ladies were bowing to the Prince on either side of her. There were whispers of greeting, and kisses being thrown, and she was naked, moving on her hands and knees as if she were only some poor animal.

But they had reached the mouth of the Great Hall, a room far more vast and shadowy than any in her own castle. An immense fire roared on the hearth, though the sun streamed warm through high narrow windows. It seemed the Lords and Ladies pressed past her, flowing silently along the walls and towards the long wooden tables. Plate and goblets were already set. The air was heavy with the aroma of the supper.

And then Beauty saw the Queen.

She sat at the very end upon a raised dais. Her veiled head was encircled with a gold crown, and the deep sleeves of her green gown were trimmed in pearls and gold embroidery.

Beauty was led forward by a quick snap of the Prince's fingers. The Queen had risen, and now she embraced her son as he stood before the dais.

"Tribute, Mother, from the land over the Mountains, and the loveliest we have received in a long time if my memory serves me. My first love slave, and I am very proud to have claimed her."

"And well you should be," said the Queen in a voice that sounded both young and cold. Beauty dared not look up at her. But it was the Prince's voice which frightened her most. "My first love slave." She remembered his puzzling commiserations with her parents, the mention of their service in this same land, and she felt her pulse quicken.

"Exquisite, absolutely exquisite," said the Queen, "but all the Court must have a look at her. Lord Gregory," she said, and made an airy gesture.

A great murmur rose from the Court gathered around. And Beauty saw a tall gray-haired man approach, though she could not see him clearly. He wore soft leather sock boots, turned down at the knees to reveal a lining of the finest miniver.

"Display the girl . . ."

"But Mother," the Prince protested.

"Nonsense, all the common people have seen her. We shall see her," said the Queen.

"And should she be gagged, your Highness?" asked this strange tall man with the fur-lined boots.

"No, that is not necessary. Though punish her surely if she speaks or cries out."

"And the hair, she is shielded by all this hair," said the man, but he was now lifting Beauty and immediately had her wrists clasped over her head. As she stood, she felt herself hopelessly revealed and could not prevent crying. She dreaded a reproof from the Prince, and she could see the Queen all the better though she did not want to see her. Black hair showed beneath the Queen's sheer veil, hanging in ripples over her shoulders, and her eyes were black as the Prince's eyes.

"Leave her hair as it is," said the Prince almost jealously.

"O, he will defend me!" Beauty thought. But then she heard the Prince himself give the order. "Mount her on the table for all to see."

The table was rectangular and stood in the center of the room. It reminded Beauty of an altar. She was forced to kneel on it facing the thrones where the Prince had taken his place beside his mother.

And quickly the gray-haired man placed a large block of smooth wood beneath her belly. She could rest her weight on it and she did, as he forced her knees wide apart and then stretched out her legs so her knees didn't touch the table at all, her ankles bound by leather to the edges. Now her wrists were treated the same. She kept her face hidden as best as she could, weeping.

"You will be silent," said the man icily to her, "or I shall see that you cannot be anything else. Do not misunderstand the Queen's leniency. She does not gag you only because it amuses the Court to see your mouth as it is, and to see you struggle with your own willfulness."

And now, to Beauty's shame, he raised her chin and placed beneath it a long thick wooden chin rest. She could not lower her head, though she lowered her eyes. And she saw all the room about her.

She saw the Lords and Ladies rising from the banquet tables. She saw the immense fire. And then she saw this man, too, with his thin angular face, and gray eyes that were not as cold as his voice, but for the moment seemed even to evince tenderness.

A long shudder went through her as she contemplated herself—spread out, yet mounted so that all could inspect even her face if they chose, and she tried to conceal her sobs by pressing her lips together. Even her hair was no covering, for it fell evenly on either side of her face and cloaked no part of her.

"Young one, little one," said the gray-haired man under his breath. "You're so frightened and it's useless." There seemed a little warmth in his voice. "What is fear, after all? It is indecision. You seek some way to resist, escape. There is none. Do not tense your limbs. It's wasted."

Beauty bit her lip and felt the tears sliding down her face, but she was soothed by his speaking to her. He smoothed back the hair from her forehead. His hand was light and cold as if he were testing for a fever.

"Now be still. Everyone is coming to see you."

Beauty's eyes glazed over, but she could still see the distant thrones where the Prince and his mother were talking to one another quite naturally. But she realized all the Court had risen and was moving towards the dais. The Lords and Ladies were bowing to the Queen and the Prince, before turning and coming towards her.

Beauty squirmed. It seemed the air itself touched her naked buttocks and the hair between her legs, and she struggled to lower her face demurely but the firm wooden chin rest would not yield and all she could do was drop her eyes again.

The first Ladies and Lords were very near and she could hear the rustle of their clothes and see the flash of their gold bracelets.

These ornaments caught the light of the fire and the distant torches, and the dim image of the Prince and the Queen appeared to flicker.

She let out a moan.

"Hush, my darling dear," said the gray-eyed man. And suddenly it was a great comfort that he was so near to her.

"Now look up and to your left," he said now, and she could see his lips spread into a smile. "You see?"

For one instant Beauty beheld what was surely an impossibility, but before she could look again, or clear the tears from her eyes, a great Lady came between her and this distant vision, and with a shock, she felt the Lady's hands upon her.

She felt the cool fingers gathering her heavy breasts, and twisting them almost painfully. She trembled, trying desperately not to cry out. For others had gathered around her, and behind her she felt a pair of very slow and calm hands parting her legs even more. And now someone touched her face, and another hand pinched the calf of her leg almost cruelly.

It seemed her body was all concentrated then in its shameful and secret places. There was a throbbing in the tips of her breasts, and those hands felt cold as if she herself were burning, and now she felt fingers examining her buttocks and prodding even at that tiny and most concealed of openings.

She couldn't help but moan, but she kept her lips tightly shut, and the tears fell down her cheeks.

And for one instant she thought of nothing but what she had glimpsed an instant ago before the procession of Lords and Ladies had intercepted her vision.

High up along the wall of the Great Hall, on a broad stone ledge, she had glimpsed a row of naked women.

It had not seemed possible, but she had seen it. They were all of them young like herself, and they stood with their hands clasped behind their necks as the Prince had taught her to do, and their eyes were down, and she could see the glow of the fire on the curl of pubic hair between each pair of legs, and the swelling, pink nipples of their bosoms.

She could not believe it. She did not want it to be so, and yet if it were so . . . well . . . again only confusion. Was she all the more terrified, or was she glad that she was not the only one enduring this unspeakable humiliation?

But she could not even think of this, shocking as it was, for the hands were all over her. She had uttered a sharp cry to feel them touching her very sex, and smoothing the hair there, and then to her horror, as her face burned and she shut her eyes tight, she felt a pair of long fingers gliding into her sex and widening it.

It was still sore from the Prince's thrusts, and though the fingers were gentle, she felt that soreness again.

But the most excruciating part was being opened like this and hearing their soft voices now as they talked of her.

"Innocent, very innocent," said one, and another that she had very lean thighs and that her skin was resilient.

That seemed to produce laughter again—that light tinkling laughter, as if all of this were but the greatest amusement, and Beauty realized suddenly that she was straining with all her might to close her legs, but it was quite impossible.

Those fingers were gone, and now someone patted her sex, and pinched shut the hidden little lips, and Beauty squirmed again, only to hear the laughter coming now from the man beside her:

"Little Princess," he said gently in her ear, leaning over so she could feel his velvet cape against her naked arm, "you cannot hide your charms from anyone."

She moaned as if she were trying to appeal to him, but his finger touched her lips.

"Now if I have to seal your lips, the Prince will be very angry. You must resign yourself. You must accept. It is the hardest lesson, compared to which the pain is really nothing."

And Beauty could feel him raising his arm so that she knew the hand that touched her breast now was his. He had imprisoned her nipple and was pressing it rhythmically.

At the same time, someone stroked her thighs and her sex, and to her shame she felt, even in the midst of this degradation, that disgraceful pleasure.

"That's it, that's it," he comforted her. "You must not resist, but rather take possession of your charms, that is, let your mind inhabit your body.

"You are naked, helpless, and all will enjoy you and what can you do? By the way, I should tell you that your squirming only makes you more exquisite. It is very lovely except that it is so rebellious. Now look again, did you see what I pointed out to you?"

Beauty made a soft sound of assent, and fearfully raised her eyes again. It was as she had seen before, the row of young women with their eyes down and their bodies as vulnerable in display as her own.

But what was it she felt? Why must she be subjected to so many confusing feelings? She had thought herself the only one so displayed and humiliated, a great prize for the Prince whom she could no longer see. And was she not displayed here in the very center of the hall?

But then who were these prisoners? Would she only

be one of them? Was this the meaning of the odd con-versation that had passed between the Prince and her father and mother? No, they could not have served like this. She felt an odd mingling of torrential jealousy and comfort.

It was a ritual, this treatment. Others had suffered it before. It was fixed and she was all the more helpless. She felt herself soften as she thought of it.

But her Lord, the gray-eyed one, was speaking: "Now, for your second lesson. You have seen the Princesses who are tributes here. Now look to your right and you shall see the Princes."

Beauty looked to the other side of the hall as best she could through the shifting figures about her, and there, on another high ledge, in the ghastly shadow-light of the fire, stood a row of naked young men, all of them in the same position.

Their heads were bowed, their hands behind their necks, and they were all of them very handsome to look at, as beautiful each in his own way as the young women of the other side, but their great difference lay in their sex, for their organs were erect and hard to a one, and Beauty could not take her eyes off this sight, for they appeared to her even more vulnerable and subservient.

She knew she had made a little noise again, because she felt the Lord's finger on her lips, and she sensed almost from the air itself that she was now being left by the Lords and Ladies.

Only one pair of hands remained and these she felt touching the tenderest flesh around her anus. She was so frightened by this—for almost no one else had touched her there—that involuntarily she struggled again, only to have the gray-eyed Lord stroke her face again gently.

There was a great commotion in the room. Beauty could just catch the aroma of cooking food, and dishes being brought in, and now she saw that most of the Lords and Ladies were seated at the tables, and there was much talking and lifting of cups, and somewhere a group of musicians had begun to play a low rhythmic music. It was full of horns and tambourines and the strumming of thick strings, and Beauty saw that the long file of naked men and women on either side was moving.

"But what are they?" she wanted to ask. "To what purpose?" But now she saw the first of them appear amid the crowd, carrying silver pitchers with which they filled the goblets at the table, always bowing when they passed the Queen and the Prince, and she watched them, forgetting herself for the moment, with great absorption.

The young men had softly curly hair, cut at the shoulders and neatly combed so that it framed their lean faces. And never did they raise their eyes, though some seemed to move in obvious discomfort from the hardness of their penises. How she could tell this discomfort, she was not sure; it was their manner, a manner of bearing tension and desire, with no expression for it.

And as she saw the first of the long-haired girls bending over the table with her pitcher, she wondered if she too felt this same softly agonizing pleasure. Beauty felt it now just looking at these slaves, and she felt a quiet relief that for a moment she herself was unobserved.

Or so she thought.

Because she could sense a restlessness in the room. Some were rising and walking about, perhaps even dancing to the music. She could not be sure. And others had gone to gather near the Queen, their goblets in hand, regaling the Prince it seemed with stories.

The Prince.

She caught a clear glimpse of him and he smiled at her. How regal he looked, his black hair glossy and full, his long, shining white boots stretched out on the blue carpet before him. He was nodding and smiling to those who addressed him, but now and then his eyes moved to Beauty.

But there was so much to see, and now she felt someone was very near her, and touching her again, and

(54)

she realized that a line of dancers was just forming to one side of her.

There was a reckless air to things. Much wine was being poured. There were great eruptions of laughter.

And then, quite suddenly, she saw far to her left a young naked boy drop his pitcher of wine, and the red liquid run out on the floor as others hastened to clean it.

At once the Lord at Beauty's side clapped his hands, and Beauty saw three exquisitely dressed Pages, no older than the naked boys themselves, rush forward and seize the boy and hold him up quickly by his ankles.

This brought a loud round of applause from those Lords and Ladies nearest the boy, and at once a paddle was produced, a very beautiful piece of gold enameling and white tracery, and the offender was smartly spanked while all looked on with the greatest fascination.

Beauty felt a fluttering in her heart. If she were to be humiliated like that, punished so immediately and ignominiously for clumsiness, she didn't know how she could bear it. To be displayed was one thing; here she had some grace.

But she could not endure the thought of being held by her ankles as the boy was. She could see only his back, and the paddle flashing down again and again on his reddening buttocks. He held his hands obediently on the back of his neck, and as he was let down on his hands and knees, the young Page with the paddle drove him quickly with a series of loud blows towards the Queen, where the young culprit, his buttocks very red, bowed his head and kissed the Queen's slipper.

The Queen had been in fast conversation with the Prince. She was a mature woman, very full blown but it was from her, obviously, that the Prince had gotten his beauty. She turned, almost indifferently, her eyes darting back to the Prince, and motioning for the young slave to rise a little, she brushed back his hair affectionately.

But then in the same indifferent manner, never withdrawing herself from the Prince, she made a motion to the Page, with a quick frown, that the boy was again to be punished.

The Lords and Ladies nearest applauded with mock scolding gestures, and then obviously enjoyed it very much as the Page put his foot on the second step of the dais before the throne, and hoisted the disobedient slave up over his knee and again, in full view of everyone, soundly spanked him.

A long row of dancers obscured the view for a moment, but again and again Beauty caught glimpses of the unfortunate boy, and she could see that as the paddle came down, he was having a more and more difficult time bearing it. He struggled just a little in spite of himself, and it was also quite obvious that the Page who delivered the paddling was very much enjoying it. His young face was flushed, and he was biting his lip slightly, and he drove the paddle down unnecessarily hard it seemed, and Beauty felt she hated him.

She could hear the Lord beside her laughing. There was a little loose crowd about her now, men and women drinking, talking idly. The dancers moved in a long chain, performing their fluid and graceful movements.

"So you see you aren't the only helpless little creature in this world," said the gray-eyed Lord, "and does it soothe you to see the Tribute that belongs to your Sovereigns? You are the first Tribute for the Prince and I think that you shall have to set a fierce example. The young slave you saw, Prince Alexi, is very much a favorite of the Queen or he wouldn't be dealt with so lightly."

Beauty saw that the paddling had stopped. Once again, the slave was on his hands and knees and kissing the feet of the Queen as the Page waited in attendance.

Now the slave's buttocks were very red. "Prince Alexi," Beauty thought. It was a lovely name, and he too was of royal blood and high birth. Why, of course, all of them were. It was a delightful thought. What if they had not been, and she were the only Princess?

She stared at his buttocks. There were obvious welts

on them and little patches that seemed much redder than the rest, and as the young slave Prince kissed the Queen's feet, Beauty could see also his scrotum between his legs, dark, hairy and mysterious.

It struck her how dreadfully vulnerable he seemed, being a boy, in ways she had never considered.

But he had been released or forgiven. He rose to his feet, and brushed his auburn curly hair out of his eyes and back from his cheek, and she saw his face stained with tears, and reddened too; yet he had about him a marvelous dignity.

He took the pitcher handed him without complaint and gracefully he moved among the standing guests, filling their goblets.

He was only a few paces from Beauty, and drawing ever closer. And she could hear how the men and women teased him.

"Another paddling and you are so wretchedly clumsy," said a very tall blond-haired Lady in a long green gown, with diamonds on her fingers, and she pinched his red cheek, as, with his eyes down, he smiled.

His penis was hard and erect as before, rising up thick and motionless from a nest of dark curly hair between his legs. Beauty could not stop herself from looking at it.

As he came nearer, she held her breath.

"Come here, Prince Alexi," said the Lord with the gray eyes. He snapped his fingers. And then taking a white handkerchief, he had the boy moisten it with the wine.

The boy was so near now Beauty might have touched him. And the Lord took the moistened handkerchief and pressed it to Beauty's lips. It felt good and cool and tantalizing.

But she could not help but look up at the obedient boy Prince who stood waiting, and she saw him looking at her.

And though his face was still slightly pink, and there were tears on his cheeks, he smiled at her.

THE PRINCE'S BED CHAMBER

BEAUTY AWOKE to new terror.

It was getting dusk; the Feast was over. The Lords and Ladies who remained were very loud and swept up in the fever of the afternoon, but she was being unbound and she did not know what would now happen to her.

Several other slaves had been soundly spanked during the course of the banquet, and it seemed finally that no offense was required, merely the decision of a Lord or Lady. The request was then granted by the Queen— and the unlucky one was thrust up over the Page's knee, his head bowed, his feet dangling off the ground, and down came the golden paddle.

Twice it had been young women.

And one of them had broken into silent sobs. But there was in her manner something that made Beauty a little suspicious. After she was spanked, she scurried all too fast to the Queen's feet, and Beauty hoped she would be spanked again until her sobs were real, and all her scurrying was real, and she found herself vaguely delighted when the Queen ordered it.

Now, as Beauty was awakened, she thought dreamily of all this, and felt sharp fear, and also some sense of drama.

Would she be sent away to some place with all these slaves? Or would the Prince take her?

She was stunned with confusion, when she realized the Prince had risen and given an order to the gray-eyed Lord to bring Beauty after him.

She was untied; she was very stiff. But the Lord now had one of those gold paddles in his hand which he tested loudly upon his palm, and giving her no time to stretch her aching muscles, he ordered her down on her knees and forward.

When she hesitated, his command came very sharp again, but he did not strike her.

She rushed to catch up with the Prince who had just reached the stairway.

And soon she was following him up and down a long corridor.

"Beauty," he stood back. "Open the doors!"

And kneeling up, she quickly opened them and forced them apart and then followed the Prince into a bed chamber.

The fire was already a great blaze on the hearth and the windows were curtained, and the bed had been turned back, and Beauty was quivering with excitement.

"My Prince, shall I begin her training at once?" asked the gray-eyed Lord.

"No, my Lord, I shall attend to it myself the first few days, possibly longer," said the Prince, "though you may of course, whenever the occasion arises, instruct her, teach her manners, the general rules that pertain to all the slaves, and so forth. She does not drop her eyes as she should, as you can see; she is so very inquisitive." And at this he smiled, though Beauty at once looked down, much as she wanted to see it.

She knelt obediently, glad her hair concealed her. And then she checked herself in this thought. She was not learning much if that was what she wanted.

She wondered if Prince Alexi had been ashamed of his nakedness. He had had large brown eyes and such a beautiful mouth, but he was much too lean to be cherubic. She wondered where he was now, and was he being punished more for his clumsiness?

"Very well, your Highness," said the Lord, "but I think you realize that firmness in the beginning is a mercy to the slave, especially when the slave is such a proud and spoilt Princess."

Beauty blushed to hear this.

The Prince gave a low, gentle laugh.

"My Beauty is very like an unstamped coin," said the Prince, "and I wish to draw in the full character. I shall take delight in training her. I wonder if you yourself are as attentive to her faults as I am."

"Your Highness?" the Lord seemed to stiffen slightly.

"You were not yourself so very strict with her in the Great Hall that you prevented her from feasting her eyes on young Prince Alexi. I rather think she enjoyed his punishment as much as her masters and mistresses."

Beauty flushed hotly. She had never dreamed that the Prince had observed her in this.

"Your Highness, she was only learning what will be expected of her, or so I thought . . ." the Lord answered very humbly. "It was I who drew her attention to the other slaves so she might profit from their obedient example."

"Ah, well," said the Prince wearily and agreeably, "perhaps I am only too enamored of her. After all, she wasn't sent to me as a Tribute, I won her and claimed her myself, and I am too jealous, it seems. Perhaps I seek for some reason to punish her. You're dismissed. Come for her in the morning, if you will, and we shall see."

The Lord, obviously worried that he had failed, left the room quickly.

Beauty was now alone with the Prince, and the Prince was sitting quietly by the fire looking at her. She was in a great state of agitation; she knew she was blushing as always, and that her breasts were heaving slightly. She rushed forward quite suddenly and pressed her lips to the Prince's boot, and it seemed to move as if it welcomed her kiss, rising slightly as over and over again she kissed it.

She was moaning. O, if only he'd give her permission to speak, and when she thought of her fascination with the punished Prince, she blushed all the more.

But her Prince had risen. He took her wrist and lifted her and drawing her hands behind her back so that he held them firmly, he spanked both her breasts hard until she cried out, feeling the heavy flesh sway and the sting of his hands on her nipples.

"Am I angry with you? Or am I not?" he asked softly.

She groaned, imploring him. And he placed her over his knee as she had seen the young Prince over the Page's knee, and with his bare hand he gave her a smart torrent of blows that had her crying aloud in an instant.

"To whom do you belong?" he demanded in a low, but angry voice.

"To you, my Prince, completely!" she cried out. It was dreadful, and then, suddenly unable to control herself she said, "Please, please, my Prince, not in anger, no . . ."

But instantly his left hand clamped over her mouth,

and she felt another terrible torrent of hot spanks until her flesh was stinging and she couldn't control her crying.

She could feel the Prince's fingers against her lips. But he would hardly be satisfied with this. He had her on her feet now and by her wrists he led her to a corner of the room between the blazing fire and the curtained window. There was a high stool there made of carved wood, and on this he sat while he stood her beside him. She was crying softly, but she dared not beg again, no matter what happened. He was angry, fiercely angry, and though she could endure any pain for his pleasure, this was unbearable for her. She must please him, must make him loving again, and then any pain at all would not be too much.

He turned her and she stood facing him as he sat inspecting her. She dared not look him in the face, and then he drew back his cloak, and laying his hand on the golden buckle of his belt said, "Unfasten this."

At once she went to obey with her teeth without being told that was how she might do it. She hoped and prayed he would be pleased. She pulled on the leather, her breath soft and fast, and then pulled the strap back so that the belt came loose.

"Now pull it off," said the Prince, "and give it to me."

She obeyed at once, even though she knew what would follow. It was a thick, wide leather belt. Maybe it would be no worse than a paddle.

Now he told her to raise her hands and her eyes, and she saw above a metal hook just over her head hanging from a chain on the ceiling.

"You see here we are not without provisions for disobedient little slaves," he said in his usual gentle voice. "Now clasp that hook, though it will put you on tiptoe, and you will not dream of letting go of it, do you understand me?"

"Yes, my Prince," she cried softly.

She had hold of it, and it seemed to stretch her out,

and the Prince moved back the stool on which he sat and appeared to make himself comfortable. He had ample room in which to swing the strap which he had made into a loop, and he was silent for a moment.

Beauty cursed herself for ever admiring young Prince Alexi. Yet she was ashamed that his very name had formed in her mind, and when she felt the first hard smack of the belt on her thighs, she let out a frightened little cry but was glad of it.

She deserved this, and she would never again make such a terrible mistake, no matter how beautiful or enticing were the slaves, and her boldness to look at them had been unforgivable.

The wide heavy leather belt struck her with a loud, frightening sound, and the flesh of her thighs, more tender perhaps than her buttocks, even sore as they were, seemed to ignite under it. Her mouth was open, she could not keep herself quiet, and suddenly the Prince ordered her to lift her knees and march in place.

"Quickly, quickly, yes, in rhythm!" he said angrily, and Beauty, astonished, struggled to obey, marching fast, her breasts moving with the effort, her heart pounding.

"Higher, faster," the Prince commanded.

She marched as he commanded, her feet slapping the stone floor, her knees coming up very high, her breasts a terrible aching weight as they swayed, and again came the belt smacking her and stinging her.

The Prince seemed in a fury.

The blows came faster and faster, as fast as she was moving her legs, and very soon, Beauty was writhing and struggling to get away from them. She was crying aloud unable to stop herself but the worst of it, the worst of it, was his anger. If only this were for his delight, if only he were pleased with her. She was crying and burying her face in her arm and the balls of her feet were burning, and her thighs felt swollen and blotched with pain as now again he took out his temper upon her buttocks.

The smacks came so quickly, she had no sense of

how many there were, only that it was a great deal more than he'd ever given her before, and it seemed he only grew more agitated, his left hand now thrusting her chin up and closing her mouth so she couldn't cry, all the while he commanded her to march faster and lift her legs higher.

"You belong to me!" he said without ever stopping the loud spanking belt. "And you will learn to please me in all things, and you will never please me with your eyes upon the male slaves of my mother. Is this clear to you? Do you understand?"

"Yes, my Prince," she struggled to say.

But he seemed at wits ends to punish her. And stopping her suddenly by lifting her around the middle, he brought her up over the stool which he had just left, so that dangling from the hook which she held for dear life, she was now thrust over it, the wooden seat of the stool pressing into her naked sex, her legs out helplessly behind her.

And then he sent his worst rain of blows on her, hard snapping spanks that made her calves quiver and sting as her thighs had done before. But no matter how he busied himself with her legs, he always returned to her buttocks, punishing them the hardest so that Beauty was choking with sobs, and felt this as endless.

Quite suddenly he stopped.

"Let go the hook," he commanded, and then he scooped her up over his shoulder and taking her across the room, he flung her down on the bed.

She fell back on the pillow, and immediately beneath her sore and swollen buttocks and thighs felt a prickling and a roughness. She had only to cast her head slightly to the side to see the jewels glittering on the coverlet. And she knew how they would torture her as soon as he had mounted her.

But she wanted him so badly. And when she saw him rise up over her, she felt not the hot throbbing pain in her body but a flood of juices between her legs and a new moan coming out of her as she opened herself to him.

She couldn't keep from lifting her hips, praying it didn't displease him.

He knelt over her, removing his erect cock from his breeches, and then he brought her up on her knees and impaled her upon it.

She cried out. Her head fell back. It was a great hard driving thing inside her sore and quivering orifice. But she felt it bathed with her juices, and as the Prince forced it in deeper and brought her down upon it, it seemed a spit that rubbed against some mysterious core in her, sending the ecstasy washing through her so she was giving great guttural moans in spite of herself. The Prince's thrusts came faster and faster and then he too gave a soft cry, and held her close to him, her breasts aching and pressed to his chest, his lips on the back of her neck, his body softening slowly.

"Beauty, Beauty," he whispered. "You have conquered me as surely as I have conquered you. Don't ever arouse my jealousy again. I don't know what I would do if you did it!"

"My Prince," she moaned and kissed him on the mouth, and when she saw the distress in his face, she covered it with kisses.

"I'm your slave, my Prince," she said.

But he would only moan and press his face into her neck, and seemed bereft.

"I love you," she implored him, and then he laid her down on the bed, and drawing up beside her, took his wine from the bedside stand and, gazing at the fire, seemed for a long time to be thinking.

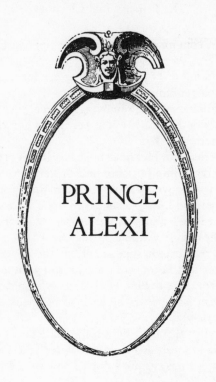

PRINCE
ALEXI

Beauty Dreamed a dream of boredom. She roamed the castle in which she had lived all her life, with nothing to do, and now and then paused in a deep window seat to watch the tiny figures of the peasants in the fields below gathering the fresh mown grass into haystacks. The sky was cloudless and she disliked the look of it, its sameness and vastness.

It seemed she could not find anything to do that hadn't been done a thousand times before, and then suddenly there came to her ears a sound she could not identify.

She followed the sound, and through a doorway saw

an old woman, bent and ugly, plying a strange contraption. It was a great turning wheel with a thread that was winding itself upon a spindle.

"What is it?" Beauty asked with great interest.

"Come see for yourself," said the old woman, who had the most remarkable voice, because it was young and strong and so unlike her visage.

It seemed Beauty had only just touched this marvelous machine with its whirring wheel when she fell down in a great swoon, and all about her heard the world weeping.

". . . sleep, sleep for a hundred years!"

And she wanted to cry out, "Unbearable, worse than death," for it seemed some great deepening of the ennui she had struggled against ever since she could remember, the wandering from room to room . . .

But she awoke.

She was not at home.

She was lying in the bed of her Prince, and she felt the prickling of the jeweled coverlet beneath her.

The room was full of the leaping shadows of the fire, and she saw the gleam of the carved posts of the bed, and the drapery fallen about her in rich colors. She felt herself animated and flushed with desire, and she rose up, so eager was she to lose the weight and texture of her dream, and she realized that the Prince was not beside her.

But there he was, by the fire, his elbow against the stone above it which bore a great crest with crossed swords. He wore his brilliant red velvet cloak still and his high turned down leather boots with their pointed toes, and his face was sharpened with brooding.

The pulse between her legs quickened. She stirred, and gave some faint little sigh so that he awoke from his thoughts and approached her. She could not see his expression in the darkness.

"All right, there is but one answer," he said to her. "You shall become accustomed to all the sights of the castle, and I shall become accustomed to seeing you accustomed to them."

He pulled the bell rope by the bed. And lifting Beauty he sat her at the end of the bed so that her legs were curled under her.

A Page entered, as innocent as the boy who had so diligently punished Prince Alexi, and like all the Pages he was extremely tall with powerful arms. Beauty was certain they had all been chosen for these endowments. She had no doubt he could have held her by the ankles had he been ordered, but his face was smooth without the slightest meanness.

"Where is Prince Alexi?" The Prince demanded. He appeared angry and resolute, and he paced back and forth as he spoke.

"O, he is in frightful trouble tonight, your Highness. The Queen is much concerned with his clumsiness. You know he must be her example to others. She has had him tied in the garden, most uncomfortably."

"Yes, well, I shall make him even more uncomfortable. Obtain my mother's permission and bring him to me and bring Squire Felix with him."

Beauty heard all this in quiet amazement. She tried to make her face as smooth as the Page's face. But she was more than alarmed. She was going to see Prince Alexi again, and she could not imagine concealing her feelings from her Prince. If only she could distract him from this.

But when she made a little whispering sound, he ordered her at once to be quiet, and to sit where she was, and to cast her eyes down.

Her hair fell around her, tickling her naked arms and her thighs, and almost with pleasure she realized there was no escaping this.

Squire Felix appeared almost immediately, and as she had suspected he was the Page who had so vigorously spanked Prince Alexi earlier. He had the gold paddle fixed to his belt so it dangled at his side as he bowed to the Prince.

"All of those who serve here are picked for their gifts," Beauty thought, looking at him, for he too was fair, and his blond hair made an excellent frame for his youthful face, though it was somewhat plainer than those of the captive Princes.

"And Prince Alexi?" the Prince demanded. His color was high, his eyes had an almost evil glitter, and Beauty became frightened again.

"We're preparing him, your Highness," said Squire Felix.

"And why should this take so long? How long has he served in this house that he should be so lacking in respect?"

At once Prince Alexi was brought in.

Beauty tried not to admire him. He was naked as before, of course, she'd expected no less, and in the light of the fire she could see that his face was flushed, and his auburn hair hung loose in his eyes which were cast down as if he dared not lift them to the Prince. They were of about the same age, surely, and about the same height, but here stood the darker Prince Alexi quite helpless and humble before the Prince who was striding back and forth before the fire, his face cold and merciless and slightly agitated. Prince Alexi's organ was rigid. He held his hands behind his neck.

"So you were not ready for me!" the Prince whispered. He drew closer, inspecting Prince Alexi. He looked at the stiffened organ and then with his hand he gave it a rough slap, so that Prince Alexi flinched in spite of himself. "Perhaps you need a little training in being . . . always . . . ready," whispered the Prince. His words came slowly and with a deliberate courtesy.

He lifted Prince Alexi's chin and looked into his eyes. Beauty caught herself staring at them both without the slightest shyness.

"My apologies, your Highness," Prince Alexi said, and his voice was low in timbre, calm, without rebellion or shame.

The Prince's lips spread slowly in a smile. Prince Alexi's eyes were larger, and they possessed the same calm as the voice. It seemed to Beauty they might even drain away the Prince's anger but this was impossible.

The Prince stroked Prince Alexi's organ and gave it another playful slap, and then another.

The submissive Prince looked down again and there was nothing in him but the grace and dignity Beauty had witnessed before.

"I must behave like this," she thought. "I must have this manner, this strength, to bear it all with the same dignity." Yet she marveled. The captive Prince must at all times show his desire, his fascination, while she could conceal this craving between her legs, and she could not stop herself from wincing as she saw the Prince pinch the tiny hardened nipples on Prince Alexi's chest, and then lift Prince Alexi's chin again to inspect his face.

Beyond them, Squire Felix watched all with obvious pleasure. He had folded his arms, his legs rather wide apart as he stood, and his eyes moved hungrily over Prince Alexi's body.

"How long have you been in the service of my mother?" the Prince demanded.

"Two years, your Highness," said the humble Prince softly. Beauty was quite astonished. Two years! It seemed to her all of her life before had not been so long, but she was more rapt with the sound of his voice than with the words. The voice made him seem more palpable and visible.

His body was a little thicker than that of the Prince, and the dark brown hair between his legs was beautiful. She could see the scrotum, no more than a shadow.

"You were sent here in Tribute by your father."

"As your mother demanded, your Highness."

"And to serve how many years?"

"As long as it pleases your Highness, and my mistress, the Queen," Prince Alexi answered.

"And you are what? Nineteen? And a model among the other Tributes?"

Prince Alexi blushed.

The Prince turned him towards Beauty with a rough blow on the shoulder, and steered him towards the bed.

Beauty drew herself up, feeling her face flushed and warm.

"And the favorite of my mother?" the Prince demanded.

"Not tonight, your Highness," Prince Alexi said with the barest trace of a smile.

The Prince acknowledged this with a soft laugh. "No, you have not comported yourself very well today, have you?"

"I can only beg forgiveness, your Highness," said Prince Alexi.

"You can do more than that," said the Prince into his ear as he pushed him nearer to Beauty. "You can suffer for it. And you can give my Beauty a lesson in willingness and perfect submission."

Now the Prince turned his gaze on Beauty, scrutinizing her mercilessly. She looked down, terrified of displeasing him.

"Look at Prince Alexi," he told her, and when she raised her eyes, she saw the beautiful captive Prince only a few inches from her. His disheveled hair partially veiled his face, and his skin appeared deliciously smooth to her. She was trembling.

Just as she feared he would, the Prince lifted Prince Alexi's chin again, and when Prince Alexi looked at her with his large brown eyes, he smiled very slowly and serenely at her for an instant the Prince could not have witnessed. Beauty drank her fill of him with her eyes because she had no choice and hoped the Prince would see no more than her distress.

"Kiss my new slave and welcome her to this house. Kiss her lips and her breasts," said the Prince. And he lifted Prince Alexi's hands from the back of his neck so they went silently and obediently to his sides.

Beauty gasped. Prince Alexi was smiling at her again, secretly as his shadow fell over her, and she felt his lips close over hers and the shock of his kiss pass through her. She could feel that misery between her legs formed into a tight knot, and when his lips touched her left breast and then her right, she bit into her lower lip so hard she might have drawn blood. Prince Alexi's hair stroked her cheek and her breasts as he carried out the command and then he stood back with that same beguiling equanimity.

Beauty put her hands to her face before she could stop herself.

But immediately the Prince took them away.

"Look well, Beauty. Study this example of the obedient slave. Become accustomed to him so that you do not see him but rather the example he sets for you," the Prince said. And roughly he turned Prince Alexi about so that Beauty could see the red marks on his buttocks.

Prince Alexi had received far worse punishment than Beauty. He was bruised and there were many white and pink welts on his thighs and on his calves. The Prince inspected all this almost indifferently.

"You will not look away again," the Prince said to Beauty, "do you understand me?"

"Yes, my Prince," Beauty said at once, only too eager to show her obedience, and in the very midst of her painful distress, an odd feeling of resignation came over her. She must look at Prince Alexi's exquisitely muscled young body; she must look at his taut and beautifully molded buttocks. If only she could hide her fascination, feign only submission.

But the Prince was no longer looking at her. He had taken both Prince Alexi's wrists in his left hand, and had taken from Squire Felix not the golden paddle, but rather a long flat leather-sheathed stick which appeared heavy and with which he struck Alexi several loud blows on his calves rapidly.

He pulled his captive to the center of the room. He placed his foot on the wrung of the stool as he had done earlier, and pushed Prince Alexi over his knee just as he had done Beauty. Prince Alexi's back was to Beauty and she could see not only his buttocks but also the scrotum between his legs, and she saw the flat leather stick land its blows in red crisscrossed marks over Prince Alexi. Prince Alexi did not struggle. He made hardly a sound. His feet were planted on the floor, and nothing in his form suggested any attempt to escape the aim of the stick as Beauty might.

Yet even as she watched, amazed, wondering at his control and his endurance, she could see the signs of strain in him. He moved ever so slightly, his buttocks rising and falling, his legs quivering and then she could hear the slightest sound from him, a whispered moan which he was obviously concealing behind his closed lips. The Prince flailed at him, the skin growing a darker red with each broad stripe from the stick, and then, when his desire seemed to have reached a crest, he ordered Prince Alexi down on his hands and knees before him.

Beauty could see Prince Alexi's face. It was stained with tears, but the composure had not broken. He knelt before the Prince, waiting.

The Prince lifted his pointed boot and thrust it under Prince Alexi, touching the tip of Prince Alexi's penis.

Then he took Prince Alexi by the hair and lifted his head.

"Open it," he said softly.

Immediately Prince Alexi moved to put his lips to the seam in the Prince's breeches. With a skill that amazed Beauty he unsnapped the hooks that concealed the Prince's bulging sex, and revealed it. The organ was enlarged and hardened, and Prince Alexi freed it from the cloth now and tenderly kissed it. But he was in great pain still and when the Prince thrust the organ into Prince Alexi's mouth he was not prepared for it. He fell backwards a little on his knees and had to reach for the Prince, caressingly, to stop himself from falling. But immediately he sucked the Prince's organ, and he did it with great back and forth motions that amazed Beauty, his eyes closed, his hands hovering at his sides ready for the Prince's command.

The Prince stopped him rather quickly. It was clear he did not want his passion brought to a pinnacle. Nothing so simple would happen.

"Go to the chest in the corner," he said to Prince Alexi, "and bring me the ring that is in it."

Prince Alexi went on his hands and knees to obey. But obviously the Prince wasn't satisfied. He snapped his finger, and Squire Felix at once drove Prince Alexi with his paddle. He drove him to the chest and continued to torment him with the paddle while he opened the chest and with his teeth removed a large leather ring and brought it back to the Prince.

Only then did the Prince send Squire Felix back to his corner, and Prince Alexi was out of breath and trembling.

"Put it on," said the Prince.

Prince Alexi was holding the leather ring not by the leather itself but by some small piece of gold attached to it. And still holding it this way in his teeth, he slipped the ring over the Prince's penis, but he did not release it.

"You serve me, you go where I go," said the Prince, and now he proceeded to walk slowly about the room, his hands on his hips as he looked down on the Prince struggling on his knees, his teeth to the leather ring, to follow him.

It was as if Prince Alexi were kissing the Prince or tethered to him. He scrambled backwards, his hands out so as not to touch the Prince disrespectfully.

The Prince with ordinary strides that took no cognizance of the difficulty of his slave approached the bed, and then turning, made his way back to the fire, his slave struggling before him.

Suddenly he turned his body hard to the left to face

Beauty, and when he did Prince Alexi had to take hold of him for balance. Prince Alexi clung to him for a moment and when he did, he pressed his forehead against the Prince's thigh, and the Prince rather idly stroked his hair. It seemed almost affectionate.

"You so dislike the ignominious position, don't you?" he whispered. But before Prince Alexi might have answered, he struck him a hard blow on the face that sent him backwards and away from him. Then he pushed Prince Alexi down on all fours.

"Back and forth across the room," he said with a snap of his fingers to Squire Felix.

As always, the Squire was only too happy to oblige. Beauty hated him! He drove Prince Alexi across the floor to the far wall and then back again to the door.

"Faster!" the Prince said sharply.

Prince Alexi moved as swiftly as he could. Beauty could not bear to hear the anger in the Prince's tone, and she raised her hands to cover her mouth. But the Prince wanted more speed. The paddle came down again and again on Prince Alexi's buttocks and the command came again and again until he was scurrying to obey the commands, and she could see his terrible misery that he had lost all grace and dignity. Now she understood the Prince's little taunt. Prince Alexi's calm and grace had obviously been his consolation.

But had he really lost them? Or was he merely calmly giving this too to the Prince? She couldn't tell. She winced with each spank of the paddle, and each time Prince Alexi turned to go back across the room, she caught a full glimpse of his tormented buttocks.

Quite suddenly, however, Squire Felix stopped. "I've drawn blood, your Highness," he said.

Prince Alexi knelt with his head down, panting.

The Prince looked at him and then he nodded.

He snapped his fingers for Prince Alexi to rise, and again he lifted his chin and looked into his tear-stained face.

"So you are reprieved for the night by virtue of that all too delicate skin of yours," he said.

He turned him towards Beauty again. Prince Alexi's hands were on the back of his neck, and his face, flushed and wet, was indescribably beautiful to her. It was full of unspoken emotion, and as he was led closer to her, she could feel her heart pounding. "If he kisses me again, I shall die," she thought. "I shall never hide my feelings from the Prince."

And if it is the rule that I can be spanked until he draws blood. . . . She had no real idea what that might mean, except a great deal more pain than she had already felt. But even that would be preferable to the Prince discovering how fascinated she remained with Prince Alexi. "Why does he do this," she thought desperately.

But the Prince thrust Prince Alexi forward.

"Put your face in her lap," he said, "and your arms about her."

Beauty gasped and sat up, but Prince Alexi obeyed immediately. Beauty looked down to see his auburn hair covering her sex as she felt his lips against her thighs, and his arms enclose her. His body was hot and pulsing; she could feel the beating of his heart, and without meaning to, she reached out to clasp his hips with her hands.

The Prince kicked Prince Alexi's legs wide apart and taking Beauty's head roughly in his left hand so that he might kiss her, he drove his organ into Prince Alexi's anus.

Prince Alexi moaned at the roughness and swiftness of the thrusts. Beauty felt the pressure against her as Prince Alexi was driven ever more quickly by it. The Prince had let her go, and she was crying. She held tight to Prince Alexi, and then the Prince gave his final thrust with a moan, his hands pressed to Prince Alexi's back, and he stood still letting his pleasure course through him.

Beauty tried to keep herself quiet.

Prince Alexi let her go, but not without a secret little kiss between her legs right on the crest of her pubic hair, and just as he was being drawn away, again, his dark eyes narrowed in a secret smile for her.

"Mount him in the passage," said the Prince to the Squire. "And see no one satisfies him. Keep him in torment. Every quarter of the hour remind him of his duty to his Prince, but do not satisfy him."

Prince Alexi was taken away.

Beauty sat staring at the open door.

But it was not over. The Prince reached out and taking her by the hair, told her to follow him.

"On your hands and knees, my dear. That is always the way you will move through the castle," he said, "unless told otherwise."

She hurried along, following him out and to the edge of the stairway.

Halfway down was a broad landing from which one might see directly into the Great Hall.

And on the landing was a stone statue that frightened Beauty. It was a pagan god of some sort with an erect phallus.

It was onto this phallus that Prince Alexi was now thrust, his legs bound apart on the pedestal of the statue. His head was laid back on the statue's shoulder. He gave another moan as the phallus impaled him and then he lay still as Squire Felix bound his hands behind his back.

The statue's right arm was upraised, the stone fingers of the hand forming a circle as if they had once clasped a knife or some other instrument. And now the Squire carefully positioned Prince Alexi's head on the shoulder of the statue beneath that hand. And through the clasped hand, he placed a leather phallus, anchoring it so that it fit into Prince Alexi's mouth.

It seemed now that the statue raped him both through his anus and through his mouth, and he was bound to it. And his organ, as stiff as before, lay thrust forward as the phallus of the statue was inside of him.

"Now you are perhaps a little more used to your Prince Alexi," said the Prince softly.

"But this is too terrible," Beauty thought, "that he must spend the night in this misery." Prince Alexi's back was painfully arched, his legs bound wide apart, and the moonlight from the window behind him made a long line down his throat, his smooth chest and his flat belly.

The Prince tugged gently on Beauty's hair which he held wrapped around his right hand and leading her back to bed, he laid her down and told her to sleep, as he would soon be doing beside her.

PRINCE
ALEXI
AND
FELIX

I<small>T WAS</small> almost dawn. The Prince lay deep asleep. And Beauty who had been waiting for his heavy sleeping breaths, slipped out of the bed, and on all fours, out of stealth, not obedience, crept into the corridor. She had lain for a long time looking at the door, seeing that it had never been really shut, and she might make her small escape without noise if she only had the courage.

She crept to the top of the steps.

The light fell full on Prince Alexi, and she could see that his organ was rigid as before, and Squire Felix was talking to him, softly. She could not hear what the Squire said, but she was furious to see him awake. She had hoped that he too would now be sleeping.

And as she watched, quite unknown to Squire Felix, she saw him come round in front of Prince Alexi, and torment the organ again with a volley of slaps that sounded very loud in the empty stairwell. The captive Prince gave a little moan, and Beauty could see his chest heave with his breath.

Squire Felix walked back and forth restlessly. Then he looked at the Prince, and it seemed he turned his head from left to right as though listening. Beauty held her breath. She was terrified she might be discovered.

Squire Felix drew near to Prince Alexi and putting his arms around his hips, he covered Prince Alexi's organ with his mouth and began sucking it.

Beauty was beside herself with frustration and anger. This was just what she had meant to do. She had imagined herself braving all dangers to do it. And now she was forced to watch as Squire Felix tormented the poor Prince. But to her surprise, Squire Felix was not merely tantalizing Prince Alexi. Squire Felix seemed quite in earnest. He was ravaging the organ with a regular rhythm and Beauty knew from the moans that Prince Alexi couldn't conceal he was now reaching the climax of his passion.

His taut, cruelly bound body shuddered with one protracted groan after another, and then he lay still as Squire Felix drew back and moved into the shadows.

It seemed he spoke to Prince Alexi then. Beauty leaned her head against the stone balustrade.

After a little while, Squire Felix told Prince Alexi to wake, and he gave the organ those tormenting slaps again and when it seemed reluctant, Squire Felix seemed fearful and became threatening. But Prince Alexi was deep asleep in his painful tethers, and Beauty was very pleased to see this.

She turned and silently made her way back to the bedroom door when she realized that someone was near her.

She was so frightened that she almost screamed, a mistake which would surely have destroyed her. But she covered her mouth, and lifting her eyes, she saw in the distant shadows the figure of Lord Gregory watching her. This was the gray-haired Lord who had wanted so to discipline her properly, who had called her spoilt.

Yet he did not move. He stood still watching her.

And when she had stopped trembling, she rushed as quickly as she could back to the Prince's bed, and slipped under the coverlet beside him.

He had never awakened.

She lay in the dark waiting for Lord Gregory to come but he did not, and she soon realized he would not dream of waking the Prince, and then she was half dozing.

She was thinking of Prince Alexi in a thousand ways, of the redness of his sore flesh after the paddle, of his beautiful brown eyes, and his strong, somewhat compact body. She was thinking of his glossy hair against her, the secret kiss he gave her thighs, and how, after this terrible humiliation, he had given her that smile which was so serene and affectionate.

The torment between her legs was no worse than before, and no better. She dared not touch it with her fingers, lest she be discovered, and it was too shameful to think of such things, and she was sure the Prince would never allow it.

THE SLAVES' HALL

I T WAS late afternoon when Beauty awoke. She realized that the Prince and Lord Gregory were in an argument. Immediately, she was afraid, but as she lay still she perceived that Lord Gregory had obviously not told the Prince what he had seen. Surely her punishment would be terrible if he had. Rather Lord Gregory was arguing only that Beauty must be taken to the Slaves' Hall and properly groomed.

"Your Highness, you are enamored of her, of course," Lord Gregory said, "but you remember, surely, your own censure of other Lords, especially your cousin, Lord Stefan, on account of his excessive love for his slave . . ."

"It is not excessive love," the Prince answered sharply, but then he stopped as if Lord Gregory had hit upon the truth. "Maybe you should take her to the Slaves' Hall," he murmured, "though only for the day."

As soon as Lord Gregory had taken her out of the room, he unfastened the paddle attached to his belt and gave her several cruel spanks as she hurried on her hands and knees before him.

"Keep your eyes down and your head down," he said coldly, "and lift your knees gracefully. Your back is to be a straight line at all times, and you are not to look to either side, is this clear to you?"

"Yes, my Lord," Beauty answered timidly. She could see a great expanse of stone before her, and though the paddle smacks had not been very hard, she found she resented them enormously. They had not come from the Prince. And it was just coming to her that now she was in Lord Gregory's power. Perhaps she'd fancied he couldn't strike her, wouldn't be allowed to, but that was obviously not the case, and she realized he might tell the Prince she had disobeyed when she had not, and she might not be allowed to speak for herself.

"Move faster," he told her. "You are always to take a rapid pace showing your eagerness to please your Lords and Ladies," he said, and again there came one of those sharp degrading little spanks that seemed suddenly quite worse than harder ones.

They had come to a narrow doorway and Beauty perceived that a long curving ramp lay before her. It was quite clever as she could not have gone down a staircase on her hands and knees, but this she could follow, and she did with Lord Gregory's pointed leather boots right beside her.

Several times he availed himself of the paddle, so that by the time they reached the door of a vast room on the lower floor, her buttocks were burning a little.

But what concerned her much more was that there were people here.

She had seen no one in the passage above. And she felt torturously shy as she realized that there were many people in this hall moving about and talking to one another.

Now she was told to sit up and back on her heels, with her hands clasped to the back of her neck.

"This will always be your position when you are told to rest," Lord Gregory said, "and keep your eyes down."

Yet even as she obeyed this command, she could see what the room was. There were deep shelves cut into the walls all along three sides of it, and on these shelves, on pallets, slept the many slaves, both male and female.

But she could not see Prince Alexi.

She did see a beautiful black-haired girl with very plump little buttocks who appeared quite deep sleep, and a blond-haired young man who appeared to be strapped on his back, though she could not tell, and others, all of whom were in a drowsy state, if not dozing.

And before her were many tables in a row, and among them pots of steaming water from which came a delicious fragrance.

"This is where you will be bathed and groomed always," said Lord Gregory in that same cold voice, "and when the Prince has had quite enough of sleeping with you as though you were his love, you shall sleep here too, and at any time when the Prince has no specific orders for you. Your groom is named Leon. He will care for you in all details, and to him you shall show the same respect and obedience you show to everyone."

Beauty saw before her the slender figure of a young man, directly beside Lord Gregory. And as he drew nearer, Lord Gregory snapped his fingers and told her to show her respect.

At once Beauty kissed his boots.

"To the lowest scullery maid you owe this respect," Lord Gregory said, "and should I ever detect the slightest haughtiness in you, I shall punish you severely. I am not as . . . shall we say, impressed with you as is your Prince."

"Yes, my Lord," Beauty answered respectfully, but she was angry. She felt she had shown no haughtiness.

But Leon's voice calmed her immediately. "Come, my dear," he said, gesturing with a pat of his hand against his thigh for her to follow him, and it seemed Lord Gregory disappeared as Leon led her into a brick-lined alcove where a large wooden tub stood steaming. The scent of the herbs was very strong.

Leon gestured for her to rise up again, and taking her hands, he lifted them over her head and told her to kneel in the tub.

She climbed into it at once and felt the delicious warm water come almost up to her sex. Leon wrapped her hair in a circle on the back of her head and fixed it with several pins. She could see him clearly now. He was older than the Page boys, but just as fair, and his hazel eyes were very appealing in their gentleness. He told her to keep her hands behind her neck and that he was going to give her a thorough cleansing and that she must enjoy it.

"Are you very tired?" he asked her.

"Not so tired, my . . ."

"My Lord will do," he said with a smile. "Even the lowliest stable boy is your Lord, Beauty," he said, "and you must always answer respectfully."

"Yes, my Lord," she whispered.

He was already bathing her, and the warm water washing down her did feel very good to her. He lathered her neck and her arms.

"Have you just awakened?"

"Yes, my Lord," she said.

"I see, but you must be tired from your long journey. The first few days slaves are always overexcited. They don't feel their exhaustion, and then after that they begin to sleep for many hours. You'll feel it soon, and there will be an aching in your arms and legs, too. I don't mean from your punishment. I mean only from your fatigue. When that happens I'll massage you and soothe you."

His voice was so gentle that Beauty warmed to him at once. His sleeves were rolled to the elbows and there was golden hair on his arms, and his fingers were very sure as he washed her ears and her face, careful not to get the soap in her eyes.

"And you have been punished very severely, haven't you?"

Beauty blushed.

He laughed softly.

"Very good, my dear, you are learning already. Never answer such a question as that. It could be taken as a complaint if you did. Any time you are asked if you have been punished too much or suffered too much, or anything of that sort, be clever enough to blush."

But even as he spoke almost affectionately, he began washing her breasts just as calmly as he had washed the rest of her, and Beauty's blushes became more painful. She could feel her nipples harden, and she was certain though she could see nothing but the soapy water before her, that he was noticing this, as his hands slowed slightly, and then he pushed at her inner thigh gently. "Spread your legs, dearest," he said.

She obeyed, kneeling with her legs farther apart, and then farther as he pushed her. He had become still, and now drying his hand on the towel at his waist, he touched her sex and she felt herself shudder.

Her sex was moist and swollen with her desire, and to her horror, his hand touched a small hard knot in which much of her craving was accumulated. She drew back involuntarily.

"Ah." He withdrew his fingers, and turning called to Lord Gregory.

"A very lovely flower, this," he said. "Have you observed?"

Beauty was crimson. Her eyes overflowed with tears. It took all her control not to drop her hands to cover her

(86)

sex as she felt Leon part her legs even wider now and gently touch the moisture there.

Lord Gregory gave a soft laugh.

"Yes, a truly remarkable Princess," he said. "I should have watched her more carefully."

Beauty gave a little muffled sob of shame and yet the driving desire between her legs would not stop, and her face was stinging as Lord Gregory spoke to her.

"Most of our little Princesses are too frightened in the first few days to show such willingness to serve, Beauty," he said in the same cold voice. "They must be awakened and educated. But I see you are very passionate and much enamored of your new masters and all they wish to teach you."

Beauty struggled against her tears. This was more humiliating surely than anything that had happened to her.

And now Lord Gregory was taking her chin as the Prince had taken Prince Alexi's chin and forcing her to look at him.

"Beauty, this is a great virtue in you. You have no cause to be ashamed. It only means that you must learn yet another form of discipline. You are awakened to the desires of your master as you should be, but you must learn to control that desire just as you see the male slaves control it."

"Yes, my Lord," Beauty whispered.

Leon withdrew and a moment later he returned with a small white tray on which were laid several little objects Beauty could not see.

But to her terror, Lord Gregory parted her legs and affixed to that little hard kernel of tormented flesh a plaster of sorts that covered it and adhered to it. He shaped it quickly with his fingers as if he did not wish to have Beauty enjoy this.

And Beauty was all the more relieved, for had she felt the ultimate pleasure, had she commenced to shudder and to blush with the final release from this torment, she would have been absolutely mortified.

But now the little plaster gave her an added torment. What could it mean?

It seemed Lord Gregory read her thoughts.

"That will prevent you from all too easily satisfying your newfound and undisciplined desire, Beauty. It will not alleviate it. It will merely prevent, shall we say, *accidental* release, until you have gained the proper control of yourself. I had not thought to commence this detailed instruction so soon, but I shall tell you now that you are never allowed to experience full pleasure save at the whims of your master or mistress. Never, never, must you be caught touching your private parts with your own hands, nor trying more secretly to alleviate your obvious . . . misery."

"Well-chosen words," Beauty thought, "for all his coldness to me."

But he was immediately gone, and once more Leon was bathing her.

"Don't be so frightened and so ashamed," he said. "You don't realize what a great advantage it is. To be taught to feel such pleasure is very difficult, and far more humiliating. And your passion gives a bloom to you that cannot be achieved otherwise."

Beauty cried softly. The little plaster between her legs made her all the more conscious of her feelings there. Yet Leon's hands and voice were soothing her.

Finally he told her she must lie down in the bath and he must wash her long beautiful hair for her. She let the warm water close over her and thought for a moment that she was covered by it and that felt extremely good to her.

As soon as she had been rinsed and dried, Beauty was put down on one of the beds nearby, and arranged on her face so that Leon could rub an aromatic oil into her skin.

It felt delicious to her.

"Now, surely," he said as he was massaging her shoulders, "there must be questions that you should like to ask me. You may do that if you like. It is not good for you to be confused about things unnecessarily. There is enough for you to fear without fears that are imaginary."

"I may . . . talk to you then?" Beauty asked.

"Yes," he said. "I'm your groom. In a way, I belong to you. Each slave, no matter how he or she ranks or pleases or displeases, has a groom, and that groom is devoted to that slave, to that slave's needs and wishes, as well as preparing the slave for the master. Now, of course, there will be times when I shall have to punish you, not because I take pleasure in it, though I can't imagine punishing a more beautiful slave than you, but because your master may order it. He may order you punished for disobedience, or merely readied for him with some blows. But I will be doing it only because I have to . . ."

"But do you . . . do you take pleasure in it?" Beauty asked timidly.

"It is difficult to resist beauty such as yours," he said, rubbing the oil into the backs of her arms and into the crevices of her elbows. "But I should much rather groom you and care for you." He put down the oil and gave her hair another brisk rub with the towel, adjusting the pillow under her face.

It felt so good to be lying here, with his hands working on her.

"But as I was saying before, you may ask me questions when I give you leave. Remember, when I give you leave, and I have just given it."

"I don't know what to ask," she whispered. "There is so much to ask . . ."

"Well, surely you must know already that all punishments here are for the pleasure of your masters and mistresses . . ."

"Yes."

"And that nothing shall ever be done which truly

harms you. You will never be burned, nor cut, nor *injured*," he said.

"Ah, that is a great relief," Beauty said, but in truth she had understood these limits without being told. "But the other slaves," she asked. "Are they here for various reasons?"

"Sent as Tributes mostly," Leon answered. "Our Queen is very powerful and commands many allies. And of course, all Tributes are well fed, well guarded, well treated just as you are well treated."

"And . . . what happens to them?" Beauty asked tentatively. "I mean, they are all young and . . ."

"They're returned to their Kingdoms when the Queen so wishes, and obviously very much better off for their service here. They're not so vain any longer, they have great self-control, and often a different view of the world, one which enables them to achieve great understanding."

Beauty could scarcely guess what this meant. Leon massaged the oil into her sore calves and the tender flesh behind her knees. She felt drowsy. The sensation was growing ever more delicious, and she resisted it slightly, unwilling to let that craving between her legs torment her. Leon's fingers were strong, almost a little too strong, and they moved to her thighs which the Prince had reddened with his strap as much as her calves and buttocks. She shifted slightly against the soft, firm bedding. Her thoughts slowly cleared.

"Then I might be sent home," she asked, but it had no meaning for her.

"Yes, but you must never mention it, and certainly never ask for it. You are the property of your Prince. You are his slave entirely."

"Yes . . ." she whispered.

"And to beg to be released would be a terrible thing," Leon continued. "However in time you will be sent home. There are different agreements for different slaves. Do you see that Princess there?"

In a great hollow in the wall, on a shelf-like bed, lay

a dark-haired girl whom Beauty had noticed. She had olive skin, richer in tone than that of Prince Alexi who was also dark, and her hair was so long it lay in rippling strands over her buttocks. She slept with her face to the room, her mouth slightly open on the flat pillow.

"Now, she is Princess Eugenia," said Leon, "and she must be returned in two years by agreement. Her time is almost up and she is broken-hearted. She wants to remain on the condition that her continued slavery will save two slaves from having to come here. Her Kingdom might agree to these terms to keep back two other Princesses."

"You mean she wants to stay?"

"O yes," Leon said. "She is mad for Lord William, the Queen's eldest cousin, and can't bear the thought of being sent home. But there are others who are ever rebellious."

"Who are they?" Beauty asked, but before he could answer, she added quickly, though trying to sound indifferent, "Is Prince Alexi one of those who is rebellious?"

She could feel Leon's hand moving towards her buttocks, and now suddenly all those welts and sore places were brought to life as his fingers touched them. The oil burned slightly as Leon added droplets of it generously, and then those strong fingers commenced to work the flesh, with no regard for its redness. Beauty winced, but even this pain had its pleasure. She felt her buttocks shaped by his hands, lifted, separated, and then smoothed again. She blushed to think that it was Leon doing this who had been talking to her in such a civilized manner, and when his voice went on, she felt a new variant of agitation. "There is no end to it," she thought, "the ways of being humiliated."

"Prince Alexi is the Queen's favorite," said Leon. "The Queen cannot bear to be separated from him for very long, and though he is a model of good behavior and devotion, he is, in his own way, relentlessly rebellious."

"But how can that be?" Beauty asked.

"Ah, you must put your mind on the pleasing of your Lords and Ladies," Leon said, "but I shall say this: Prince Alexi appears to have surrendered his will as a fine slave must, but there is a core in Prince Alexi that no one touches."

Beauty was enthralled by this answer. She thought of Prince Alexi on his hands and knees, his strong back and the curve of his buttocks as he had been driven back and forth across the Prince's bedroom; she thought of the beauty of his face. "A core in him no one touches," she mused.

But Leon had turned her over now, and when she saw him bending down, so close to her, she felt bashful and closed her eyes. He was rubbing the oil into her belly and into her legs, and she pressed her legs together and tried to turn to the side.

"You'll become very accustomed to my ministrations, Princess," he said. "You will think nothing of being groomed in time." And firmly he pressed her shoulders to the pallet. His swift fingers smoothed the oil into her throat and into her arms.

Beauty opened her eyes cautiously to see him intent on his work. His pale eyes moved over her without passion but with an obvious absorption.

"Do you . . . derive pleasure from it?" she whispered, and was shocked to hear herself speak these words.

He emptied some oil into the palm of his left hand, and putting the bottle down beside him, he rubbed the oil into her breasts, lifting them and squeezing them as he had done her buttocks. She closed her eyes again, biting her lip. She felt him roughly massaging her nipples. She almost let out a little cry.

"Be still, my dear," he said matter-of-factly. "Your nipples are tender and must be slightly toughened. You've been subjected to very little sport so far from your love-stricken master."

Beauty was frightened by this. Her nipples felt painfully hard to her; she knew her face had colored darkly. It seemed all the feeling in her breasts swelled and pumped towards those tiny hard nipples.

Mercifully, Leon let go of her breasts with a hard squeeze. But then he parted her legs and rubbed the oil into her inner thighs, and this was even worse for her. She could feel her sex throbbing. She wondered if it gave off heat that he could feel with his hands.

She hoped he would be quick.

Yet even as she lay, red faced and trembling, he pushed her legs farther apart, and to her horror, parted the lips of her sex with his fingers as though inspecting her.

"O, please . . ." she whispered, turning her head from side to side, her eyes stinging.

"Now Beauty," he scolded gently, "you must never never plead for anything from anyone, not even from your loyal and devoted groom. I must inspect you to see if you are sore, and as I thought, you are. Your Prince has been rather . . . devoted."

Beauty bit her lip and closed her eyes as he widened the orifice and now oiled it. She felt as if she were being pulled apart, and even under the plaster that tiny knot of feeling throbbed above the opening Leon's fingers had broadened. "If he touches it, I shall die," she thought, but he was quite careful not to do that, though she felt his fingers entering her, and massaging the lips of her vagina.

"Poor darling slave," he whispered to her with feeling. "Now sit up. If I were to have my way, you would rest. But Lord Gregory wants you to see the rest of the Training Hall and the Hall of Punishments. Let me finish your hair quickly."

He began to brush Beauty's hair and arrange it in coils on the back of her head as she sat, still trembling, her knees drawn up, and her head bowed.

THE
TRAINING
HALL

BEAUTY WASN'T certain that she hated Lord Gregory. Perhaps there was something comforting in his air of command. What would it be like to be here without someone who directed her so completely? But he appeared obsessed with his duties.

As soon as he took her out of Leon's hands, he gave her two gratuitous blows with the paddle before ordering her to her knees and to follow him. She was to keep close to the heel of his right boot, and she was to observe all that was around her.

"But you must never look at the faces of your masters and mistresses, you must never try to meet their eyes, and there is not to be a sound out of you," he directed, "save your answers to me."

"Yes, Lord Gregory," she whispered. The stone floor beneath her was swept very clean and polished, but it hurt her knees nevertheless because it was stone. Yet she followed him at once past the other beds on which slaves were being groomed, and the baths in which two young men were being bathed, just as she had been bathed, their eyes flashing over her with mild curiosity as she risked a glance at each of them.

"All handsome," she mused.

But when a stunningly beautiful young woman was driven across her path, she felt a hot flush of jealousy. This was a girl with a mane of silvery hair much fuller and curlier than Beauty's, and as she was on her knees, her huge and magnificent breasts hung down showing their large pink nipples to great advantage. The Page who drove her with the paddle seemed very engaged with her, laughing at her little cries, and forcing her to move faster with the force of his blows as well as the mocking and cheerful commands he gave her.

Lord Gregory paused as if he, too, enjoyed the sight of this girl as she was brought up, and into the bath, her legs forced apart as Beauty's had been. Beauty could not help but notice her breasts again, and how large were the pink nipples. The girl's hips were ample for her size, and to Beauty's amazement, she was not really crying as she was lowered into the water. Her moans were more complaints as the paddle still smacked her.

Lord Gregory made some approving sound. "Lovely," he said so that Beauty could hear him. "And three months ago she was as wild and untamed as a nymph from the forest. The transformation is quite exquisite."

Lord Gregory turned sharply to his left and when Beauty did not at once realize it, he gave her a sound spank and then another.

"Now, Beauty," Lord Gregory said, as they passed through a doorway into a long room, "do you wonder how others are trained to show the passion you exhibit with such abandon?"

Beauty knew her cheeks were crimson. She could not bring herself to answer.

The room was dimly lit by a nearby fire, but its doors were open to the garden. And here Beauty saw that many captives were positioned on tables as she had been in the Great Hall, each with a Page in attendance. And all the Pages worked diligently taking no note of cries or commotion at any other table.

Several young men knelt with their hands strapped behind them. They were paddled steadily while at the same time their penises were also being given pleasure. Here a Page stroked the engorged penis as he worked the paddle. Here two Pages attended the same Prince mercilessly.

Beauty could understand what was happening even when Lord Gregory did not explain it to her. She saw the confusion and misery of the young Princes, their faces caught between struggle and surrender. The Prince nearest her was on all fours, his penis tormented slowly. As soon as the paddling commenced, he went soft. So the paddling ceased, and the hands attended to him again, hardening him.

Along the walls were other Princes, spread-eagled, their ankles and wrists bound to the bricks, their organs being taught obedience with touching and kisses and suckling.

"O, it is worse for them, much worse," Beauty thought, but her eyes and her mind were too filled with their exquisite endowments. She looked at the rounded buttocks of those made to kneel; she loved their polished chests, the lean muscularity of their limbs, and above all, perhaps, the nobility of suffering in their handsome faces. She thought of Prince Alexi again and she wanted to shower him with kisses. She wanted to kiss his eyelids and the nipples of his chest; she wanted to suckle his organ.

Now she saw a young Prince brought over on his hands and knees to suck the penis of another. And as he performed the act with great enthusiasm, he in turn was paddled by the Page who seemed, as all others, to take delight in inflicting torment. The Prince's eyes were closed, he drew on the powerful sex of the other with long caresses of his lips, his own buttocks flinching with each blow, and as the poor Prince whom he suckled seemed on the edge of culminating passion, the suckler was pulled back by the Page who took his obedient slave to yet another erect penis.

"Here, as you can see, the young slave Princes are taught their manners," Lord Gregory said, "to be ever in readiness for their masters and mistresses. A hard lesson to learn and one which you are, in general, spared. It is not that readiness isn't required of you; it is that you are spared having to make such a display of it."

He led her on closer to the female slaves who were being worked in a different manner. Here Beauty saw a lovely red-haired Princess with her legs held apart by two Pages who with their hands massaged that little nodule between her legs. Her hips rose and fell; it was clear she could not control her own movement. She begged to be allowed peace, and just as her face flushed and it seemed she could not control herself, she was let alone, legs held apart so that she groaned miserably.

Another very lovely girl was being spanked and stroked at the same time by a Page who used his left hand between her legs to work her.

And to Beauty's horror several were mounted on phalluses against the wall on which they worked themselves with wild contortions while the Pages in attendance wielded merciless paddles.

"You see each slave receives simple instructions. She is to work herself on the phallus until she achieves satisfaction. Only then will the paddling cease, no matter how sore she is. She soon learns to think of the paddle and pleasure as one in the same, and she soon learns to achieve her pleasure in spite of the paddle. Or on command, I should say. Of course she shall seldom be allowed such satisfaction by her masters and mistresses."

Beauty gazed at the row of struggling bodies. The girls' hands were bound over their heads, their feet below. They had little room for moving on the leather phalluses. They twisted, trying to undulate as best they could, the inevitable tears spilling down their faces. Beauty felt pity for them, yet she so craved the phallus. She knew with deep shame it would not have taken her long to please the Page paddling her. As she watched the nearest Princess, a girl with red ringlets, she saw her finally achieve her goal, her face blood red, her whole body gone to violent quivering. The Page spanked her all the harder. She went limp finally as though too weary to feel shame, and the Page gave her a gentle approving pat and left her.

Everywhere Beauty looked she saw some form of training.

Here a young girl with hands clasped above her head was being taught to kneel still while her private parts were stroked and not to put her hands down to cover herself. Another was being forced to feed her breasts to the Page who suckled them, holding them for him while yet another examined her. Lessons in control, lessons in pain and pleasure.

The voices of the Pages were some of them stern, some of them tender, the dull whacking of the paddle everywhere. And there were the inevitable spread-eagled girls being now and then tormented to awaken them and teach them what they could feel if they did not know it.

"But for our little Beauty such lessons are not necessary," Lord Gregory said. "She is too accomplished as it is. And perhaps she should see the Hall of Punishments, how those disobedient slaves are chastised using the very pleasure they have learned to feel here."

THE
HALL
OF
PUNISH-
MENTS

A̲ᴛ ᴛʜᴇ door of the new
hall, Lord Gregory signaled one of the busy Pages.

"Bring Princess Lizetta here," he said raising his voice
slightly. "Sit back on your heels, Beauty, with your hands
behind your neck and observe all that's presented for your
benefit."

The unfortunate Princess Lizetta was apparently just
being brought in, and Beauty saw at once that she
was gagged but rather simply so. A small cylinder covered with leather and shaped like a dog's bone was forced
into her mouth and back so far between her teeth that
it was rather like a bit, and apparently she could not

have dislodged it with her tongue if she had wanted to.

She was crying angrily and kicking, as the Page who held her hands behind her back gestured for yet another Page to take her about the waist and carry her to Lord Gregory.

She was placed on her knees right before Beauty, her black hair falling down in front of her face, her dark breasts heaving.

"Petulance, my Lord," said the Page rather wearily. "She was to be quarry in the Hunt in the Maze when she refused to give her Lords and Ladies good sport. The usual nonsense."

Princess Lizetta tossed her black hair over her shoulder and let out a little contemptuous growl from behind the gag, which astonished Beauty.

"Ah, and impudence as well," said Lord Gregory. He reached down and lifted her chin. Her dark eyes evinced nothing but anger as she looked up at him and she turned her head so sharply that she was soon free of him.

The Page gave her several hard spanks but she showed no contrition. Her little buttocks looked hard in fact.

"Double her, for punishment," said Lord Gregory. "I think a real punishment is in order."

Princess Lizetta gave several high-pitched groans. They seemed both anger and protest. She seemed not to have bargained for this, and as she was carried ahead of Beauty and Lord Gregory into the Hall of Punishments, the Pages quickly affixed leather cuffs to her wrists and ankles, each cuff with a heavy metal hook imbedded in it.

Now she was raised, struggling, to a great low beam that spanned the room, her wrists hung from a hook above her head and then her legs brought straight up in front of her so that her ankles were fixed to the same hook. She was, in fact, bent double. Her head was then forced between her calves, so that Beauty could see her face clearly. And a leather strap was bound around her, securely pressing her upturned legs against her torso.

But the most cruel and frightening aspect of it for Beauty was the exposure of the Princess's secret parts, for she was hung so that anyone could see her full sex with its pink lips and its dark hair even to the tiny brown orifice between her buttocks. And all this just below her scarlet face. Beauty could imagine no worse exposure and she looked down timidly, glancing up again and again to the girl whose suspended body moved slightly as with a current in the air, the leather links at her wrists and ankles creaking.

But she was not alone. Beauty realized that only yards away, other doubled bodies hung from the same beam just as helplessly.

Princess Lizetta's face remained colored with rage, but she had quieted somewhat and now she turned and tried to conceal her expression against her leg, but the Page nearby adjusted her face forward.

Quickly Beauty looked at the others.

Not very far to the right a young man was mounted in the very same fashion. He appeared very young, no more than sixteen at best, and he was blond with curly hair, and his pubic hair was slightly reddish. His organ was erect, its tip glossy, and there exposed to all the world was his scrotum and again the tiny opening of his anus.

There were more of them, another young Princess and another Prince, but these first two engaged Beauty completely.

The blond Prince was moaning painfully. His eyes were dry, but he appeared to struggle, to shift as he hung from the black leather manacles, and he caused his body to turn a little to the left as he did so.

A young man, meantime, looking somewhat more impressive than the Pages, and differently costumed in dark blue velvet, came down the line of doubled and manacled slaves and appeared to inspect each face and each configuration of mercilessly exposed organs.

He smoothed back the hair from the young Prince's forehead. The young Prince moaned. It seemed he tried to thrust himself forward, and this man in blue velvet stroked the Prince's penis causing the Prince to moan all the louder and more with the sound of one imploring.

Beauty bent her head but she continued to watch the man in velvet as he approached the Princess Lizetta.

"Stubborn one, most difficult," he said to Lord Gregory.

"A day and night of punishment will subdue her," Lord Gregory answered. And Beauty was shocked to think of being exposed for so long, and so uncomfortably. She knew at once she would do anything to prevent this punishment, yet she had the terrible fear that despite all her efforts it might befall her. She at once imagined herself hung in this position, and she let out a little gasp, though she pressed her lips together to stop it.

But to her amazement, the man in velvet had begun to stroke Princess Lizetta's sex with a small instrument that was, as so much here, covered in smooth black leather. This was a three-pronged rod that somewhat resembled a hand, and as soon as he teased the helpless Princess, she began to struggle in her bonds.

Beauty understood at once what was happening. The Princess's pink sex, terrifying to Beauty as it hung so unprotected, appeared to swell, to ripen. Beauty could see tiny droplets of moisture appear on it.

And even as she watched, she felt her own sex ripening in this same manner. She felt the hard plaster that had been placed over the kernel of feeling there, and it seemed to do nothing to prevent the increased throbbing.

As soon as the helpless Princess had been so awakened, the man in velvet left her with an approving smile, and continued his movement back down the row of slaves, stopping again to tease and torment the young blond-haired Prince who without pride or dignity pleaded from behind his leather bone gag.

The Hall of Punishments

The victim beside him, another Princess, was even more abandoned in her wordless entreaties for satisfaction. Her sex was small, thick lipped, a mouth amid a thicket of brown curls, and she twisted her entire body struggling to gain some greater contact from the Lord in velvet who left her now to tease and torment yet another.

Lord Gregory snapped his fingers.

Beauty went down on her hands and knees again and followed him.

"Need I tell you that you are well-suited for that sort of punishment, Princess?" he asked.

"No, my Lord," Beauty whispered. She wondered if it was within his power to punish her this way for nothing. She longed for the Prince, and for the time when he alone had power over her. She could think of nothing but the Prince, and why had she ever displeased him by looking at Prince Alexi? Yet she had only to think of Prince Alexi and she was pitched into helpless misery. But if she could be in the Prince's arms, she would think of no one but him. She craved his tender punishment.

"Yes, my dear, you would speak?" Lord Gregory asked, but there was something ruthless in his tone.

"Only tell me how to obey, my Lord, how to please, how to avoid this discipline."

"To begin with, my precious," he said angrily, "stop admiring the male slaves so very much, staring at them at every opportunity. Don't revel so much in all I show you to frighten you!"

Beauty gasped.

"And never, never again think of Prince Alexi."

Beauty shook her head. "I will do as you say, my Lord," she said anxiously.

"And remember, the Queen is none too pleased with her son's passion for you. A thousand slaves have surrounded him ever since he was a young boy, and in none of them has he found an object of devotion such as you. The Queen does not like it."

"O, but what can I do?" Beauty cried softly.

"You can show perfect obedience to all your superiors, and do nothing to make yourself seem rebellious or unusual."

"Yes, my Lord," Beauty said.

"You know that I saw you watching Prince Alexi last night," he said, his voice now a menacing whisper.

Beauty winced. She bit her lip and tried not to cry.

"I could tell this to the Queen at any moment."

"Yes, my Lord," she gasped.

"But you are very young and lovely. And for such an offense as that you would face the most terrible punishment; you would be sent out of the castle to the village, and that would be more than you could bear . . ."

Beauty trembled. "The village"—what could this mean? But Lord Gregory continued:

"And no slave of the Queen or the Crown Prince should ever be condemned to such disgraceful punishment, and no favorite slave ever has." He took a deep breath as if to cool his anger. "And when you are properly trained, you shall be a splendid slave. And there is no reason finally why the Prince should not enjoy you, why everyone here should not enjoy you. I am here, therefore, to make something of you, not to see you destroyed."

"You are most kind and gracious, my Lord," Beauty whispered, but the words, *the village,* made their indelible impression. If only she might ask . . .

But a young Lady had come into the room, passing through the door in a great rush, her long yellow hair in thick braids, her dress a rich burgundy color trimmed in ermine. Before Beauty remembered to look down, she caught a full glimpse of the Lady with her ruddy cheeks and large brown eyes which swept the Hall of Punishments now as if searching for someone.

"O, Lord Gregory, how nice to see you," she said, and as Lord Gregory bowed, she curtsied gracefully. Beauty was stunned by her loveliness, and then overcome with her own shame and vulnerability. She stared at the Lady's pretty silver slippers and the rings on the fingers of her right hand which gathered her skirts easily.

"And how may I serve you, Lady Juliana?" asked Lord Gregory. Beauty felt desolate. She was thankful the Lady never looked at her, and then again she felt abysmal. She was nothing to this woman who was dressed and a Lady and free to do all that she pleased, while Beauty was an abject naked slave who could do nothing but kneel before her.

"Ah, but there she is, that wicked Lizetta," said the Lady, and the cheerfulness went out of her face as her lips quivered slightly. There were two little dots of color in her cheeks as she drew near the doubled Princess. "And she has been so spoilt and bad today."

"Well, she is being severely punished for it, my Lady," said Lord Gregory. "Thirty-six hours here should greatly improve her disposition."

The Lady took several delicate steps forward and peered at Princess Lizetta's exposed sex. And to Beauty's amazement, Princess Lizetta did not try to hide her face but stared into the Lady's eyes imploringly. She gave several imploring groans as clearly supplicating as the earlier moans of the Prince beside her. And as she writhed on her hook, her body rocked slightly forward.

"You're a bad girl, you are," whispered the Lady as though reproving a small child. "And you disappointed me. I had prepared the Hunt for the amusement of the Queen and chosen you specially."

Princess Lizetta's groans grew more insistent. She seemed now without hope or pride or anger. Her face was knotted and pink, and her gag looked most painful, her huge eyes flashing as they implored the Lady.

"Lord Gregory," the Lady said, "you must think of something special." Then to Beauty's horror, the lady reached out delicately and fastidiously and pinched Princess Lizetta's pubic lips hard so that they exuded moisture. Then she pinched the right lip and the left, and the girl winced with pain and misery.

Lord Gregory had meantime snapped his fingers for

the Lord with the iron clawlike hand, and whispered something Beauty could not hear. "It will strengthen her punishment."

And now the Lord appeared with a little pot and a brush and as the Lady stepped back, he took the brush and bathed Princess Lizetta's naked organ in a heavy syrup. A few droplets fell to the floor, and the Princess again made known her misery. She sobbed softly behind her gag, but the Lady only smiled rather innocently and shook her head. "It will attract any flies we have about," Lord Gregory said, "and if we have none it shall produce its inevitable itching as it dries. It is quite uncomfortable."

The Lady did not seem satisfied. Her pretty and innocent face was smooth however and she sighed. "I suppose it will do for now, but I wish she were bound with her legs apart to a stake in the garden. Then let the flies and the little insects of the air find her honeyed mouth. She deserves it."

She turned to express her thanks to Lord Gregory, and again Beauty was struck by her bright ruddy face. Her braids were done with tiny pearls and thin strands of blue ribbon.

But Beauty, almost lost in her contemplation of all this, was suddenly shocked to realize the Lady was looking at her.

"Oooooh, yes, it is the Prince's lovely one," she said, and now she advanced, and Beauty felt the Lady's hand lifting her face. "And how sweet she is, how truly beautiful."

Beauty shut her eyes, trying to restrain her heaving breaths. She did not believe she could endure the imperious touch of this young Lady. And yet there was nothing she could do.

"O, I should so like to have her take Princess Lizetta's place, it would be a treat for everyone," said the Lady.

"But that is impossible, my Lady," said Lord Gregory. "The Prince is most possessive of her. I cannot allow her to participate in such a spectacle."

"But surely we'll see more of her. Will she be run on the Bridle Path?"

"I feel certain, in time," said Lord Gregory. "There is no accounting for the whim of the Prince. But here, you may examine her if you wish. There is no rule prohibiting it."

He lifted Beauty by her wrists and forced her hips forward with the handle of the paddle. "Open your eyes and keep them down," he whispered. Beauty could not bear to see this lovely Lady's hands as they moved towards her. But Lady Juliana touched her breasts, and then her smooth stomach.

"Why she is radiant and so full of tender spirit."

Lord Gregory laughed softly. "Yes, she is, and you are so discerning to value it."

"They turn out all the better for that," said Lady Juliana with quiet wonder. She pinched Beauty's cheek as she had Princess Lizetta's secret lips. "O, what I would give for a quiet hour alone with her in my chambers."

"In time, in time," said Lord Gregory.

"Yes, and I bet she fights the paddle so, with her tender spirit."

"Only with her spirit," said Lord Gregory. "She is obedient."

"I can see that. Well, my girl, I must leave you. Be confident that you are exquisite. I wish I had you over my knee. I'd paddle you until sundown. You'd play a lot of little games running from me in the garden, you would." And then she kissed Beauty warmly on the mouth, and left as quickly as she had come, in a flurry of burgundy velvet and flying braids.

Just before Beauty took the sleeping potion from Leon she begged to know the meaning of what she had heard. "What is the Bridle Path?" she asked in a whisper, "and the village, my Lord, what does it mean to be sent there!"

"Never speak of the village," Leon cautioned her calmly. "That punishment is for incorrigibles and you are the slave of the Crown Prince himself. As for the Bridle Path, my lovely, you shall know soon enough."

He laid her down in her bed, strapping her ankles and wrists far away from her so that not even in sleep could she touch herself. "Dream," he said to her, "for tonight the Prince will want you."

DUTIES IN THE PRINCE'S CHAMBER

THE PRINCE was finishing his supper when Beauty was brought to him. The castle hummed with life, torches flaring in the long, high, vaulted corridors. And the Prince sat in a library of sorts, eating alone at a narrow table. Several ministers were about with papers for him to sign, and there was the sound of their soft leather sock boots on the floor, and the crackling of the scrolls of parchment.

Beauty knelt by his chair, listening to the scratch of his pen, and when she was sure he would not see, she looked up at him.

He appeared radiant to her He wore a blue velvet

surcoat trimmed in silver and emblazoned with his coat of arms above a heavy silk girdle. The sides of the surcoat were loosely laced and through them Beauty could see his white shirt, and she admired as well the firm muscles of his legs in the long tight fustian breeches.

He took a few more bites of his meat as a plate was set down on the stones for Beauty. And quickly she lapped up the wine he poured in a bowl for her, and ate the meat as delicately as she could without using her fingers. It seemed he was watching her. He gave her bits of cheese and more fruit, and she heard him give some little sound of satisfaction. She cleaned her plate with her tongue.

She would have done anything to show him how pleased she was to be with him again, and quite suddenly she remembered she had not kissed his boots, and she made up for this immediately. The smell of the clean, polished leather was delicious to her. She felt his hand on the back of her neck, and when she looked up, he fed her a handful of grapes one by one, lifting each one a little higher so that she had to rise off her heels to get it.

He tossed the last grape in the air. She darted up to catch it in her mouth and succeeded. Then overcome with shyness she bowed her head. Was he pleased? After all she'd witnessed during the day, he seemed her savior. She could have wept for happiness now that she was with him.

Lord Gregory had wanted her to dine with the slaves. He had shown her the hall. There were two long rows of Princes and Princesses, all on their knees, hands clasped behind their backs, eating with their quick little mouths from plates on a low table before them. They were bent over so that, as she passed, she saw the row of sore buttocks and felt herself shocked by the sight of so many of them. They were all alike, and yet each body was different. The Princes showed less of themselves if their legs were together, as the scrotum couldn't be seen; but the girls could do nothing to hide their pubic lips. It had alarmed her.

But the Prince had wanted her immediately in his chamber. And now she was with him. Leon had removed the small sealing wax from her secret core of pleasure, and she felt the first stirring of desire. She did not care about the servants moving about, or the last minister waiting nearby with his petition. She kissed the Prince's boots again.

"It's very late," the Prince said. "You've had a long rest, and I see you are much improved for it."

Beauty waited.

"Look at me," he said.

And when she did, she was shocked by the beauty and ferocity of his black eyes. She felt her breath catch in her throat.

"Come," he said, rising and dismissing the minister. "Time for lessons."

He walked fast towards his bed chamber and she followed on her hands and knees, rushing before him as he waited for her to open the door, then going in behind him.

"If only she could sleep here, live here," she thought. And yet she was afraid as she saw him turn with his hands on his hips. She remembered the whipping last night with the strap and she shuddered.

Beside him was a high pedestal table, and he reached into a cloth-covered casket there, and took out what seemed a handful of little brass bells. "Come here, my spoilt dear," he said softly. "Tell me, have you ever attended a Prince in his chamber, dressed him, groomed him?" he asked.

"No, my Prince," Beauty said, and she hurried to his feet.

"Kneel up," he said. She obeyed, hands behind her neck and then she saw the little brass bells he held and that each was fixed to a little spring clamp.

Before she could protest, he applied one very carefully to the nipple of her right breast. It was not tight enough to hurt; nevertheless it bit down on her nipple, pinching her, and causing the nipple to harden. She watched as he clamped the other to her left breast, and then without meaning to, she took a deep breath that made the bells ring ever so faintly. They were heavy. They pulled on her. And she flushed, desperately wishing to shake them loose. They weighted her breasts, made her painfully conscious of them.

But he was telling her to stand up and spread her legs. And as she obeyed she saw another pair of brass bells taken from the casket. They were as large as walnuts. And, whimpering slightly, she felt his hands between her legs as he clamped these bells to her pubic lips quickly.

It seemed she felt parts of herself of which she had been unconscious. The bells touched her thighs. They tugged on the lips and cut into the flesh tightly.

"O, come now, it isn't so dreadful, my little maid," he whispered, and he rewarded her with a kiss.

"If it pleases you, my Prince . . ." she stammered.

"Ah, that is lovely," he said. "And now to work, my beautiful one. And I want to see you work fast, yet gracefully. I want to see you do all things correctly, yet with some artfulness. In my closet on a hook you will see my red velvet scapular and gold girdle. Bring these things to me quickly and lay them out on the bed. You are going to dress me."

Beauty rushed to obey.

She had the clothing down from its hooks and hastened to bring it back, moving on her knees, the clothing in her arms. She laid it out on the foot of the bed, and turned waiting.

"Now undress me," said the Prince. "And you must learn to use your hands only when you cannot accomplish something otherwise."

Obediently Beauty took the leather lacings of his surcoat in her teeth, pulled loose the knot and saw them open. The Prince pulled the coat over his head and gave it to her. And now as he seated himself on a stool by the fire, she went to work unfastening his many buttons. It seemed she met with one obstacle after another. She was conscious of his body, its perfume and warmth, and his strange preoccupation. Soon she had the shirt off with his help, and then she must remove his long breeches.

Now and then he would aid her, but most tasks she performed herself, taking the upper lip of his velvet-lined boots carefully in her teeth as she pulled at the heels with her hands until they slipped off easily.

It seemed a long time that she labored, learning every detail of his wear. And now she must dress him.

She placed the white silk undershirt on him with both hands as he slipped his arms into it. And though she laid the placket of buttonholes in place with her hands, she drew each button through with her mouth so that he was very pleased and commended her.

She grew tired; her breasts ached from the heavy brass bells, and she felt the weight of the others between her legs, and that maddening stroking of her thighs and the jingling sound which never quite died away. But when she was finished, and he had just pulled on his new boots to help her, he gathered her in his arms and kissed her.

"As time passes, you will learn to work faster. It will be nothing for you to dress or undress me, to perform any small task I ask of you. I shall have you sleep in my chambers, and attend to everything."

"My Prince," she whispered, and she pressed her breasts against him, aching for him. She kissed his boots quickly, and all she had seen during the day came back to haunt and tantalize her: Princess Lizetta's cruel punishment, the Princes being trained, and then the one she had not seen, but never forgotten, Prince Alexi—all of this came together in her mind, stoking her passion and at the same time frightening her. O, if she could only sleep in the Prince's quarters now. Yet when she thought of all those male slaves she had seen in the Hall . . .

But the Prince, as if he sensed her mind was not as attentive to him as it should have been, began kissing her roughly.

Then he ordered her to go down on her hands and knees with her forehead pressed to the floor so that he might see her buttocks turned to him. She obeyed, the cruel little bells reminding her of all the naked parts of her.

"My Prince," she whispered to herself. She felt some change in her heart which she did not fully understand. Yet she was afraid as always.

He ordered her to rise, and again he gathered her into his arms, and this time he said:

"Kiss me as you desire to kiss me."

And overjoyed she kissed the cold smoothness of his forehead, kissed the dark locks of his hair, his eyelids and his long eyelashes. She kissed his cheeks, and then his open mouth. And his tongue passed into her mouth and she weakened all over so that he had to support her.

"My Prince, my Prince," she murmured knowing that she disobeyed. "I am so afraid of all of it."

"But why, beautiful one? Isn't it clear to you now? Isn't it simple?"

"O, but how long will I serve? Will this be all of my life now?"

"Listen to me." He became grave but not angry. He held her by the shoulders, and then he looked at her swollen breasts. The little brass bells shivered as she breathed. She felt his hands between her legs, and then his fingers inside of her, stroking her in an upward motion that caused her to twist her body with the pleasure of it.

"This is all you are to think about, this is all you are to be," he said. "In some former life, you were many things, a lovely face, a lovely voice, an obedient daughter. You've shed that skin as if it were a cloak of dreams, and now you think of these portions of yourself only." He stroked her pubic lips, he widened her vagina. And then he squeezed her breasts almost cruelly. "This is you now, all of you. And your lovely face, only because it is the lovely face of a naked and helpless slave."

Then, as if he could not resist, he embraced her and carried her to the bed. "In a little while, I must take wine with the Court, and you will serve me there, demonstrating your obedience to everyone. But that can wait . . ."

"O, yes, my Prince, if it pleases you," she breathed the words so low he might not have heard. She was lying on the jeweled coverlet, and though her buttocks and legs were not as raw as they had been the night before, she felt the painful prickling of the jewels.

The Prince knelt over her straddling her, and then opened her mouth with his fingers, and showing her his hard penis, drove it into her mouth with a quick downward motion. She sucked on it, drew on it. Yet all she need do was lie back helpless for he made the strong thrusts himself, into her, and she closed her eyes, smelling the delicious fragrance of his pubic hair, and tasting the saltiness of his skin, the penis nudging the back of her throat again and again as it all but bruised her lips.

She was moaning in time with its movements, and when suddenly he drew himself out, she gasped, her hands up to embrace him. But he had lain down on her full length, parted her legs, and pulled away the brass bells. Her pubic lips ached as he did so.

He drove into her. She felt herself explode with pleasure, her back arched so rigidly that she lifted his weight with her. Her body was drenched in pleasure. She thrust with her hips in almost a snapping motion, and when he came at last, he gave her cruel thrusts until he lay exhausted.

It seemed she slept; she dreamed. And then she heard him say to someone standing there:

"Take her away, wash her, adorn her. And send her to me in the upstairs parlor."

SERVING
MAID

BEAUTY COULD not believe
her bad luck when, entering the upstairs parlor, she saw
the lovely Lady Juliana was playing chess with the Prince,
and that other beautiful Ladies were seated about at various chessboards, and that there were several Lords as
well, including an old man with white hair that flowed
down over his shoulders.

Why did it have to be this Lady Juliana, so full of
airy gestures and sunshine, her thick braids done tonight
with crimson ribbon, her breasts beautifully molded by
her velvet gown, and her laughter already filling the air
as the Prince whispered to her some little witticism.

Serving Maid

Beauty did not know what she felt. Was it jealousy? Was it merely the usual humiliation?

And Beauty had been adorned so cruelly by Leon, it was better to be naked.

First Leon had scrubbed away all the Prince's fluids, then he had braided only a thick lock of Beauty's hair on either side, pinning back these braids so that most of her hair still hung free. Then he had put little jeweled clamps on her nipples, but these were connected to each other by two strands of fine gold chain like a necklace.

The clamps hurt and the chains moved as the bells had with Beauty's every breath. But she had been quite horrified to discover this was not all.

Leon's quick, graceful fingers had probed her navel, then smoothed into it a paste in which he set a glittering brooch, a fine jewel surrounded by pearls. Beauty had gasped. She felt as if someone were pressing her there, trying to enter her, as if her navel had become a vagina. And the feeling continued. She could feel it now.

Then her ears must be hung with heavy jewels on tight gold clamps that stroked her neck when she moved, and her pubic lips of course could not be spared but must wear the same adornment. There were snake bracelets for her upper arms, and jeweled cuffs for her wrists, the effect to make her feel all the more exposed. Adorned and yet exposed. It was mystifying. About her neck finally a choker of jewels, and then on her left cheek a little jewel in paste like a beauty mark.

It caused her such annoyance. She wanted to wipe it away and could imagine it glittering. It seemed she could even see it out of the corner of her eye. But then she had been quite frightened when Leon tipped her head back, and put a delicate little gold ring on the side of her nostril. Its prongs pierced her though not deeply, only enough to hold it in place, but she almost cried because she wanted so to wipe it away like the jewel, indeed, to pull all these adornments loose, though Leon was complimenting her.

"Ah, when they give me something truly beautiful to work with, then I can show my skill," he sighed. He gave her hair a brisk brushing and then said she was ready.

Now she entered this vast shadowy parlor on her hands and knees and hurried to the Prince's side, kissing his boots immediately.

The Prince did not look up from his chessboard, and to Beauty's scalding shame, it was the Lady Juliana who greeted her:

"Ah, but if it isn't the darling one, and how lovely she looks. Kneel up, my precious," she said in that gay, carefree voice, tossing one of her braids back over her shoulder. She laid her hand on Beauty's throat, examining the jewel necklace. It seemed her fingers caused a tingling through Beauty's flesh, but she did not even try to steal a glance at the young woman's face.

"Why am I not sitting there as she is sitting, exquisitely dressed and free and proud," Beauty thought. "What has become of me, that I must kneel here before her and be handled as something less than human? I am a Princess!" And then she thought of all the other Princes and Princesses and felt foolish. "Do they think these thoughts?" This woman, more than any other, tormented her.

But Lady Juliana was not satisfied. "Stand up my dear so that I can have a look at you and don't make me tell you to put your hands behind your neck and spread your legs."

Beauty heard laughter from behind her and someone remarking to someone else that yes, the Prince's slave was well named. And realizing suddenly that there were no other slaves in this room, Beauty felt all the more bereft.

She shut her eyes as she had before when Lady Juliana had inspected her. And she felt the Lady's hands on her thighs and then pinching her buttocks. "O, why can she not leave me alone, doesn't she know what I suffer?" Beauty thought, and through her narrowed eyelids she looked down to see the Lady beaming at her.

"And what does her Highness think of her?" Lady Juliana asked with genuine curiosity, glancing at the Prince who was still deep in contemplation.

"She does not approve," the Prince murmured. "She accuses me of passion."

Beauty tried to remain composed, standing as she was in attendance. She heard laughter and conversation about her. She heard the rumbling of the old man's voice, and a woman say that the Prince's girl should serve the wine, should she not, so they might all see her?

"And haven't they seen me," Beauty thought. Could it be worse than the Great Hall, and what if she spilled the wine?

"Beauty, go to the sideboard and take the pitcher. Serve carefully and well, and come back to me," said the Prince, again without looking at her.

Beauty moved through the shadows to find the gold pitcher on the sideboard. She could smell the fruity aroma of the wine, and she turned, feeling awkward and graceless, and approached the first table. "A common serving girl, slave," she thought, more keenly than she had thought anything when she had been displayed.

With trembling hands she poured the wine slowly into goblet after goblet, and through her glazed vision saw smiles and heard whispered compliments. Now and then some haughty man or woman was quite indifferent to her. She was shocked once by a pinch on her rear and gasped to a general round of laughter.

As she bent over the tables, she felt the nakedness of her belly, saw the chains shimmering as they connected her pinched nipples. Each common gesture made her feel more hopeless.

She backed away from the last table, from a man who sat back with his elbow on the arm of his chair and smiled at her.

And then she filled Lady Juliana's goblet and saw those bright round eyes looking up at her.

"Lovely, lovely, O, I do wish you weren't so possessive of her," said Lady Juliana. "Put the pitcher down, my dear, and come here to me."

Beauty obeyed and returned to the Lady's chair. When she saw the Lady snap her fingers and point to the floor, Beauty blushed. She fell to her knees, and then in a strange impulsive moment, she kissed the Lady's slippers.

It seemed to happen very slowly. She found herself bending down towards the silver slippers and then she touched them with her lips fervently.

"Ah, what a darling," said the Lady Juliana. "Give me only an hour with her."

And Beauty felt the woman's hand on the back of her neck, caressing her, stroking her, and then gathering her hair back and smoothing it tenderly. Tears came to Beauty's eyes. "I am nothing," she thought. And there was that awareness again of some change in her, some quiet despair, except that her heart was racing.

"I would not even have her here," said the Prince under his breath, "save my mother commands it, that she be treated like any other slave, that she be enjoyed by others. Given my own will, I would chain her to my bedpost. I would beat her. I would watch every tear, every change of color."

Beauty felt her heart in her throat like a little fist knocking there faster and faster. "I would make her my wife, even . . ."

"Ah, but you are in the grip of madness."

"Yes," said the Prince, "she has done that to me. Are others blind?"

"No, of course not," said Juliana, "she is lovely. But

each seeks his own love, you know that. Would you have everyone else equally mad for her?"

"No," he shook his head. And without looking away from the chessboard, he reached out to caress Beauty's breasts, lifting them, squeezing them, so that she winced.

But suddenly everyone was rising.

Chairs slid back on the stones; the assemblage stood bowing.

Beauty turned.

The Queen had come into the room. Beauty glimpsed her long green gown, the girdle of gold embroidery about her hips and that sheer white veil that hung down her back to her hem, only thinly concealing her black hair.

Beauty went down low on her hands and knees not knowing what she must do. Her forehead touched the stones and she held her breath. Yet she could see the Queen approaching. The Queen stood right before her.

"Be seated everyone," said the Queen, "and return to your games. But you, my son, how do you fare with this new passion?"

The Prince was obviously at a loss for an answer.

"Pick her up, display her," said the Queen.

And Beauty realized she was being lifted by her wrists. She rose up quickly, her arms being twisted behind her, her back forced into a painful arc, and suddenly she was standing on her toes moaning. The clamps seemed to tear at her nipples, the jewels between her legs to pull her open. Behind the jewel in her navel, she felt her heart beat, and she felt it too in the lobes of her clamped ears and in her eyelids.

She was looking at the floor but all she could see was that shimmering chain and some great indistinct form that was the Queen standing over her.

Then suddenly the Queen's hand struck Beauty's breasts so hard that Beauty cried out, and at once felt the Page's fingers over her mouth tightly.

She moaned in panic. She felt her tears come, the

Page's fingers biting into her cheek. And without meaning to, she struggled.

"There, there, Beauty," whispered the Prince. "You do not show my mother your best disposition."

Beauty tried to calm herself, but the Page forced her forward more harshly.

"She is not so bad," said the Queen, and Beauty could feel the iron in her voice, her cruelty. No matter what the Prince did to her, she did not sense in him such pure cruelty.

"She is only afraid of me," said the Queen. "And I wish you were more afraid of me, my son."

"Mother, be gentle with her, please, I beg you," said the Prince. "Allow me to keep her in my chambers, and to train her myself. Don't send her back to the Hall of Slaves tonight."

Beauty tried to smother her own crying. It seemed the Page's hand over her mouth only made it more difficult for her.

"My son, when she has proven her humility, we shall see," said the Queen. "Tomorrow night, the Bridle Path."

"O, but Mother, it is so soon."

"Such rigor will be good for her; it will make her malleable," said the Queen.

And turning with a broad gesture that loosened the train of her gown and made it fall behind her, the Queen left the parlor.

The Page released Beauty.

And the Prince at once took her wrists in his hand and urged her out into the corridor, Lady Juliana coming beside him.

The Queen was gone, and the Prince moved Beauty angrily along ahead of him, Beauty's sobs echoing under the dark vaulted ceilings.

"O, dear, poor exquisite dear," said the Lady Juliana.

At last they reached the Prince's apartments, and to Beauty's misery, the Lady Juliana came in as if this were nothing to enter the Prince's chamber.

"Have they no propriety and restraint among them-selves," Beauty thought, "or are they degraded with each other as we are degraded?"

But she soon realized it was only the Prince's study, and Pages were about. And the door remained open.

The Lady Juliana took Beauty now from the Prince, her soft cool hands urging Beauty down on her knees before her chair.

Then from somewhere in the folds of her gown, the Lady produced a long narrow silver-handled brush and she commenced to brush Beauty's hair lovingly. "This will soothe you, my poor precious one," she said. "Don't be so frightened."

Beauty broke into fresh sobs. She hated this lovely Lady. She wanted to destroy her. She felt such savage thoughts, and yet she wanted at the same moment to cling to her, to sob against her breast. She thought of friends she'd had at her father's Court, her Ladies in waiting, and how many times they had been easily affectionate with one another, and she wanted to abandon herself to the same affection. The brushing of her hair produced a tingling all through her scalp and through the flesh of her arms as well. And when the Lady's left hand covered her breasts and gently patted them, she felt herself defenseless. Her mouth went slack and she turned towards the Lady Juliana and laid her forehead against her knee, defeated.

"Poor, darling one," said the Lady. "But the Bridle Path is not so dreadful. You will be grateful afterwards that you were used rigorously in the beginning, for it will all the sooner soften you."

"Familiar sentiments," Beauty thought.

"Perhaps," the Lady Juliana went on with the rhythmic stroking of the brush, "I shall ride beside you."

What could this mean?

And then the Prince said:

"Take her back to the Hall now."

Without explanations, without farewells, without tenderness!

Beauty turned and rushed to him on her hands and knees and gave his boots fervent kisses. Again and again she kissed them both, hoping for what she did not know, one real embrace from him perhaps, something to allay her fears of the Bridle Path.

The Prince received her kisses for a long time, and then he lifted her and turned her to Lady Juliana who clasped Beauty's hands behind her back.

"Be obedient, beautiful one," she said.

"Yes, you ride beside her," said the Prince. "But you must make a good show of it."

"Of course, I should very much enjoy making a good show of it," said the Lady Juliana, "and it is best for you both. She is a slave, and all slaves desire a firm mistress and master. If they cannot be free, then they do not like for there to be ambivalence. I shall be most firm with her, but always loving."

"Take her back to the Hall," said the Prince. "My mother will not allow me to keep her here."

THE
BRIDLE
PATH

As soon as Beauty opened her eyes from sleep, she could feel a new excitement in the castle.

Torches everywhere brilliantly illuminated the Slaves' Hall, and all about her Princes and Princesses were receiving elaborate preparation. The hair of the Princesses was being combed and studded with flowers. The Princes were being polished with oil, their stiff curls combed just as carefully as those of the young women.

But Beauty was hastily taken from bed by Leon who seemed uncommonly excited.

"It's Festival Night, Beauty," he said, "and I've

allowed you to sleep a long time. We must hurry."

"Festival Night," she whispered.

But she was already being placed on the table for grooming.

At once he parted her hair and started to braid it. She felt the air on her neck and hated it, and she realized he had started the braids very high on her head so she would look even more girlish than Lady Juliana. A long black leather thong was braided into the hair on both sides, and knotted around the ends with a little brass bell affixed to it. When Leon dropped the braids they were heavy against Beauty's breasts and her neck was exposed as well as all of her face.

"Charming, charming," Leon mused with his usual air of satisfaction. "But now your boots."

And slipping her into a pair of high black leather boots he told her to stand in them while he bent to lace them tightly to her knees and then smooth the leather around her ankles until it was cleaving like a glove there.

Not until Beauty lifted her foot did she realize each boot was fitted at toe and heel with a horseshoe. And the tops were hard and strong so that nothing could hurt her toes.

"But what is happening, what is the Bridle Path?" she asked in a great fluster.

"Shhhhh . . ." Leon said, pinching and prodding her breasts to give them as he said, "some color."

He then glossed Beauty's eyelids and eyelashes with oil and smoothed a little rouge into her lips and into her nipples. Beauty drew back instinctively but his touch was sure and quick and he took no notice of her.

But what bothered her most was that her body felt cool and vulnerable. She could feel the sheathing of leather against her calves, and all the rest of her felt worse than naked. It was more terrible than any of the smaller adornments.

"What is going to take place?" she asked again, but

Leon had thrust her over the end of the table and now oiled her buttocks vigorously. "Well healed," he said. "The Prince must have guessed last night you would run tonight and he spared you."

Beauty felt his strong fingers plying her flesh and a dread came over her. So they would spank her, but they always did. Only it would be in the presence of many others?

Every humiliating spank she had received before the eyes of others had cost her dearly, though she knew now she would suffer any amount of paddling for the Prince, but she had not really been given a hard, thorough spanking for the pleasure of others since the Inn on the road where the Innkeeper's daughter had spanked her for the soldiers and the common people at the windows.

"But it must come," she thought. And a vision of the Court watching it as some ritual caused her to feel an undeniable curiosity that soon enough gave way to panic. "My Lord, please tell me . . ."

Amid the crowd about her, she saw other girls with braided hair and boots. So she was not alone. And there were Princes being fitted with boots also.

Through it all there moved a handful of young Princes on their hands and knees polishing boots as quickly as they could, their own buttocks raw, their necks encircled by a little cord of leather to which was attached a sign that Beauty could not read.

But now as Leon brought her up standing again and gave some finishing touches to her lips and eyelashes, one of these Princes was now buffing her boots though he was weeping. His buttocks were as red as it could have been. And she saw the sign about his neck said, "I am in Disgrace," in small letters.

A Page approached and gave the Prince a sound crack with a belt to hurry him on to another.

But Beauty had no time to think of it. Leon had affixed the accursed little brass bells to her nipples.

She shuddered almost instinctively but they were firmly attached, and he told her to fold her arms behind her back tightly.

"Now forward, only you are to bend your knees slightly and to march, lifting each knee high," he told her.

She started, awkwardly, reluctant to obey, but then she saw all about her other Princesses marching in an almost sprightly manner, their breasts bouncing gracefully as they moved into the corridor.

She hurried, the heavy boots difficult for her to lift with any decorum, but soon she had fallen into a rhythm and Leon was walking beside her.

"Now, darling," he said, "the first time is always difficult. Festival Night is frightening. I had thought some easier duty would be yours this first time, but the Queen has ordered you especially for the Bridle Path, and the Lady Juliana will drive you."

"Ah, but what . . ."

"Shhhh, or I shall have to gag you and that will very much displease the Queen as well as make your mouth quite ugly."

All the girls were now in a long room, and through narrow windows on one wall, Beauty could see the garden.

Torches flared in the dark trees, throwing an uneven glare on the leafy boughs above them. The line of girls formed right beside these windows, and Beauty was now able to see more of what lay beyond them.

There was a great roar as of many people conversing, laughing. And then to her shock Beauty saw slaves all through the garden positioned in various ways for their torment.

On high stakes here and there were strapped Princes and Princesses painfully contorted, their ankles bound to the stakes, their shoulders bent over the tops of them. They seemed no more than ornaments, the torchlight causing their twisted limbs to glow, the hair of the Princesses falling free in the air behind them. Surely they could see only the sky above, though all could see their miserable contortions.

And everywhere beneath were the Lords and Ladies, the light falling upon a long embroidered cloak here, a pointed hat there with a veil trailing airily from it. There were hundreds in the garden, these tables placed far back into the trees, as far as Beauty could see in all directions.

Beautifully adorned slaves moved about, pitchers in hand, little gold chains fixed to their breasts, the Princes adorned with gold rings on their erect organs. They hurried to fill the goblets, pass the platters of food, and as in the great hall there was music.

The line of girls before Beauty grew restless. Beauty could hear one girl crying as her groom tried to comfort her, but most of the others were obedient. Here and there a groom rubbed more oil into plump buttocks or whispered in a Princess's ear, and Beauty's sense of apprehension deepened.

She did not want to look into the yard; it frightened her too much, but she could not prevent herself. And each time she saw some new horror. A great wall to the left, was adorned with spread-eagled slaves, and on a huge serving cart she saw slaves fixed to the giant wheels, turned upside down over and over as the cart was moved forward.

"But what will happen to us?" Beauty whispered. The girl in line before her who could not be quieted was now hanging by her ankle from the hand of a strong Page who punished her swiftly. Beauty gasped to see her spanked, her braids falling to the floor beneath her.

"Shh, it is best for her," Leon said, "it will exhaust her fear and drain her slightly. And she will be all the more free on the Bridle Path."

"But tell me . . ."

"You must be still. You will see the others first and understand, and as we draw nearer to your turn I shall instruct you. Remember this is a special night of high festivity, but the Queen will be watching. And the Prince will be furious if you fail him."

Beauty's eyes returned to the garden. The great cart of steaming food had moved along, and for the first time she saw the distant fountain. Here too were bound slaves, their arms linked as they stood knee deep in the water, surrounding the central pillar, its sparkling flow pouring down over them. Their bodies glistened under the water.

The groom beside the girl in front of Beauty laughed softly and said that someone was miserable to be missing Festival Night but it was her own fault.

"Surely," Leon agreed when the groom glanced back to him. "They are talking about Princess Lizetta," he told Beauty, "who is still in the Hall of Punishments, and cursing no doubt to miss the excitement."

To miss the excitement! But in spite of her fear, Beauty nodded at this as if it were perfectly natural. A calm descended upon her in which she heard her own heart and felt her body as if there were limitless time in which to know it. She felt the sheathing of the leather boots, the click of her horseshoes on the stones, the air on her neck, her belly. And she thought, "Yes, this is what I am, so I should not wish to miss it either. Yet I rebel in my soul; why do I rebel?"

"O, I despise that miserable Lord Gerhardt, why must he drive me?" asked the girl before her in a low voice. The groom said something that made her laugh. "But he's so slow," she said, "savoring every moment. And I like to run!" The groom laughed at her. She went on, "and what do I get out of it?—the most miserable spanking. I could take the spanking if I could only cut loose and run . . ."

"You want everything!" said the groom.

"And what do you want? Don't tell me you don't like it when I'm covered with welts and almost blistered!"

The groom laughed. He had a cheerful face, and was small of build, keeping his hands clasped behind his back, though his chestnut hair fell down over his eyes slightly.

"My dear, I love everything about you," he said.

"And so does Lord Gerhardt. Now say something to comfort Leon's little pet, she's so frightened."

The girl turned and Beauty saw her pert face, eyes slanting at the ends somewhat like the eyes of the Queen, but they were smaller, with no cruelty. She smiled with full little red lips. "Don't be frightened, Beauty," she said, "but you have no need for comfort from me. You have the Prince. I have only Lord Gerhardt."

A great current of laughter passed through the garden. The musicians were playing loudly, with much strumming of their lutes and tapping of the tambourines, and then Beauty quite distinctly heard the thunder of hooves approaching. A rider shot past the windows, his cape flying out behind him, his horse bridled in silver and gold which made a streak of light as he rushed forward.

"O, at last, at last," said the girl in front of Beauty. Other riders were coming, and they were making a line all along the wall that almost blocked Beauty's view of the garden. She could not bear to look up at them, but she did and saw they were splendid Ladies and Lords, and each held the reins of the horse in his or her left hand, and in the right a long rectangular black paddle.

"Now, into the room," said Lord Gregory, and the slaves who had waited in a long line were ushered into the next chamber where they stood directly facing the arched door to the garden. Beauty could see now that a young Prince was first in line, and she saw that mounted Lord, his horse pawing the dirt before the archway.

Leon moved Beauty a little to the side. "Now you can see better," he said.

And she saw the Prince clasp his hands behind his neck and step forward.

A trumpet sounded, catching Beauty off guard so she gasped. And a cry rose from the crowd behind the archway. The young slave was forced out and at once greeted by the black leather paddle of the Lord on horseback.

Immediately the slave commenced to run.

The mounted Lord rode right beside him, and the sound of the paddle came loud and distinct as the murmur of the crowd seemed to rise and mingle itself with faint ripples of laughter.

Beauty was aghast as she saw the two figures disappear down the path together. "I cannot do it, I cannot," she thought. "I cannot be made to run. I will fall. I will fall to the ground and cover myself. To be tied, to be bound in front of so many was dreadful enough, but this is impossible . . ."

But another rider was already in place, and a young Princess was forced suddenly forward. The paddle found its mark, the Princess let out a little cry and was immediately running desperately fast along the Bridle Path, the rider after her, spanking her fiercely.

Before Beauty could take her eyes off them, another slave was on the way, and her eyes blurred as she saw far ahead a dim line of torches outlining the path that seemed to go on and on through the trees, past an endless vista of feasting Lords and Ladies.

"Now, Beauty, you see what is required, and don't cry. If you're crying it will be harder. You must put your mind on running fast, keeping your hands on your neck. Here, place them there now. And you must lift your knees high, and try not to squirm to escape the paddle. It will catch you no matter what you do, but I warn you, no matter how many times I tell you that, you will find yourself trying to run away from it. That is the trick, but remain graceful."

Another slave was running, and then another.

And the young girl who had cried earlier was upended again, dangling, as she was spanked.

"Dreadful of her," said the Princess in front of Beauty. "She'll be spanked hard enough in a moment."

Suddenly there were only three slaves before Beauty and the archway.

"O, but I can't . . ." she cried to Leon.

The Bridle Path

"Nonsense, my darling, follow the path. It will un-
wind slowly before you, you will see its turns well in
advance, and stop only if you see the slave before you
stopped. Now and then the line is stopped, for as the
slaves come before the Queen, they must stop for praise
or condemnation. She is on a great pavilion to your right,
but don't glance at her when you step out or the paddle
will catch you off guard."

"O, please, I shall faint, I can't, I can't . . ."

"Beauty, Beauty," said the pretty Princess in front
of her, "just follow my example."

And Beauty realized with horror there was no one
left but this girl.

But then that one who had just been spanked was
placed before her, and ushered out to the waiting paddle.
The girl was frantic, sobbing, but she kept her hands on
her neck, and soon she was running beside her laughing
rider, a tall young Lord who lifted his arm way back as
he spanked her.

Suddenly another rider appeared, the elderly Lord
Gerhardt, and as Beauty watched in terror, the pretty
Princess ran out to receive the first blows and run with
graceful lifts of her knees beside him. But for all her
complaints, the Lord's horse seemed to move terribly fast
and the paddle was loud and merciless.

Beauty was forced to the threshold of the garden.
For the first time she stared at the true immensity of the
Court, the dozens upon dozens of tables that sprawled
out on the green and appeared in great numbers in the
forest beyond it. Everywhere were servants and naked
slaves. It was perhaps three times the size she had judged
from the windows.

She felt tiny, insignificant, for all her terror. Lost
and without a name or a soul suddenly. "What am I now,"
she might have thought, but she could not think. And as
if in nightmare, she saw all the faces of those at the nearest
tables, Lords and Ladies twisted to see the Bridle Path,

and far to her right loomed the pavilion of the Queen, canopied and festooned with flowers.

She was gasping for breath, and when she looked up and saw the splendid mounted figure of Lady Juliana, her eyes filled with tears of gratitude that it was she, though she knew Lady Juliana would spank her perhaps all the harder to do her duty.

The lovely Lady's braids were done with the same silver that threaded her shapely gown. She seemed made for the sidesaddle in which she sat and the handle of her paddle was laced to her wrist. She was smiling.

There was no time to see more, to think more. Beauty was running forward, feeling the crunch of the Bridle Path under her horseshoes, hearing the stomp of hooves beside her.

And though she thought it was not possible to endure such degradation, she felt the first cracking blow to her naked buttocks. It was so forceful it almost knocked her off balance. The stinging pain spread out from it like a warm fire and Beauty realized she was rushing forward.

The stomp of hooves deafened her. And the paddle caught her again and again, almost lifting her and forcing her forward. She realized she was crying out loud through her clenched teeth, her tears making a blur of the torches that clearly defined the path before her. And she was running, running fast towards the enclosing trees, though she could not escape the paddle.

It was as Leon had warned her; it caught her over and over and each time there was some hideous surprise because she was trying to outrun it. She could smell the horse, and when she widened her eyes and gasped for breath, she saw everywhere on either side of her those torchlit and abundantly decked supper tables. Lords and Ladies drank, supped, laughed, turned to glance at her perhaps, she did not know, she was sobbing and running frantically from the blows, which came harder and harder.

"O, please, please, Lady Juliana," she wanted to cry out, but she did not dare to ask for mercy. The path had turned and she was following it only to see more and more Nobles banqueting and dimly before her the figure of the other rider and slave who had greatly outdistanced her.

Her throat was burning as much as her sore flesh.

"Faster, Beauty, faster, and lift your legs higher," Lady Juliana sang out over the wind. "Ah, yes, better, my darling." And there came another shock of pain, and another. The paddle found her thighs with a hard uplifting slap, and then seemed to scoop up her buttocks.

Beauty gave an open-mouthed cry because she could not stop it, and soon she heard her own wordless pleas as clearly as the horse's hooves pounding the cinders.

Her throat constricted, even the soles of her feet burned, but nothing hurt as much as the quick, strong paddling.

Lady Juliana seemed possessed of some evil genius, catching Beauty from one angle and then another, lifting her up again with the blows, smacking her hard and then three or four times in rapid succession.

The path had made another turn, and far ahead Beauty saw the walls of the castle. They were returning now. They would soon reach the Queen's canopied pavilion.

Beauty felt as if all the breath had gone out of her, yet mercifully Lady Juliana slowed her pace as did the riders before her. Beauty ran more slowly, knees high, and felt a great relaxation course through her. She could hear her own choking sobs, and feel the tears slipping down her face, and yet a puzzling sensation was passing over her.

She felt suddenly calmed in some way. She did not comprehend it. She felt no rebellion suddenly, though the obligation to rebel prodded her. Perhaps she was only exhausted. But she knew only that she was a naked slave of the Court and anything might be done to her. Hundreds of Lords and Ladies watched her with amusement. It was nothing to them, as she was only one of many, and it had all been done a thousand times, and would be done again, and she must do her best or take her place tethered to that beam in the Hall of Punishments suffering for the amusement of no one.

"Lift your knees, my precious darling," Lady Juliana said to her as they were moving slowly now. "And O, if you could only see how exquisite you are, you have done splendidly."

Beauty tossed her head. She felt the heavy braids fall against her back, and suddenly when the paddle struck her she felt herself move so languidly with it. It was as if this strange relaxation were softening her all over. Is that what they had meant when they said that the pain would soften her? Yet she feared this relaxation, this despair . . . was it despair? She did not know. She had no dignity in this moment. She saw herself as Lady Juliana must surely have seen her, and it seemed she almost preened as she imagined this, tossing her head again, pushing her breasts out proudly.

"That's it, lovely, lovely," Lady Juliana called out. The other rider had disappeared.

The horse picked up its pace; the paddle struck Beauty violently again and drove her through the clustered tables as the crowd grew thicker, the castle coming closer, and suddenly they had stopped before the pavilion.

Lady Juliana turned her mount to the side, and with small prodding spanks brought Beauty beside her to attention.

Beauty did not look up but she could see the long garlands of flowers, the dim white vision of the canopy ballooning gently in the breeze, and a host of figures seated behind the festooned railing of the pavilion.

Her body seemed consumed with fire. She could not catch her breath, and then she could hear the conversation above, the Queen's pure icy voice and others laughing. Her throat was raw, her buttocks pulsing with pain, and now Lady Juliana whispered:

"She's pleased with you, Beauty, now kiss my boot quickly and drop down on your knees and kiss the grass before the pavilion. Do it with spirit, my girl."

Beauty obeyed without hesitation, and as if it were water washing through her, she felt again that calm, that sense of what was it? Release? Resignation?

"Nothing can save me," she thought. All the sounds about her mingled in a din. Her buttocks seemed to glow with pain, and she imagined a great light emanating from them.

And then she was back on her feet, and another hard blow sent her crying into the dark cellar chamber of the castle.

Slaves everywhere were thrown over barrels, their sore bodies being washed quickly with cool water. Beauty felt its flow over her abraded flesh, and then the soft toweling.

At once, Leon had her on her feet. "You've pleased the Queen marvelously. Your form was magnificent. You were born for the Bridle Path."

"But the Prince . . ." Beauty whispered. And she felt dizzy, and mistakenly envisioned Prince Alexi.

"Not tonight for you, lovely one, he is quite busy with a thousand amusements. And you must be placed where you can serve and rest, as the exertion of the Bridle Path is quite enough in one night for a novice."

He unfastened her braids and brushed out her hair in ripples. She was breathing deeply and evenly now and bent her forehead against his chest.

"Was I truly graceful?"

"Pricelessly beautiful," he whispered, "and Lady Juliana is thoroughly in love with you."

But now he ordered her down on her knees and told her to follow him.

She was suddenly out in the night again, on the warm grass with the noisy crowd all about her. She saw the table legs, the gathered gowns, hands moving in the shadows. There was a shriek of laughter nearby and then she saw before her a long banquet table covered with sweets, fruit and pastries. Two Princes attended it and decorative pillars stood at both ends to which slave girls were affixed, their hands above their heads, their feet chained slightly apart at the bottom.

One of these was removed as Beauty approached and she was quickly fastened in the girl's place, standing firmly, her head and swollen buttocks pressed back against the pillar.

She could see the whole feast around her, even with her lids lowered, and she felt herself quite firmly bound in place, unable to move, and it did not matter. The worst was over.

Even when a passing Lord stopped to smile at her and pinch her nipples, she did not care. She was amazed to see the little brass bells had been taken away. She was so weary she hadn't noticed.

Leon was still nearby, at her ear, and she was about to murmur some question as to how long she would be here, when quite distinctly in front of her she saw Prince Alexi.

He was as beautiful as she had remembered, his auburn brown hair curling against the hollows of his handsome face, his soft brown eyes fixed on her. His lips spread easily in a smile though he drew up to the table and gave his pitcher to be filled to one of those in attendance.

Beauty stared furtively out of the corner of her eye. She saw his thick hard sex and the lush hair around it. The vision of the Page, Felix, sucking it filled her with sudden passion.

She must have moaned or stirred because Prince Alexi, glancing up at the distant pavilion before he bent over the table to gather some sweet, suddenly kissed her on the ear, brushing Leon aside as if he were nothing.

"You behave yourself, you wicked Prince," said Leon, but it was not playful.

"I shall see you tomorrow night, my dearest," Prince Alexi whispered with a smile. "And don't be frightened of the Queen for I shall be with you."

Beauty's mouth quivered on the verge of a cry, but he was gone, and now Leon had drawn up to her ear again, cupping his hand as he whispered:

"You're to see the Queen tomorrow night for a few hours in her Quarters."

"O, no, no . . ." Beauty wailed, tossing her head from side to side.

"Don't be foolish. This is very good. You could not wish for better," and as he spoke, he slipped his hand between her legs and pinched her lips gently.

She felt herself grow warm there.

"I was on the pavilion while you were running. The Queen was impressed in spite of herself," he went on, "and the Prince said you had always shown such form and spirit. And again, he pleaded for you, and that the Queen should not censure his passion. He agreed then not to see you tonight but to have a dozen or so new Princesses paraded before him . . ."

"Don't tell me any more!" Beauty cried softly.

"No, but don't you see, the Queen was enthralled with you and he knew it. She watched you closely as you ran, impatient for you to come to the pavilion. And it was she who said perhaps she should taste your charms herself to see if you were not as spoilt and vain as she had supposed. She will have you in her Quarters tomorrow night after supper."

Beauty cried softly, too spiritless to answer.

"But, Beauty, this is a great privilege. There are slaves here who serve years without ever being noticed by the Queen. You shall have your full opportunity to enchant her. And you shall, my dear, you shall, you cannot fail to do so. And the Prince has been clever for once. He has not worn his heart for all to see it."

"But what will she do to me!" Beauty whimpered. "And Prince Alexi, will he see all of it? O, what will she do?"

"O, she shall only make a plaything of you, of course. And you shall try to please her."

THE
QUEEN'S
CHAMBER

H ALF THE night was gone
before the Queen came.

Beauty had dozed, then awakened again and again,
to find herself still chained in the ornate bedchamber as
if in a nightmare. She was bound to the wall, her ankles
cuffed in leather, her wrists up over her head, her buttocks
pushed against the cold stone behind her.

At first the stone had felt good. Now and then she
twisted to let the air touch the soreness. Of course the
abraded flesh was much healed from last night's ordeal
on the Bridle Path, but she still suffered, and she knew
tonight she was surely destined for more torment.

Not the least of it, however, was her own passion. What had the Prince awakened in her that after one night of no satisfaction, she should feel so wanton? It was the stirring between her legs that first brought her out of sleep in the Slaves' Hall, and now and then she felt it as she stood waiting.

The room itself lay in shadow and unbroken stillness. Dozens of thick candles burned in their heavy gilded holders, the wax spilling in rivulets through the traceries of gold. The bed with its tapestried draperies appeared a gaping cavern.

Beauty closed her eyes. She opened them again. And when she was again on the verge of dream, she heard the heavy double doors thrown open and suddenly saw the tall, slender figure of the Queen materialized before her.

The Queen moved to the center of the carpet. Her blue velvet gown cleaved to her girdled hips before flaring gently to cover her black pointed slippers. She gazed at Beauty with narrow, black eyes tipped up at the ends to give her a cruel expression, and then she smiled, her white cheeks dimpling though an instant before they had seemed as hard as white porcelain.

Beauty had lowered her eyes at once. Petrified, she watched covertly as the Queen moved away from her and seated herself at an ornate dressing table, her back to a high mirror.

With an off-handed gesture she dismissed the Ladies who stood at the door. A figure remained there, and Beauty, afraid to look, was certain it was Prince Alexi.

So her tormentor had come, Beauty thought. Her heart pounded in her ears, becoming a roar rather than a pulse, and she felt the bonds holding her helpless so that she could not have defended herself against anyone or anything. Her breasts felt heavy, and the moisture between her legs greatly agitated her. Would the Queen discover it and use it to further punish her?

Yet mingled with her fear was some sense of her helplessness which had come over her the night before and never left her. She knew how she must appear, she was afraid, but she could do nothing and she was accepting it.

Maybe this was a new strength, this acceptance. And she needed all her strength, for she was alone with this woman who had no love for her. Without words, she evoked a memory of the Prince's love, of Lady Juliana's affectionate touch and warm words of praise, even of Leon's caressing hands.

But this was the Queen, the great powerful Queen who ruled all and who felt nothing but coldness and fascination for her.

She shivered against her will. The throbbing between her legs seemed to slacken and then to grow slightly more intense. Surely the Queen was staring at her. And the Queen could make her suffer. And there would be no Prince to witness it, no Court, no one.

Only Prince Alexi.

She saw him now, moving out of the shadows, a naked form exquisitely proportioned, the dark golden skin making him seem a polished statue.

"Wine," said the Queen. And he was moving to pour it for her.

He knelt at her side and he placed the two-handled cup in her hands, and as she drank, Beauty looked up and saw Prince Alexi smiling directly at her.

She was so startled, she almost made a little gasp. His large brown eyes were full of the same gentle affection he'd shown her last night when he passed her at the banquet table. Then he made his mouth into a silent kiss before Beauty looked away in consternation.

Could he feel affection for her, real affection, even desire, as she felt desire for him when she first saw him?

O, how she ached suddenly to touch him, to feel just once for an instant that silken skin, that hard chest, those dark, rose-colored nipples. How exquisite they were on that flat chest, those little nodules that seemed so unmasculine, giving him a touch of feminine vulnerability.

How had the Queen punished them, she wondered? Were they ever clamped and adorned as her breasts had been?

They were piquant, those little nipples.

But the throbbing between her legs warned her, and it took an act of will for her not to move her hips.

"Undress me," the Queen said.

And from beneath her half-mast lids, Beauty watched as Prince Alexi obeyed the command skillfully and deftly.

How clumsy she had been two nights ago and how patient the Prince had been with her.

He used his hands but seldom. His first duty was with his teeth to unsnap the hooks of the Queen's dress and this he did, quickly gathering it as it fell down around her.

Beauty was astonished to see the Queen's full white breasts naked under a thin chemise of lace. And then Prince Alexi removed her ornate mantle of white silk to show the Queen's black hair hanging loose in ripples over her shoulders.

He took the garments away.

Then he came back to remove with his teeth the Queen's slippers. He kissed her naked feet before he took the shoes out of sight, and then he brought back to the Queen a sheer nightgown trimmed in white lace, the fabric a lustrous cream color. It was very full and pressed into a thousand pleats.

And as the Queen rose, Prince Alexi pulled down the chemise that she wore, and rising to his full height put the nightgown over the Queen's shoulders. She slipped her arms into the deep pleated bag sleeves, and the garment fell about her like a bell.

And then with his back to Beauty, Prince Alexi on his knees again tied a dozen little bows of white ribbon to close the front of the gown to its hem above the Queen's naked insteps.

As he bent over for the last of these, the Queen's hands played idly with his auburn hair, and Beauty found herself staring at his reddened buttocks where he had obviously been recently punished. His thighs, his tight, hard calves, all of this enflamed her.

"Pull back the curtains of the bed," the Queen said. "And bring her to me."

Beauty's pulse deafened her. It seemed there was a pressure in her ears, in her throat. Yet she heard the tapestries being drawn back. She saw the Queen recline on the coverlet amid a nest of silk pillows. The Queen looked younger now that her hair was free, and her face was without a trace of age as she stared at Beauty. Those eyes were as placid as if they had been painted in her face with enamel.

Then with a shock of unwelcome pleasure, Beauty saw Prince Alexi before her. He obliterated the vision of the menacing Queen. He bent to untie her ankles and she felt his fingers deliberately caress her. When he rose in front of her again, his hands up to free her wrists, she smelled the perfume of his hair and skin, and there seemed something utterly lush about him. For all his hardness, the squareness of his build, he seemed some great spicy delicacy to her, and she found herself staring right into his eyes. He smiled and let his lips touch her forehead. And they stayed secretly pressed to her forehead until her wrists were entirely free and he was holding them.

Then he pushed her gently down on her knees and gestured to the bed.

"No, simply bring her," said the Queen.

And Prince Alexi lifted Beauty and threw her over his shoulder as easily as a Page might have done, or the Prince himself when he took her from her father's castle.

His flesh felt hot beneath her, and thrown over his back as she was, she boldly kissed his sore buttocks.

Then she was laid down on the bed and realized she was beside the Queen, looking up into her eyes, as the Queen, who rested on her elbow, looked down at her.

Beauty's breath left her in rapid gasps. The Queen seemed quite enormous to her. And now she perceived a great resemblance to the Prince, only as always the Queen seemed infinitely colder. Yet there was about her red mouth something which might have once been called sweetness. She had thick eyelashes, a firm chin, and as she smiled dimples showed in her cheeks. Her face was heart shaped.

Flustered, Beauty closed her eyes, biting her lip so hard she might have cut it.

"Look at me," said the Queen. "I want to see your eyes, naturally. I want no modesty from you now, do you understand me?"

"Yes, your Highness," Beauty answered.

She wondered if the Queen might hear her heart beat. The bed was soft beneath her, the pillows soft, and she found herself staring at the Queen's great breasts, the dark circle of a nipple beneath the gown, before she looked at the Queen's eyes again obediently.

A shock passed through her, collecting in a knot in her belly.

The Queen merely studied her in great absorption. Her teeth showed perfectly white between her lips, and those eyes, slanted, long, were black to the core and revealed nothing.

"Sit there, Alexi," the Queen said without looking away.

And Beauty saw him take his position at the foot of the bed, with his arms folded on his chest, and his back to the bedpost.

"Little plaything," the Queen said under her breath to Beauty. "And now I understand perhaps why Lady Juliana is so enraptured over you."

She ran her hand over Beauty's face, her cheeks, her eyelids. She pinched Beauty's mouth. She smoothed back her hair, and then she slapped Beauty's breasts to the right and to the left and again.

Beauty's mouth quivered but she made no sound. She kept her hands still at her sides. The Queen was like a light that threatened to blind her.

If she thought about it, lying here so near the Queen, she would be overcome with panic.

The Queen's hand moved over her belly and her thighs. It pinched the flesh of her thighs and then the backs of her legs at the calves. And in spite of herself Beauty felt a tingling everywhere she was touched as if the hand itself had some dreadful power. She felt hatred for the Queen suddenly, more violently than she had felt it for Lady Juliana.

But then the Queen commenced to examine, slowly, Beauty's nipples. The fingers of the Queen's right hand turned each nipple this way and that, testing the soft circle of skin around it. Beauty's breath became uneven, and she felt the moisture between her legs as though a grape had been squeezed there.

It seemed the Queen was monstrously bigger than she, and as strong as a man, or was it only that to struggle against the Queen was unthinkable? Beauty tried to regain some calm, to think of her feeling of release on the Bridle Path, but it eluded her. It had been fragile all along. Now it was nothing.

"Look at me," the Queen commanded gently again, and Beauty realized as she looked up that she was crying.

"Spread your legs," the Queen ordered.

At once Beauty obeyed. "Now she will see," Beauty thought. "It will be as bad as when Lord Gregory saw. And Prince Alexi will see."

The Queen laughed. "I said spread your legs," she said, and gave Beauty's thighs fierce stinging slaps. Beauty spread her legs much wider and felt graceless as she did so. When her knees were pressed down to the coverlet on either side, she thought she could not endure the ignominy of it. She stared at the coffered ceiling of the bed above her and realized that the Queen was opening her sex as Leon had done. Beauty bit down on her cries. And Prince Alexi witnessed all of it. She remembered his kisses, his smiles. The lights of the room shimmered, and she felt her own shuddering as the Queen's fingers felt the moisture in this secret, exposed spot, playing with Beauty's pubic lips, smoothing the pubic hair, and finally catching a lock of it to pull and tease idly.

It seemed the Queen took both her thumbs and wrenched Beauty open. Beauty tried to keep her hips still. She wanted to rise to escape, like some miserable Princess in the Training Hall who could not endure being so examined. Yet she did not protest; her whimpers were faint and uncertain.

The Queen commanded her to turn over.

Blessed concealment, that she could hide her face in the pillows.

But those cool, commanding hands were playing with her buttocks now, opening them, touching her anus. "O, please," she thought desperately, and she knew that her shoulders shook with her silent crying. "O, this is dreadful, dreadful!"

With the Prince, finally, she had known what was wanted.

On the Bridle Path, finally, she had been told what was wanted. But what did this wicked Queen want of her, that she suffer, that she cringe, that she offer herself or merely endure? And the woman despised her!

The Queen massaged her flesh, prodding it, testing it as if for thickness, softness, resilience. She tested Beauty's thighs in the same manner, and then pushed Beauty's knees so far apart and high on the bed that Beauty's hips rose and she felt she was squatting, sprawled apart, over the coverlet, her sex protruding, hanging down, her buttocks surely split so that she resembled a ripe fruit.

The Queen's hand was under her sex as if weighing it, feeling the roundness and heaviness of the lips, pinching them.

"Arch your back," said the Queen, "and lift your buttocks, little cat, little cat in heat."

Beauty obeyed, her eyes flooded with tears of shame. She was trembling violently as she took a deep breath, and against her will felt the Queen's fingers commanding her passion, squeezing the flame so it burned hotter. Surely Beauty's pubic lips were swelling, their juices flowing, no matter how bitterly she struggled against it!

She did not want to *give* anything to this wicked woman, this witch of a Queen. To the Prince she would yield; to Lord Gregory, to nameless and faceless Lords and Ladies who showered her with compliments, but to this woman who despised her . . . !

But the Queen had sat back on the bed beside Beauty, and hastily she gathered up Beauty as if she were a floppy doll and threw her over her lap, her face away from Prince Alexi, her buttocks surely still exposed to his scrutiny.

Beauty gave an open-mouthed moan, her breasts rubbed against the coverlet, her sex throbbing against the Queen's thigh. It was as if she were some toy in the Queen's hands.

Yes, it was exactly like being a toy, only she was alive, she breathed, she suffered. She could imagine how she appeared to Prince Alexi.

The Queen lifted her hair. She ran a finger down Beauty's back to the tip of her spine.

"All the rituals," the Queen said in a low voice, "the Bridle Path, the stakes in the garden, the wheels, and then the Hunts in the Maze, and all the other clever games devised for my pleasure, but do I ever know a slave until I have this intimacy with the slave, the intimacy of the slave over my lap ready for punishment? Tell me, Alexi. Shall I spank her with my hand only to sustain this intimacy? Feel her stinging flesh, its warmth, as I watch it change color? Shall I use the silver-back mirror, or one of a dozen paddles that are all excellent for the purpose? What do you prefer, Alexi, when you are over my lap? What is it you hope for even as you are crying?"

"You may hurt your hand if you spank her that way," came Prince Alexi's calm answer. "May I get you the silver mirror?"

"Ah, but you do not answer my question," the Queen

said. "And do get me the mirror. I shall not spank her with it. Rather I shall see her face with it as I spank her."

In a blur, Beauty saw Prince Alexi move to the dressing table. And then before her, propped against a silk pillow, was the mirror, tilted so she could see the Queen's smooth white face in it distinctly. The dark eyes terrified her. The Queen's smile terrified her.

"But I shall show her nothing," Beauty thought desperately, shutting her eyes, the tears squeezed out down her cheeks.

"Surely, there is something superior about the open hand," the Queen was saying, her left hand on Beauty's neck, massaging it. She slipped it down under Beauty's breasts, and pushing them closer to one another, touched both nipples with her long fingers. "Have I not spanked you with my hand as hard as any man, Alexi?"

"To be sure, your Highness," he answered softly. He was behind Beauty again. Perhaps he had taken his place against the bedpost.

"Now clasp your hands in the small of your back and keep them there," said the Queen. And she closed her hand over Beauty's buttocks just as she had closed her other hand over Beauty's breasts. "And acknowledge my commands to you, Princess."

"Yes, your Highness," Beauty struggled to respond, but to her further shame her voice broke into sobs and she shivered trying to restrain them.

"And be quieter than that," said the Queen sharply.

The Queen commenced to spank her. One great hard slap after another fell on her buttocks, and if a paddle had ever been worse she could not remember it. She tried to be still, to be quiet, to show nothing, nothing, as she repeated that word over and over in her mind, but she could feel herself writhing.

It was as Leon had said with the Bridle Path; you always struggle as if you could escape the paddle, squirm away from it. And she heard herself crying out suddenly in gasps as the slaps stung her. The Queen's hand seemed immense and hard and heavier than the paddle. It shaped itself to her as it spanked her, and she realized she was frantic, full of tears, and cries, and all of this for the Queen to see in her cursed mirror. Yet she could not stop it.

And the Queen's other hand pinched her breasts, stretched her nipples one at a time, letting them go, and stretching them again, as the spanks went on and on until Beauty was sobbing.

Anything would have been better. Rushing through the hall at the end of Lord Gregory's paddle, the Bridle Path, even the Bridle Path, was better for there was some escape in the movement, and here there was nothing but the pain, her enflamed buttocks laid bare for the Queen who now sought out new spots, spanking on the left buttock and then the right, and then covering Beauty's thighs with smacks while Beauty's buttocks seemed to swell and throb unbearably.

"The Queen must tire. The Queen must stop," Beauty thought, but she had thought this only moments before and it went on, so that Beauty's hips were rising and falling, and she found herself squirming to the side only to be rewarded with sounder blows, more rapid blows, as if the Queen were growing ever more violent. It was as when the Prince had beaten her with the strap. It was becoming more frenzied.

Now the Queen worked on the very bottom of her buttocks, that portion which Lady Juliana had so deliberately lifted on her paddle, and she spanked hard and long on either side before moving up again and to the side, and then to Beauty's thighs and back again.

Beauty clenched her teeth to stifle her cries. She opened her eyes in frantic silent pleas seeing only the Queen's hard profile in the mirror. The Queen's eyes were narrowed, her mouth twisted, and then suddenly she gazed through the mirror at Beauty though she never ceased punishing her.

Beauty's hands broke their firm clasp and struggled

to cover her buttocks, but the Queen at once moved them aside.

"You dare!" she whispered, and Beauty clasped them tight again, sobbing into the coverlet as the spanking continued.

Then the Queen's hand lay on the burning flesh without motion.

It seemed the fingers were still cold, yet they burned. And Beauty could not control her racing breath or her tears, and she would not open her eyes again.

"You shall tender me your apology for that little slip of decorum," said the Queen.

"I . . . I . . . " Beauty stammered.

" 'I am sorry, my Queen.' "

"I am sorry, my Queen." Beauty whispered frantically.

" 'I deserve only your punishment for it, my Queen.' "

"I deserve only your punishment for it, my Queen."

"Yes," the Queen whispered. "And you shall have it. But all and all . . ." The Queen sighed. "Was she not good, Prince Alexi?"

"Very well behaved, your Highness, I should think, but I await your judgment."

The Queen laughed.

She pulled Beauty up roughly.

"Turn around and sit in my lap," she said.

Beauty was astonished. She at once obeyed and realized she was facing Prince Alexi. But he did not matter to her in these moments. Shaken, sore, she sat shivering on the Queen's thighs, the silk of the Queen's gown cool under her burning buttocks, the Queen's left arm cradling her.

The Queen's right hand examined her nipples, and Beauty looked down through her tears to see those white fingers again pulling the nipples.

"I had not thought to find you so obedient," said the Queen, pressing Beauty to her ample breasts, Beauty's hip against the Queen's smooth stomach. Beauty felt tiny as well as helpless, as if she were nothing in this woman's arms, nothing but something small, a child perhaps, no, not even a child.

The Queen's voice grew caressing.

"You are sweet, sweet as Lady Juliana told me you were," she said softly in Beauty's ear.

Beauty bit her lip.

"Your Highness . . ." she whispered, but she did not know what to say.

"My son has trained you well, and you show great perception."

The Queen's hand plunged down between Beauty's legs and felt the sex which had never grown cold or dry during all of the worst of the spanking, and Beauty shut her eyes.

"Ah, now why are you so afraid of my hand when it touches you gently?"

And the Queen bent and kissed Beauty's tears, tasting them on Beauty's cheeks and on her eyelids. "Sugar and salt," she said.

Beauty broke into a fresh shower of sobs. The hand between her legs massaged the most moist portion of her, and she knew that her face was flushed, and the pain and the pleasure mingled. She felt overpowered.

Her head fell back against the Queen's shoulder, and her mouth went slack, and she realized the Queen was kissing her throat, and she murmured some strange words that were not words to the Queen, some plea.

"Poor little slave," said the Queen, "poor little obedient slave. I wanted to send you home to get rid of you, to rid my son of his passion for you, my son who is now as enchanted as you were before, under the spell of the one whom he released from the spell, as if all life were a series of enchantments. But you are as perfect in temperament as he said you were, as perfect as more trained slaves, and yet you are fresher, sweeter."

Beauty gasped as the pleasure between her legs washed

through her, mounting and mounting. She felt her swollen breasts might burst, and her buttocks, as always, throbbed so that she felt every inch of the abraded flesh relentlessly.

"Now, come, did I spank you so very hard, tell me?"

She took Beauty by the chin and turned her so that Beauty looked into her eyes. They were huge and black and fathomless. The lashes curled upwards, and there seemed a great casing of glass over the eyes, so deep they were, so brilliant.

"Well, answer me," said the Queen with her red lips, and she placed her finger in Beauty's mouth and tugged on her lower lip. "Answer me."

"It was . . . hard . . . hard, my Queen . . ." Beauty said meekly.

"Well, yes, perhaps for such fresh little buttocks. But you make Prince Alexi smile with your innocence."

Beauty turned as if bidden to do so but when she gazed at Prince Alexi she did not see him smiling. Rather he was merely looking at her with the strangest expression. It was both remote and loving. And then he looked to the Queen without haste or fear and let his lips lengthen in a smile as she seemed to wish of him.

But the Queen had tipped back Beauty's head again. She kissed Beauty. The Queen's rippling hair fell down around her, full of perfume, and for the first time, Beauty felt the velvety white skin of the Queen's face, and she realized the Queen's breasts were pressed against her.

Beauty's hips moved forward, she started to gasp, but just before it became too much for her, this shock penetrating to her wet, throbbing sex, the Queen suddenly pushed her down and drew back smiling.

She held Beauty's thighs. Beauty's legs were open. And the hungry little sex wanted for all the world for the legs to be crushed closed against it.

The pleasure subsided slightly, back into that great never ending rhythm of craving.

Beauty moaned, her brows knit in a frown, and the

Queen suddenly pushed her off, slapping Beauty's face so hard that Beauty cried out before she could stop herself.

"My Queen, she is so young and tender," said Prince Alexi.

"Don't try my patience," the Queen answered.

Beauty lay facedown on the bed crying.

"Rather ring for Felix and have him bring Lady Juliana. I know how young and tender is my little slave, and how much she has to learn, and that she must be punished for her small disobedience. But that is not what concerns me. I should see more of her, more of her spirit, her efforts to please, and . . . well, I have promised Lady Juliana."

It did not make any difference how hard Beauty cried, they would proceed, and Prince Alexi could not stop them. Beauty heard Felix come, she heard the Queen walking about the room, and finally when Beauty's tears were now a steady silent flow, the Queen said, "Get down from the bed, and prepare yourself to greet Lady Juliana."

LADY JULIANA IN THE QUEEN'S CHAMBER

Lady Juliana came into the room exactly as she had come into the Hall of Punishments, her steps light and springing, her round face full of prettiness and animation. She wore a rose pink gown, and there were pink roses threaded through her long thick braids with pink ribbon.

She seemed too full of light and gaiety for the vast shadowy chamber with the torches throwing huge uneven shadows on the high arched ceiling. The Queen sat in the corner on a great chair that resembled a throne, her foot on a plump green velvet cushion. Her arms rested on the chair, and she smiled faintly when Lady Juliana bowed to her. Prince Alexi, sitting on his heels at the Queen's feet, very politely kissed the pretty Lady's slippers.

Beauty knelt in the center of the flowered carpet, still much shaken and tear-stained, and as soon as Lady Juliana approached her she kissed her slippers as Alexi had done, only perhaps a little more fervently.

Beauty was surprised at her response to Lady Juliana. She had been appalled to hear her name, and yet she almost welcomed her. She felt some connection with her. Lady Juliana had, after all, showered Beauty with affectionate attention. She felt almost as if Lady Juliana were on her side, though she had little doubt that she would now be punished by her. Lady Juliana's paddle had been too diligent on the Bridle Path for Beauty to have any doubt of that. Yet she felt almost as if this were a girlhood friend of great confidence and strength, coming to embrace her.

Lady Juliana was beaming at her.

"Ah, Beauty, sweet Beauty, is the Queen pleased?" And as she stroked Beauty's hair and pushed her back to sit on her heels, Lady Juliana glanced at the Queen politely.

"She is all that you said she would be," answered the Queen. "But I wish to see more of her to judge properly. Use your imagination, lovely one. Do as you please, for me."

At once Lady Juliana motioned to the Page. He opened the door to admit yet another young man who carried a great flower basket filled with pink roses.

Lady Juliana took the basket over her arm, and the two Pages retired to the shadows. They stood as still as guards, and Beauty wondered that their presence meant so little to her. For all she cared, there might have been a row of them there. It did not matter.

"Look up, precious, with those beautiful blue eyes of yours," said Lady Juliana, "and see what I have prepared to amuse the Queen, and further demonstrate your lovliness." She lifted a rose which had a rather short stem, no more than eight inches. "No thorns, my pet, and this I show you so you fear only what you should fear, and not carelessness or blunders."

Beauty could see the basket was heaped with such carefully prepared flowers.

The Queen gave a cheerful laugh and shifted in her chair. "Wine, Alexi," she said, "sweet wine, this room is rather permeated with sweetness."

Lady Juliana burst into soft laughter as though this were a wonderful compliment, and she danced about the room, twirling her rose-colored skirts, her braids swinging.

Beauty watched her in wonder, her vision still unclear from her crying, and the woman seemed, like the Queen, immense and powerful. She turned her smiling face on Beauty like a light. And the glare of the torches flashed in the deep red brooch she wore at her throat, and in the jewels sewn skillfully into her heavy girdle. Her pink satin slippers had silver heels and she danced up to Beauty and kissed the top of her head lovingly.

"But you look so forlorn and that is not good. Now kneel up, fold your arms behind your back to show your exquisite breasts, that's it, and arch your back more becomingly. Her hair, Felix, brush it."

And as the Page hastened to obey, gently untangling Beauty's long locks down her back, Beauty saw the Lady Juliana take from a chest nearby a long oval paddle.

It was very like the paddle used on the Bridle Path, but nothing as big or as heavy. In fact it was so flexible that Lady Juliana, setting down her basket of flowers, could make it vibrate when she pressed the tip of it with her thumb. It was white, smooth, and limber.

It will sting, Beauty realized, but it will not truly hurt as badly as the Queen's hand, and it will hurt nothing as badly as that weapon on the Bridle Path, yet she realized her buttocks were so thoroughly welted that each light blow would enkindle a certain amount of pain in her.

Lady Juliana, laughing, whispering with the Queen in her girlish manner, turned back as Felix finished. Beauty knelt waiting.

"And so our gracious Sovereign spanked you over her lap, did she? And you have had the Bridle Path, and you have learned something of grooming. And then there has been your Lord and Master's temper and demands, and now and then a little routine smacking from your groom or Lord Gregory."

"My groom has never smacked me," Beauty thought crossly, but she merely replied, "Yes, my Lady . . ." as was expected.

"But now you shall learn some actual discipline, for in the little game I devise your will to please is direly tested. And don't think you shan't profit from it. Now . . ." She lifted a handful of roses from the basket. "I shall scatter these about the room, and do you know what you shall do, my precious girl, you shall run very fast to gather each one in your teeth and place in the lap of your Sovereign. And when she has quite finished with you, you shall go to fetch another, and another, and another. And you shall do that as fast as you can, and do you know why, because you are commanded to do so, and you shall be much punished if you do not rush to obey as we command you."

She raised her eyebrows, smiling at Beauty.

"Yes, my Lady," Beauty replied, unable to think, though the thought of having to hurry to obey struck a strange new note of apprehension in her. Gracelessness. She dreaded it. On the Bridle Path there had been much gracelessness when she was running so fast and out of breath. . . . O, but she must not think of anything save what she had to do now.

"And on your hands and knees of course, my girl, and be very very quick!"

Lady Juliana at once scattered the little pink rose-buds with their waxed stems everywhere.

Beauty bent forward and was grasping the nearest in her teeth when she realized that Lady Juliana was right behind her. The handle of the oval paddle was so long, Lady Juliana did not even bend over as she spanked Beauty and with a start, Beauty dropped the flower.

"Pick it up at once!" Lady Juliana cried out, and Beauty's lips scraped the carpet before she had it.

The paddle came down with a fearful zinging sound, smacking her sore welts as she rushed on her hands and knees to the Queen, and Lady Juliana managed some seven or eight good blows before Beauty had dropped the flower in the Queen's lap obediently.

"Now turn around at once," commanded the Lady, "and off you go." But she was already spanking Beauty fiercely as Beauty ran in search of another flower. As soon as she had it in her lips, she ran to the Queen, but the blows followed her. And Beauty wanted to cry out for patience as she went for another.

She gathered a fourth, a fifth, a sixth, depositing each in the Queen's lap, yet there was no escape from the paddle, from its persistence, nor Lady Juliana's voice urging her on crossly.

"Quickly, my girl, quickly, get it in your lips and back again." It seemed her flaring pink skirt was everywhere in Beauty's eyes, and Beauty was surrounded by the flashing of her little silver-heeled slippers. Beauty's knees burned from the rough wool of the carpet, yet she went breathlessly on in her search seeing the tiny pink roses everywhere.

And yet no matter how she gasped for breath, no matter how moist were her face and her limbs, she could not blot from her mind the thought of what she was doing. She could see her own buttocks splotched with white welts, her reddened thighs, and her breasts dangling between her arms as she rushed across the floor like a pitiable animal. There was no mercy for her, and the worst of it was that she could not please Lady Juliana, Lady Juliana goaded her, even kicked her now with the toe of her slipper. Beauty's cries were wordless pleas, but Lady Juliana's tone was angry, unsatisfied.

It was dreadful to be struck in anger.

"Hurry! Do you hear me!" Lady Juliana sounded almost contemptuous, spanking Beauty all the harder, and making little tisks now of impatience. Beauty's nipples scraped the carpet as she bent to obey, and with a shock she felt the toe of Lady Juliana's slipper in her pubis. She gave a startled cry and rushed back to the Queen with the rose as all about her it seemed was the muted laughter of the Pages and the Queen's higher laughter. But Lady Juliana had found the tender spot again, forcing that long pointed satin slipper right into Beauty's vagina.

Suddenly as Beauty turned and saw yet more roses scattered before her, her sobs went into muffled shrieks and she turned to Lady Juliana even as the paddle spanked her thighs and her calves, and kissed and kissed those pink satin slippers.

"What?" Lady Juliana said with genuine outrage. "You dare beg me for mercy before the Queen? Wretched, wretched girl!" She smacked Beauty's buttocks, but she had Beauty by the hair with her left hand and pulled her up, snapping her head back so that Beauty's knees went wide apart to keep her balance.

Beauty's open-mouthed sobs were choked and uneven. And she saw the paddle being passed to one of the Pages who offered the Lady a heavy broad leather belt immediately.

The belt struck Beauty's buttocks with a resounding wallop. Again it struck her. "Take another rose, another, two, three, four in your mouth at once and give them to your Queen immediately!"

Beauty ran to obey, and it seemed for a moment all perception left her. She was frantic to obey, to outdistance

Lady Juliana's anger. It was hotter, more frenzied than the Bridle Path at its worst, and as she turned to gather more of the little roses, she felt the Queen catch her face in both hands and hold her still so that Lady Juliana could beat her.

It did not matter. She could not please. She deserved to be beaten. She quivered with every blow of the strap, yet, drenched with tears, she even lifted her buttocks to receive the punishment.

But the Queen was not satisfied still, and she turned Beauty around, her hand on Beauty's hair to pull her head back, as Lady Juliana now smacked Beauty's breasts and her belly and made the wide leather strap lick at her pubis.

The Queen held Beauty's hair fast.

"Open your legs!" Lady Juliana commanded.

"Oooooh . . ." Beauty sobbed aloud, but she obeyed, and desperately she thrust her hips forward to receive the angry punishment. She must please Lady Juliana, she must show her that she had tried. Her sobs came hoarse and brokenhearted.

And the strap smacked her pubic lips again and again, and she did not know what was worse, the little shock of pain, or the violation of it.

Her head was pulled so far back she was now resting it in the Queen's lap, and she felt her own sobs rising up out of her chest and out of her lips almost languidly.

"I am defenseless, I am nothing," she found herself thinking as she had thought it on the Bridle Path in the midst of the worst exhaustion. The belt licked her breast. It was no more than she could bear, and it did not even occur to her to lift her arms, though her pubis was flooded with warm pain. Her sobs had a delicious release for her.

She felt herself growing limp, yielding. She felt the Queen's hand caressing her chin, and then she realized Lady Juliana had dropped down before her in a flurry of pink silk and was kissing her throat and her shoulders.

"There, there," said the Queen, "my brave little slave . . ."

"There, there, my girl, my virtuous, lovely girl," said Lady Juliana at once as if given permission. The blows had stopped. Beauty's cries filled the room. "And you were good, very good, you tried very hard, and you struggled so hard to be graceful."

The Queen moved Beauty forward into Lady Juliana's arms, and Lady Juliana rose to her feet pulling Beauty up in her embrace, her hands pressed into Beauty's enflamed buttocks.

Lady Juliana's arms were soft and her lips were tickling Beauty, stroking her, and Beauty felt her breasts against Lady Juliana's plump breasts, and then Beauty seemed to lose all awareness of her own weight, her sense of balance.

She was drifting in Lady Juliana's arms, feeling the delicious cloth of the Lady's gown, and her rounded limbs beneath it.

"O, sweet little Beauty, my Beauty, you are so good, so very good," the Lady whispered to her. And her lips pried open Beauty's lips, and her tongue touched the inside of Beauty's mouth as her fingers pressed harder into Beauty's buttocks. Beauty's wet sex was pressed against Lady Juliana's gown, and then she felt the hard mound of Lady Juliana's sex. "Blessed Beauty, O, you do love me, don't you, I love you dearly."

Beauty could not stop herself from throwing her arms about Lady Juliana's neck. She felt the prickling of those blond braids, but Lady Juliana's skin was plump and soft, and her lips strong and silken.

They sucked at Beauty's mouth, plump lips, while Lady Juliana's teeth bit here and there as if tasting Beauty.

And then Beauty looked into Lady Juliana's eyes, so large and innocent and full of tender concern. Beauty moaned and laid her cheek against Lady Juliana's cheek.

Lady Juliana in the Queen's Chamber

"That is enough," said the Queen coldly.

Slowly, slowly, Beauty felt herself being released. She was being forced down, and languidly she let herself droop, until she sat on her heels on the floor, her legs parted slightly, her sex nothing but craving and pain to her.

She bowed her head. She feared above all that she would lose control of this mounting pleasure. She would blush, she would pant, she would writhe with it, unable to disguise it from those before her. So she parted her legs, feeling her pubis open and close like a hungry little mouth desperate for satisfaction.

Yet she did not care. She had known there would be no release for her.

It was enough to feel the rough wool of the carpet against her itching, stinging buttocks, and all life seemed but gradations of pain and pleasure. Her breasts seemed to be tipped with weights, and she let her head fall to the side, and a great ripple of relaxation ran through her. What more could they do to her with their games, it did not matter. "Do it," she thought, and her eyes melted into tears, the torchlight a glare before her.

She looked up.

Lady Juliana and the Queen stood side by side, the Queen's arm about Lady Juliana's shoulder. And they were both looking down at Beauty as Lady Juliana unbraided her hair and the little rosebuds fell free at her feet unheeded.

The moment seemed to go on forever.

Beauty rose to her knees again. She moved silently forward. She bent down with great delicacy and picked up one of the tiny rosebuds in her teeth, and she lifted her head in offering.

She felt the rose taken from her. And then the gentle cool kisses of both women.

"Very good, my darling," said the Queen with the first true affection.

Beauty pressed her lips to their slippers.

She heard through her drowsiness the Queen's command that she be taken by the Pages and chained to the wall of the dressing room nearby until morning.

"Spread her, and spread her wide," said the Queen.

And Beauty knew with a sweet despair that her craving would not for a long time leave her.

WITH
PRINCE
ALEXI

THE QUEEN slept surely. Maybe Lady Juliana slept in her arms. The whole castle slept, and beyond it the villages and the towns, the peasants in their cottages and hovels.

And through the high, narrow window of the dressing room, the sky gave a moon-white light on the wall where Beauty was shackled, her ankles far apart, her wrists spread equally wide apart above her. She lay her head to the side, gazing at the long row of magnificent gowns, the mantles on their hooks, the circlets of gold and embroidery, the beautiful ornamental chains, and heaps upon heaps of lovely slippers.

And here she was among these things as if she were but an adornment, a possession, kept with other valuable possessions.

She sighed, and she deliberately rubbed her rear against the stone wall, wanting somehow to punish it more so that after a few seconds she could feel the relief when she stopped doing this.

Her sex would not stop its throbbing. It was sticky with its own wetness. Poor Princess Lizetta in the Hall of Punishments, did she suffer worse than this? At least she was not alone in the darkness, and suddenly even those who must pass her, taunting her, teasing her, stroking her swelling sex, seemed to Beauty a desirable company. She strained and twisted her hips. It was no comfort to her, and she did not understand why she felt this craving when only a little while ago her pain had been so great she had kissed Lady Juliana's slippers. She flushed to think of Lady Juliana's angry words, those reproving spanks that somehow hurt her worse than the others.

And how the Pages must have laughed when a dozen Princesses had probably played the little gathering game with the roses and done it better.

But why, why had Beauty at the very end picked up that last rosebud, and why had she felt her breasts swollen with warmth when Lady Juliana took it from her lips? It had seemed in that moment that Beauty's nipples were cruel little caps that prevented pleasure from breaking loose in her. Strange thought. They seemed too tight for her then, her nipples, and her sex gaped and hungered and the moisture trickled down the inside of her thighs, and when she thought of Prince Alexi's smile, and Lady Juliana's brown eyes, and her Prince's beautiful face, and even the Queen, yes, even the Queen's red lips, she felt herself burning in agony.

Prince Alexi's sex was thick and dark, like all of him, and his nipples a dark, dark rose color.

She tossed her head, rolled it against the wall. But

why had she picked up the rose, offered it to pretty Lady Juliana?

She stared forward in the darkness, and hearing a creaking sound very near to her, she thought she was imagining it.

But in the darkness of the near wall, a seam of light appeared and widened. The door had been opened, and Prince Alexi slipped into the dressing room. Unbound, free, he was standing before her, and very gently, he pushed the door closed behind him.

Beauty held her breath.

He did not move, as if he must accustom himself to the darkness, and then immediately he came forward and released Beauty's wrists and ankles.

She stood trembling. And then her arms were about him. He held her against his chest, his stiff organ prodding her thighs, and she felt the silken skin of his face, and then his mouth opened over hers, hard, yes, savoring her.

"Beauty," he gave a deep sigh and she knew he was smiling. Her hand went up to feel his eyelashes. In the light of the moon she saw the planes of his face, his white teeth. She touched him all over hungrily, desperately. And then she descended upon him with loud kisses.

"Wait, wait, my lovely one, I am as anxious as you are," he whispered. But she couldn't keep her hands off his shoulders, his neck, his satin flesh.

"Come with me," he said and though it seemed an effort to disengage himself, he opened another door and took her down a long, low-roofed passage.

The moon entered windows that were no more than narrow slices out of the wall, and then he paused before one of many heavy doors, and she found herself descending a twisting stairway.

Beauty grew afraid.

"But where are we going? We'll be caught, and what will happen to us?" she whispered.

But he had opened a door and led her into a little chamber.

One little square of window gave them light, and Beauty saw a heavy straw bed covered with a white blanket. A servant's robe hung upon a hook, but all was neglected as if the room had long ago been forgotten.

Alexi bolted the door. No one could possibly open it.

"I thought you meant to escape," Beauty sighed with relief. "But will they find us here?"

Alexi was looking at her, the moon full on his face and his eyes that were filled with that strange serenity.

"The Queen sleeps every night of her life until the break of day. Felix has been dismissed. If I'm at the foot of her bed at dawn, we won't be discovered. But there is always the chance, and then we shall be punished."

"O, I don't care, I don't care." Beauty said frantically.

"Neither do I," he started to say, but his mouth was buried in Beauty's neck as Beauty flung her arms about him.

At once they were on the straw bed, against the soft blanket. Beauty's buttocks felt the prickles of the straw, but they meant nothing to her so much as Alexi's wet, hard kisses. She pressed her breasts to his chest, she wrapped her legs about his hips and strained against him.

All the long night's teasing and tormenting of her was maddening her. And then he drove into her that thick sex she had desired from the first instant she had seen it. His thrusts were brutal, strong, as if he too were overcome with denied passion. Her aching sex was filled, her tight nipples throbbing, and she snapped her hips, lifting him as she had lifted the Prince, feeling him fill her, pinion her.

At last she rose up crying out in her relief, and she felt him come with a last driving motion. Hot fluids filled her, and she lay back gasping.

She lay against his chest. He cradled her, rocked her, never stopped kissing her.

And when she sucked his nipples, bit at them playfully with her teeth, he was hard again and pushing against her.

He rose to his knees and lifted her down on his organ. She whispered her assent and then he moved her back and forth, jabbing her, working her. She had her head thrown back, her teeth clenched. "Alexi, my Prince!" she cried. And again her wet sex, stretched wide over him, throbbed in a frenzied rhythm until she was all but screaming with release as again he filled her.

It was not until after a third time that they lay still.

Yet she bit at his nipples, her hands feeling his scrotum, his penis. He rested on his elbow and smiled down at her, and let her do as she wished, even when her fingers probed his anus. She had never felt a man in this manner before. She sat up, and made him roll on his face, and then she examined all of him.

And then, overcome with shyness, she lay beside him again, nestled into his arms and buried her head in his warm, sweet smelling hair, and welcomed his gentle, deep, affectionate kisses. His lips played with hers. He whispered her name in her ear, and laying his hand between her legs sealed her tight with his palm as he clung to her.

"We must not fall asleep," he said. "I fear that for you the punishment might be too terrible."

"And not for you?" she asked.

He appeared to reflect, and then he smiled. "Probably not," he answered. "But you are a fledgling."

"And do I do so badly?" she asked.

"You are incomparable in all things," he said. "Don't let your cruel masters and mistresses deceive you. They are in love with you."

"Ah, but how should we be punished?" she asked. "Would it be the village?" She dropped her voice as she said it.

"And who has told you about the village?" he asked, a little surprised. "It could be the village . . ." he was thinking . . ."but no favorite of the Queen or the Crown Prince has ever been cast out into the village. But we won't be caught, and if we are I shall say I gagged you, forced you. You should suffer at most a few days in the Hall of Punishments, and what happens to me does not matter. And you must swear to me you will let me take all the blame, or I shall gag you, and carry you back and chain you up immediately."

Beauty bowed her head.

"I brought you here. I shall be punished if we're caught. That must be a rule between us. No arguments from you."

"Yes, my Prince," she whispered.

"No, don't say this to me," he pleaded. "I had not meant to command you. I'm Alexi to you, and nothing more than that, and I am sorry if I was harsh, only I cannot lead you into terrible punishment. Do as I ask because . . . because . . ."

"Because I adore you, Alexi," she said.

"Ah, Beauty, you are my love, my love," he answered. He kissed her again. "Now you must tell me, what are your thoughts, why do you suffer so?"

"Why do I suffer? But don't you see it with your own eyes? Did I ever forget for one moment that you were watching me tonight? You see what was done to me, what is done to you, what is . . ."

"Of course I watched you and was glad of the pleasure of it," he said. "Did you *not* enjoy seeing me paddled by the Crown Prince and did you *not* enjoy seeing me punished in the Great Hall when you were first brought in? What would you do if I told you I spilt the wine that first day so that you would notice me?"

She was stunned.

"I ask you why you suffer. I don't mean what you suffer from the paddle, or the relentless games of our Lords and Ladies. I mean what do you suffer in your heart? Why are you in such conflict? What prevents you from yielding?"

"Have you yielded?" she demanded, slightly angry.

"Of course," he said easily. "I adore the Queen and I adore pleasing her. I adore all those who torment me, because I must. It is profoundly simple."

"And you feel no pain, no humiliation?"

"I feel much pain and much humiliation. And that will never stop. If it did, even for a little while, our endlessly clever masters and mistresses would think of some new way to make us feel it. Do you think I was not humiliated in the Great Hall to be upended by Felix and spanked before an entire Court, and so casually, and for so little? I am a powerful Prince, my father is a powerful King. I never forget it. And surely it was painful to be so roughly treated by the Crown Prince for your benefit. And he thought it would make you love me less!"

"He was wrong, so wrong!" Beauty said, but she sat up and put her hands to the sides of her head in consternation. She loved them both, that was the misery of it, the Crown Prince whom even now she could envision with his lean white face and those immaculate hands and those dark eyes so full of turbulence and dissatisfaction. It had been an agony to her that he had not taken her to his bed after the Bridle Path.

"I want to help you because I love you," Alexi said. "I want to guide you. You are in rebellion."

"Yes, but not always," she admitted in a vague whisper, looking off, as if she were suddenly ashamed to admit it. "I have . . . so many feelings."

"Tell me," he said with authority.

"Well, tonight . . . the rose, the last little pink bud . . . why did I pick it up in my teeth and offer it to Lady Juliana? Why? She had been so cruel to me."

"You wanted to please her. She is your mistress. You are a slave. The highest thing that you can do is please, so you sought to do it, and not only in response to her paddling and her commands, but in that moment *of your own will*."

"Ah, yes," said Beauty, that was it. "And . . . on the

Bridle Path, how can I confess it, I felt some release in myself as if I were no longer locked in struggle, I was just a slave, a poor, desperate slave who must strive, strive *purely*."

"You are eloquent," he said with feeling. "You know much already."

"But I don't want to feel this. I want to rebel in my heart, I want to steel myself against them. They torment me endlessly. My Prince, were he the only one . . ."

"But even if he were, he would find new ways to torment you, and he is not the only one. But tell me why you don't wish to give in to them."

"Well, surely you know. Didn't you rebel? Don't you? Why, Leon said of you there is a core in you which no one touches."

"Nonsense. I merely know and accept everything. There is no resistance."

"But how can it be?"

"Beauty, you must learn it. You must accept and yield, and then you shall see everything is simple."

"I would not be here with you if I yielded because the Prince . . ."

"Yes, you could be here with me. I adore my Queen and I am here with you. I love you both. I yield to that entirely as well as everything else and even the knowledge I may be punished. And when I am punished, I shall dread it, and suffer it and understand it and accept it. Beauty, when you accept you will flower in the pain, you will flower in your suffering."

"There was a girl ahead of me in line last night who ran the Bridle Path just before me. She was resigned, wasn't she?" Beauty asked.

"No, forget about her, she is nothing, that is Princess Claire and she is silly and playful and always was and feels nothing. She has no depth, no great mystery. But you have these and you will always suffer more than she does."

"But does everyone sooner or later acquire this ability to accept?"

"No, some never do, but it is very hard to tell who has attained it. I can tell, but our masters are not always so wise, I can assure you. For example, Felix told me that yesterday you saw Princess Lizetta strung up in the Hall of Punishments. Do you think she is resigned?"

"Certainly not!"

"Ah, but she is, and she is a great and valuable slave Princess. But Princess Lizetta adores being bound up, being unable to move, and when she is greatly bored, she endures the displeasure of her betters, the better to amuse them by letting them punish her."

"Ah, no, you can't be serious."

"Yes, I can. That is her way. All slaves have their way. And you must find yours. It will never be easy for you. You will suffer much before you know it, but don't you see that on the Bridle Path and tonight when you gave the rose to Lady Juliana you felt the beginnings of it. Princess Lizetta is a struggler. You shall be a yielder, much as I am. That shall be your way, exquisite and personal devotion. Great calm, great serenity. In time perhaps you will see other slaves who are exemplary in this. Prince Tristan, for example, the slave of Lord Stefan, is incomparable. His Lord is in love with him as the Prince is with you, which makes it both difficult and simple."

Beauty gave a deep sigh. She was flooded suddenly with the sensation of kneeling before Lady Juliana and offering her the rose. She felt herself running on the Bridle Path, and the breeze touching her, and her body burning all over with her striving.

"I don't know, I feel ashamed when I give in, I feel as if I have truly lost myself."

"Yes, that is it. But listen. We have the night here together. I want to tell you the story of how I came here and how I attained the path I speak of. When I am finished, if you still feel rebellious, I ask you to think on it. I shall go on loving you, no matter, and go on striving for moments to see you in secret. But if you listen to me, you shall see that you can conquer everything about you.

"Don't try to understand all that I say at once. Merely listen and see if the story in the end does not soothe you. Remember, you cannot possibly escape this place. No matter what you do the Court will find ways to wring amusement from you. Even a wild, teeth-gnashing slave can be bound and used in an abundance of different ways to amuse everyone. So accept this limit; and then try to understand your own limits and how you must broaden them."

"O, if I know you love me I can accept, I can accept anything."

"I do love you. But the Prince loves you, too. And even so, you must seek your path of acceptance."

He embraced her, then gently forcing his tongue between her lips, kissed her violently.

He suckled her breasts until they were almost sore, as she arched her back moaning again, her passion rising. He lifted her under him and once again he drove his organ into her, turning her gently so they lay on their sides facing one another.

"They shan't rouse me tomorrow for anything and for that alone I'll be punished." He smiled. "But I do not care. It's worth it, to have you, to hold you, and to be with you."

"But I can't bear to think of you punished."

"Be comforted that I shall deserve it, and the Queen must be satisfied, and I belong to her, just as you belong to her and you belong to the Prince, and should he catch you he would have every right to punish me further."

"But how can I belong to him and to you?"

"As easily as you might belong as well to the Queen and Lady Juliana. Did you not give Lady Juliana the rose? I wager that before the month is out, you will be mad to please Lady Juliana. You will dread her displeasure; you will hunger for her paddling just as you fear it."

Beauty turned her face away and buried it in the straw because it was already true. Tonight she had been glad to see Lady Juliana. And this was the way she felt about her Prince.

"Now, listen to my story and you will understand more. It is not a neat explanation. But you will see something of a mystery unfolded."

PRINCE
ALEXI
TELLS OF
HIS CAPTURE
AND
ENSLAVE-
MENT

W<small>HEN IT</small> came time to send
Tributes to the Queen," Prince Alexi said, "I was not at
all resigned to be chosen. There were other Princes who
were brought forward to go with me, and we were told
that our service with the Queen would last no more than
five years at most, and that we would return greatly enhanced in wisdom, patience, self-control, and all virtues.
Of course I had known others who had served, and though
they are all forbidden to speak of what happens, I knew
it was an ordeal and I cherished my freedom. So when
my father told me I must go, I ran away from the castle
and went roaming through the villages.

(176)

Prince Alexi Tells of His Capture and Enslavement

"I don't know how my father received this news. It was a party of the Queen's soldiers who raided the village where I was and carried me off with a number of the common boys and girls for other forms of service. These were given to minor Lords and Ladies to serve in their own manor houses. Princes and Princesses such as we serve only at the Court, as I'm sure you realize.

"It was a brilliantly sunny day. I was walking alone in a field south of the village writing poetry in my mind when I saw the Queen's soldiers. I had my broadsword, of course, but I was at once surrounded by some six horsemen. As soon as I realized they meant to take me as a slave I knew they belonged to the Queen. They threw a net over me and quickly disarmed me. I was stripped on the spot, and thrown over the Captain's saddle.

"That alone was enough to infuriate me and make me fight for my freedom. You can imagine it, my ankles tied with coarse rope, my naked buttocks in the air, my head dangling. The Captain laid his hands on me often enough when he was idle. He pinched and prodded as suited him, and seemed to enjoy his advantages."

Beauty winced at all this. She could well picture it.

"It was a long journey to the Queen's Kingdom. I was handled roughly like so much baggage, bound at night to a pole outside the Captain's tent and though no one was allowed to violate me, I was tormented by the soldiers. They would take reeds and sticks and prod my organs, touch my face, my arms and legs, whatever they could. My hands were tied over my head; I stood all that while, sleeping on my feet. The nights were warm enough but it was quite miserable.

"However, all of this had a wisdom to it. I was promised to the Queen herself, by virtue of her treaty with my father. And of course I was eager to be rid of these coarse soldiers. Each day's ride was the same, over the Captain's saddle. He often whipped me with his leather gloves playfully. He let the villagers come near the road when we passed. He taunted me, and tousled my hair, and called me pet names. But he could not really use me."

"Were you thinking of escape?" Beauty asked.

"Always," said the Prince. "But I was in the midst of the soldiers at all times, and completely naked. Even had I managed to reach a villager's cottage or a serf's hut, I would have been overpowered and returned for the ransom money. More humiliation and more degradation. I rode, bound hand and foot and ignominiously thrown over the horse, in a state of fury.

"But finally we reached the castle. I was scrubbed, then oiled and brought before her Highness. She was coldly beautiful. This made its impression upon me at once. I had never seen such pretty eyes, yet such cold eyes. And when I refused to be silent or to obey, she laughed. She ordered me gagged with a leather bit. I'm sure you've seen it. Well, mine was bound in place so I couldn't remove it. And then she had me shackled in leather so that I could not rise from my hands and knees. I could move as told, but not rise, the leather collar around my neck securely linked by leather chains to the leather cuffs on my wrists, and those to the cuffs on my legs above the knees. My ankles were linked so they couldn't be spread very wide apart. It was all quite clever.

"And then the Queen took her long lead—as she calls it—to drive me. It was a rod with a leather-encased phallus on the end of it. I shall never forget the first moment I felt it drive into my anus. She thrust it forward, and in spite of myself I moved ahead of her like an obedient pet as she commanded me. And when I lay down and refused to obey, she only laughed at this, and commenced her work with the paddle.

"Well, I was fiercely rebellious. The more she paddled me, the more I growled and refused to obey. So she had me hung upside down and paddled on and off for hours. You can well imagine the misery of it. But understand, other slaves were looking at me in utter confusion. Being stripped, being cuffed, being ordered about with the paddle was quite enough to make them obey, coupled as it was with the knowledge that they could not escape and they must serve for several years, and they were helpless.

"Yet nothing worked its magic with me. When I was taken down I was sore from the paddle on my buttocks and my legs, but I did not care. And all attempts to rouse my organ had failed. I was too stubborn.

"Lord Gregory lectured me at length. The paddle was far easier to bear with an erect organ, he told me; with passion coursing through my veins, I should see the rhyme and reason of pleasing my mistress. I wouldn't listen.

"The Queen still found me amusing. She told me I was more beautiful than any other slave sent to her. She had me bound to the wall in her chambers night and day so that she might watch me. But more truly, it was so that I might watch her and desire her.

"Well, at first, I did not look at her. But by and by I grew to studying her. I learned every detail of her, her cruel eyes, and her heavy black hair, her white breasts and her long legs, and the way that she lay abed or walked about, or ate her food so daintily. Of course, she had me paddled regularly. And a strange thing commenced to happen. The paddlings were the only things that broke the boredom of this time, aside from watching her. So that watching her and being paddled became of interest to me."

"O, she is devilish!" Beauty gasped. She could understand all this perfectly.

"Of course she is, and infinitely sure of her own beauty.

"Well, all this while, she went about the business of the Court, coming and going. I was often alone with nothing to do but struggle, and curse behind the gag. Then she would return, a vision of soft tresses and red lips. My heart started to pound when she was undressed. I loved the moment when her mantle was released from its folds

and I saw her hair. Then, when she was naked and step-
ping into her bath, I was beside myself.

"All this was secret. I did my best to display nothing
of it. I quieted my passion. But I am a man, so in a matter
of days my passion commenced to build, to show itself.
The Queen laughed at this. She tormented me. Then she
would tell me how much less I would suffer if I were over
her lap obediently accepting her paddle. This is the Queen's
favorite sport, the simple spanking over the lap, as you
learned painfully enough tonight. She loves the intimacy
of it. All her slaves are her children."

Beauty puzzled over this, but she didn't want to
interrupt Alexi, who went on.

"As I told you, she would have me paddled. And
always in a most uncomfortable and cold manner. She
would send for Felix, whom I then despised . . ."

"You don't now?" Beauty asked. But then with a
flush she remembered the scene she had witnessed on
the stairway, Felix suckling the Prince so tenderly.

"I don't despise him now at all," Prince Alexi answered. "He is, of all the Pages, one of the more *interesting*. One comes to treasure that here. But in those days,
I despised him as much as I did the Queen.

"She would give the order for me to be spanked.
He would have me removed from the shackles that held
me to the wall, as I kicked and struggled frantically. Then
I'd be thrown over his knee, my legs kicked wide apart,
and the spanking would go on until the Queen was tired
of it. It hurt very much as I'm sure you know, and it only
further humiliated me. But as I became more and more
desperately bored in my hours of solitude, I commenced
to look upon it as an interlude. I began to think about
the pain, the various stages of it. There were the first few
cracks of the paddle, not so painful at all. Then, as they
came on harder and harder, the aching, the stinging, I
found myself wriggling and trying to escape the blows,
though I'd sworn I wouldn't. I'd remind myself to be still
only to slip into writhing again, which amused the Queen

immensely. When I was very sore, I felt very tired, tired of the struggle, and the Queen knew then I was most vulnerable. She would touch me. Her hands felt very delicious on my welts though I hated her. Then she'd stroke my organ, telling me in my ear what ecstasies I might enjoy in serving her. I would receive her full attention, she said, and be bathed and babied by the grooms, instead of roughly scrubbed and hung on the wall. I would weep sometimes because I couldn't stop myself. The Pages would laugh. The Queen thought it all quite laughable, too. Then I would be returned to the wall to be broken down by more interminable boredom.

"Now all this time, I never saw the other slaves punished by the Queen. She would carry out her pleasures and games in her many parlors. Sometimes I would hear cries and blows through the doors, but seldom.

"But, as I began to exhibit an erect and craving organ in spite of myself, and began to actually look forward to the terrible spankings . . . in spite of myself . . . these two interludes not being connected as yet in my mind . . . she brought in a slave now and then for her amusement.

"I can't tell you the rages of jealousy I felt the first time I had to witness a slave punished. This was a young Prince Gerald, whom she adored in those days. He was sixteen, and had the roundest, smallest buttocks. They were irresistible to the Pages, and the grooms, as yours are . . ."

Beauty blushed at this.

"Don't count yourself unlucky. Listen to what I say about the boredom," Alexi said, and he kissed her tenderly.

"As I was saying, this slave was brought in and the Queen stroked and teased him shamelessly. She placed him over her lap and proceeded to deliver a naked-handed spanking as she did to you, and I could see his erect penis, and how he tried to keep it away from her leg for fear he would spill his passion and displease her. He was utterly compliant and devoted to her. He had no dignity in his surrender at all, but scampered to obey her every command, his beautiful little face always flushed, his skin pink and white and full of blushes where he'd been punished. I couldn't take my eyes off him. I thought I can never be made to do these things. Never—I should die first. Yet I watched him, and I watched her punish him and prod him and kiss him.

"And when he had pleased her well, how she rewarded him! She had brought in six Princes and Princesses from whom he must choose with whom he would couple. Of course his choices were to please her. He chose the Princes always.

"And as she presided over him with the paddle, he would mount one of these who knelt for it obediently enough and, receiving the Queen's blows, he would achieve ecstasy. It was a tantalizing spectacle. His own plump little buttocks being soundly spanked, the red-faced submissive slave on his knees to receive Prince Gerald, and the boy's erect cock going in and out of the undefended anus. Sometimes the Queen spanked the little victim first, gave him a merry chase about the room, a chance to escape his fate if he could fetch a pair of slippers for her in his teeth before she could achieve ten good cracks of the paddle. The victim would scurry to obey. But seldom was he able to find the slippers and bring them to the proper place before the Queen had soundly paddled him. So he had to bend over for Prince Gerald, who was too well endowed for sixteen surely.

"Of course I told myself all this was disgusting and beneath me. I should never play such games." He laughed softly, and squeezed Beauty against his chest with his arm, kissing her forehead. "I've played them enough since," he said.

"But now and then, too, Prince Gerald did choose a Princess. This angered the Queen, though only slightly. She had the little girl victim perform some hopeless tasks in the hope of escape, the same game with the slippers, or the getting of a hand mirror or the like, all the while driving her mercilessly with the paddle. Then she would be thrown down on her back and taken by the lusty little Prince for the Queen's amusement. Or she might be doubled and hung as in the Hall of Punishments.

Beauty winced at this. To be taken in such a position hadn't occurred to her. But a Princess would surely be ripe and open for it.

"As you can imagine," Alexi went on, "these spectacles became a torture. In my hours alone, I longed for them. As I watched, I could feel the blows on my buttocks as if I too were being spanked, and I felt my penis stir against my will at the sight of the little girls being chased, or even Prince Gerald being stroked and sometimes suckled by a Page for the Queen's amusement.

"I should add that Prince Gerald found this very hard. He was an anxious Prince, ever striving to please the Queen, and punishing himself in his own mind, dreadfully, for failure. He never seemed to realize that many of the tasks and games were deliberately made too difficult for him. The Queen would have him brush her hair with the brush fixed in his teeth. This is most difficult. And he would be weeping when he could not brush her hair in long enough strokes, nor thoroughly enough. Of course she was annoyed. She'd throw him over her lap, and with a leather-handled brush flail at him. He wept, full of shame and misery, and feared her worst wrath: that he be given over to others for pleasure and chastisement."

"Does she ever give you to others, Alexi?" Beauty asked.

"When she's displeased with me, she gives me to others," he continued. "But I have surrendered and accepted this. It saddens me but I accept it. I am never in the frenzy in which Prince Gerald always found himself. He would beseech the Queen with silent kisses all over her slippers. It was never any use. The more he pleaded, the more she punished him."

"What became of him?"

"The time came for him to be sent back to his Kingdom. That time comes for all slaves. It will come for you, too, though when, no one can say, on account of the Prince's passion for you, and that he awakened you and claimed you. Your Kingdom was a legend here," said Prince Alexi.

"But Prince Gerald went home richly rewarded and I think most relieved to be let go. He was of course beautifully dressed before he left, and received by the Court, and then we were assembled to see him ride out. It's the custom. I think it was as humiliating for him as anything else. It was as if he remembered his nakedness and his subjugation. But other slaves suffer just as much when they are released for many reasons. Who knows, however. Maybe Prince Gerald's endless worries saved him from something worse. It's impossible to tell. Princess Lizetta is saved by her rebellion. It was *interesting* to Prince Gerald surely . . ."

Prince Alexi paused to kiss Beauty again and soothe her. "Don't try to understand all I say just now. That is, don't try to find immediate meaning in it," he said. "Merely listen and learn and perhaps what I tell you shall save you some mistakes, give you different paths for the mind later. Ah, you are so tender to me, my secret flower."

He would have embraced her again, perhaps become carried away by his passion again, but she stopped him with a touch of her fingers to his lips.

"But tell me, when you were shackled to the wall, what did you think of . . . when you were alone, did you daydream, and what did you dream?"

"What a strange question," he said.

Beauty seemed very serious. "Did you think of your former life, and wish you were free for this or that pleasure?"

"Not really," he said slowly. "I thought rather of what would happen to me next, I suppose. I don't know. Why do you ask this?"

Beauty didn't reply, but she had dreamed three times since she had come and each time her old life to her had seemed grim and fraught with tiny worries. She remembered hours with her embroidery, and the endless bowing at Court to the Princes who kissed her hand. She remembered sitting quite still for hours at interminable banquets where others talked and drank, and she had felt only boredom.

"Please continue, Alexi," she said gently. "But to whom does the Queen give you when she's displeased?"

"Ah, that is a question with several answers," he said. "But let me proceed. You can well imagine what my existence was, the hours of boredom and solitude broken only by these three diversions: the Queen herself, Prince Gerald's punishment, or the fierce paddling from Felix. Well, soon, in spite of myself and my rage, I commenced to show my excitement whenever the Queen came into the chamber. She ridiculed me for it, but she marked it. And now and then, I could not conceal it when I saw Prince Gerald so boldly erect and taking his pleasure of one of the other slaves, or even taking the paddle. The Queen observed all this, and each time she saw that my organ was stiff and beyond my will, she would have Felix at once deliver a hard spanking to me. I struggled, I tried to curse her, and at first these spankings quelled my passion, but very soon they did not quell it. And the Queen added to my misery with her own hands, slapping my penis, stroking it, and then slapping it again at the very moment that Felix was punishing me. I twisted, struggled. It was no use. Very soon, I so craved the Queen's hands that I was moaning aloud and in one of these great tormented states, I did all that I could by gesture and manner to show that I would obey her.

"Of course I had no intention of doing so. I did so only long enough to be rewarded. And I wonder if you can imagine how difficult this was for me. I was put free on my hands and knees, and told to kiss her feet. It was as if I had only just been stripped naked. Never had I obeyed any command; nor been made to obey while free of shackles. And yet so tortured was I for relief, my sex so swollen with desire, that I forced myself to kneel at her feet and kiss her slippers. I shall never forget the magic of her hands when she touched me. I could feel the shock of passion through me, and as soon as she stroked and toyed with my sex, my passion was at once released, which greatly angered her.

" 'You have no control,' she said crossly to me, 'and for this you will be punished. But you have tried to submit and that is something.' But at that moment, I rose up and tried to run from her. I'd never had any intention of submitting to anything.

"Of course the Pages apprehended me at once. You must never think yourself safe from them. You may be in a vast, dimly lit chamber alone with a Lord. You may think yourself quite free when he falls asleep with his wine cup. But should you try to rise and escape, at once the Pages appear to subdue you. Only now that I am the Queen's trusted valet am I allowed to sleep alone in her chamber. The Pages dare not enter the darkened room where the Queen sleeps. So they have no way of knowing that I am here with you. But this is rare, most rare. And even now we might be discovered . . ."

"But what happened to you," Beauty pressed. "They apprehended you," she said fearfully.

"The Queen gave little consideration to how I should be punished. She sent for Lord Gregory and told him I was most incorrigible. That in spite of my fine hands and skin, and royal birth, I should be taken at once to the kitchen, there to serve for as long as she should decree . . . and indeed, she hoped she would remember I was there and send for me.

"I was carried down to the kitchen, protesting as usual. Mind you, I had little idea what was to happen to me. But very soon I saw that I was in a dark and dirty place, full of the grease and soot of the cooking where the pots were always boiling and dozens of menials were at work at the chopping of vegetables and the cleaning or plucking of the fowl, and all the other tasks that go to produce the banquets served here.

"No sooner was I brought in than they rejoiced to have a little amusement. I was surrounded by the crudest beings I had ever seen. 'But what is this to me,' I thought. 'I obey no one.'

"But in moments, I realized these creatures were no more interested in my compliance than they were interested in the compliance of the fowl they slaughtered, or the carrots they scrubbed, or the potatoes they threw in the pot. I was a plaything to them and seldom did they even address me as though I had ears to hear or sense to comprehend what they said about me.

"I was at once collared in leather, this collar linked to the cuffs on my wrists, and my wrists to my knees so that I could not rise from a hands-and-knees position. A bit with a bridle was placed in my mouth, and bound so securely to my head that I might be pulled forward by leather straps with little ability to resist, my limbs reluctantly allowing me to follow.

"I refused to stir. I was dragged about on the dirty kitchen floor while they howled with laughter. They had their paddles out, and were soon punishing me mercilessly. Nothing was spared, of course, but my buttocks in particular delighted them. And the more I bucked or struggled, the more they found it hilarious. I was no more than a dog to them. And that was precisely how they treated me. But this was only the beginning. I was soon unshackled enough to be thrown over a great barrel. And there I was raped by one and all of the men, the women looking on with laughter. I was sore from this, and so dizzy from the motion of the barrel that I was sick, but this again they thought most amusing.

"But when they were done with me, and had to return to their work, they shackled me above the open hogshead that received the garbage. My feet were deposited firmly in the waste of cabbage leaves and carrot tops, onion peels, and chicken feathers that made up the refuse of the day's work and, as they added to it, it rose around me. The stench was terrible and when I writhed and struggled, again they laughed, and thought of other ways to torment me."

"O, this is too dreadful," Beauty gasped. Each person who had handled her or punished her had in some way admired her. And when she thought of her beautiful Alexi treated this way, she felt weak with fear.

"Of course I did not know this was to be my regular station. I was taken out hours later when after the evening meal was served they again chose to rape me. Only this time I was thrown down and spread out on a large wooden table. And for their pleasure they paddled me again this time with coarse wooden paddles, saying the leather paddles they had used earlier were now too good for me. They held my legs wide apart, they lamented they could not torture my private parts without risking punishment. But by this they did not mean my penis which they punished a great deal with slaps, and rough handling.

"I was frantic by this time. I cannot explain it. There were so many of them, they were so crude, and my movements or sounds were nothing to them. The Queen had noticed my smallest change of expression. She had scoffed at my growls and struggles, but she had savored all of it. These crude cooks and kitchen boys rubbed my hair, lifted my face, slapped my buttocks and spanked me as if I had no sense whatsoever.

"They would speak of me, 'What plump buttocks,' and 'Look at those strong legs,' and that sort of thing as if I were a mere animal. They pinched me, poking me, jabbing me as they pleased, and then they set to raping me. They greased me well with their cruel hands as they had done before, and when they had finished, they flushed me out with some crude piping attached to a wineskin filled with water. I cannot tell you the mortification of this, to be washed inside and out by them. The Queen had at least allotted to me privacy in these matters, as the needs of our bowels and bladders do not interest her.

But to be emptied by this violent stream of cold water and in front of these piggish men made me weak and spiritless.

"I was limp when they hung me back in the refuse. And in the morning my arms ached, and I was sickened by the stench that rose around me. Roughly they pulled me out and shackled me on my knees again and threw down for me some food on a plate. It had been a day since I had eaten; yet I did not wish to eat for their amusement, as they would not allow me the use of my hands. It was nothing to them. I refused the meals until the third day when I could endure it no longer and I lapped up the gruel they gave me like a hungry puppy. They never took the slightest notice. When I finished my meals it was back to the heap of refuse until they had some time to make sport of me.

"In the meantime I hung there. And when they passed, they would perhaps give me some strong slap, twist the nipples of my chest, spread my legs wider with one of their paddles.

"It was an agony beyond anything I had known in the Queen's chamber. And soon, in the evening, the stable boys received word that they might come and use me as they wished. So I had them to satisfy as well.

"They were better dressed, but they smelled of the horses. They came in and took me out of the hogshead, and one of them thrust the long rounded leather handle of his whip into my anus. Lifting me up by this, he forced me into the stable. I was then laid over a barrel again and raped by all of them.

"It seemed unendurable, and yet I endured it. And as in the Queen's chamber, I could feast my eyes on my tormentors all day long though in between their wants they took little notice of me.

"One evening however, when all of them had had much to drink and had been congratulated for a very good meal upstairs, they turned for more imaginative play with me. I was terrified. I had no thoughts of dignity anymore and began to groan behind my gag as soon as they approached me. I squirmed and twisted to resist their hands.

"The games they chose were as degrading as they were disgusting. They spoke of decorating me, of improving my appearance, that I was altogether too clean and too fine an animal for my lodgings. And, spread-eagling me in the kitchen, they soon cut loose their fury on me with a dozen concoctions they made from the honey, the eggs, the various syrups and mixtures at their disposal. I was soon covered with these egregious liquids. They painted my buttocks, and laughed as I struggled. They painted my penis and balls. They decorated my face with it, and stuck back my hair with it. And when they had finished, they took the feathers from the fowl and pasted these to my body.

"I was terror-stricken, not of any real pain, but merely of their vulgarity and their meanness. I could not bear the humiliation of such disfigurement.

"Finally, one of the Pages came in, to see what was the noise, and he took pity on me. He had them release me and told them to wash me. Of course they scrubbed me roughly, and they took to paddling me again. It was then that I knew I was losing my senses. I was down on my hands and knees, though I was not shackled, and running desperately to hide from their paddles. I struggled to get under the kitchen tables, and everywhere I sought a moment's rest, they sought me out, moving the tables and chairs if need be to get at my buttocks with their paddles. Of course if I tried to rise, they pushed me down. I was desperate.

I found myself scurrying to the Page and kissing his feet just as I had seen Prince Gerald do with the Queen.

"But if he told the Queen, it was of no use to me. The next day I was shackled as before, and awaiting the boredom and restlessness of the same mistresses and masters. Sometimes passing me, they stuffed into my anus some bit of food rather than throw it away, carrots, other roots, whatever they thought liken to a penis. I was raped over and over by these things, and had to expel them with great effort. They would not have spared my mouth, I suppose, had they not been commanded to leave me gagged as all such slaves are gagged.

"And whenever I caught a glimpse of a Page I found myself pleading with him by all my gestures and manner of groaning.

"I had no real thoughts during this time. Perhaps I had begun to think of myself as the half human thing that they thought I was. I don't know. To them I was a disobedient Prince sent to them because I deserved it. Any abuse was their duty. If the flies were bad, they would paint my penis and balls with honey to attract them and think that very clever.

"Much as I feared the leather whip handles of the stable boys forced up my anus, I came to look forward to being taken to the cleaner, cooler places in the stable. Those boys at least thought it quite marvelous that they had a real Prince to torment. They rode me quite long and hard, but it was better than the kitchen.

"I don't know how long it went on. Every time they unshackled me I was terrified. They soon took to throwing about the refuse on the floor and making me gather it up as they chased me with their paddles. I had lost all sense of the wisdom of merely keeping still, and flustered and in panic I ran this way and that to finish the task as they spanked me. Prince Gerald had never been so frantic.

"Of course I thought of him as I found myself doing this. And I thought bitterly, 'He is amusing the Queen in her chambers, and I am here in this filthy place.'

"Why, to me the stable boys were royalty. And one of them in particular had become quite fascinated with me. He was big, very strong. He could mount me on his whip handle so that my feet barely touched the ground, and force me along, my back arched, my hands bound, almost carrying me. He delighted in doing this, and one day he took me off to a part of the garden alone. I tried once to struggle against him, and he simply flipped me over his knee effortlessly. He forced me down in the grass, and told me that with my teeth I was to pick the little white flowers there for him or he would take me back to the kitchen. I can't tell you how willingly I obeyed him. He kept his whip handle in me and forced me this way and that with it. And then he commenced to torment my penis. Yet even as he slapped it and abused it, he would stroke it. To my horror, I felt it swell. I wanted to stay with him forever. I thought, 'What can I do to please him?' And I was humbled by this, in despair, for I knew that this was just what the Queen had wanted in punishing me. I was convinced even in my madness that if she knew how much I suffered, she would release me. But my mind was empty of thought. I knew only that I wanted to please my stable boy lest he return me to the kitchen.

"I fetched the little flowers in my teeth and brought them back to him. He told me then I was too bad a Prince to be treated so gently by everyone, and that he knew how to punish me. He ordered me to mount a nearby table. This was a round wooden table, weathered but often draped and used when any of the Court want to take their repast in the garden.

"I obeyed at once, but I was not to kneel there, I was to squat with my legs wide apart and my hands behind my neck and to keep my eyes down. This was unbelievably degrading to me and yet all I could think of was to please him. Of course he spanked me in this position. He had a leather paddle, heavy but thin with a powerful wallop. And he commenced swatting my buttocks with it. And yet I remained there, unshackled but obedient, my legs aching as I squatted, my penis all the time swollen as he tormented me.

"It was the best thing that could have happened. Because Lord Gregory witnessed it. However, I didn't know this at the time, I knew only that others were passing near, and when I heard their voices and knew them to

be Lords and Ladies, I experienced unbelievable consternation. They would see me being humiliated by this
stable boy, me the proud Prince who had rebelled against
the Queen. And yet all I could do was to weep, and suffer,
and feel the paddle swatting me.

"I did not even think of the Queen learning of this.
I was too devoid of hope. I thought only of the moment.
Now, this, Beauty, is one aspect of yielding and acceptance, surely. I thought only of the stable boy and pleasing
him and escaping, for a little while longer, at this terrible
price, the kitchen. In other words, I thought of doing
precisely what was expected of me.

"Now, my stable boy grew tired of it. He ordered
me back down to the grass on my hands and knees and
took me deeper into the woods. I was completely unbound, yet I was under his will utterly. Now he found a
tree and told me to stand up and grasp the limb over my
head. I hung by the limb, my feet off the ground, as he
raped me. He thrust in deep and hard and repeatedly. I
thought it would never end, and my poor penis was hard
as the tree itself with suffering.

"And when he was finished, the most extraordinary
thing happened. I found myself kneeling at his feet, kissing his feet and more than that, I was twisting my hips,
and thrusting and doing all in my power to beg him to
relieve the passion between my legs, to allow me some
release, for I had known absolutely none in the kitchen.

"He laughed at all this. He pulled me up, impaled
me easily on his whip handle and drove me back towards
the kitchen. I was weeping as uncontrollably as ever in
my life.

"The vast room was almost empty. All were out
tending the vegetable gardens, or in the anterooms above
as the meals were being served, and only a young serving
girl remained, who climbed to her feet at once when she
saw us. In a moment, the stable boy was whispering to
her, and as she nodded her head, and wiped her hands
on her apron, he ordered me up onto one of the square

tables. I was to squat again with my hands behind my head. I obeyed without even thinking. More paddling, I thought, and for the benefit of this little girl with her wan face and brown braids. She meantime drew near and looked at me with what seemed wonder. Then for her the stable boy began to torment me. He had taken a soft little broom which was used to sweep out the inside of the oven. And with this he began to brush and stroke my penis. The more he stroked the more miserable I became, but each time it was almost too much for me he would withdraw the broom a quarter of an inch from my penis so that I struggled after it. It was more than I could bear, yet he would not allow me to move my feet, and paddled me immediately if I disobeyed him. I soon saw his game. I must thrust my hips forward as much as I could to keep my hungry penis in contact with the soft stroking bristles of the broom, and so I did, crying all the while as the girl gazed on with obvious delight. Finally, she begged to be allowed to touch me. I was so grateful for this I could not stop my sobs. The stable boy then put his broom under my chin and lifted my face. He said he wished to see me satisfy the young maid's curiosity. She had never really seen a young man spend his passion. And as he held me and scrutinized me and looked at my tear-stained face, she stroked my penis, and without pride or dignity, I felt my passion erupt into her hand, my face flushing with heat and blood as a shudder went through my loins relieving all of the days of frustration.

"I was weak when it was finished. I had no pride, nor thoughts of past and future. I made no resistance when I was manacled. I wished only that the stable boy would come again soon, and I was drowsy and afraid when all the cooks and kitchen boys returned and commenced their inevitable idle sport with me.

"The next few days were filled with the same terrible kitchen torments. I was paddled, chased, ridiculed and otherwise treated contemptuously. But I dreamed of the stable boy. Surely he would return. I don't think I even thought of her Highness. I felt only despair when I envisioned her.

"Finally one afternoon, the stable boy came in and he was finely dressed in rose-colored velvet trimmed in gold. I was aghast. He ordered me washed and scrubbed. I was too excited to fear the rough hands of the kitchen boys, though they were merciless as ever.

"My penis was rigid already at the mere sight of my stable boy Lord, but he told me quickly that it must be brought to perfect attention, and that I was to keep it thus, or be severely punished.

"I nodded all too vigorously. Then he took the gag bit out of my mouth and replaced it with an ornate one.

"How can I describe what I felt then? I didn't dare dream of the Queen. I was so bereft that any respite was wondrous to me. He led me now into the castle, and I who had rebelled against everyone was quickly scampering after him down the stone corridors past the slippers and boots of Lords and Ladies who all turned to take some notice of me and give some compliment. The stable boy was very proud.

"And then we entered a great high-ceilinged parlor. It seemed never in my life had I seen cream-colored velvet and gilt, and statues against the walls, nor the bouquets of fresh flowers everywhere. I felt myself born again with no thought of my own nakedness or subservience.

"And there sat the Queen in a high-backed chair, resplendent in purple velvet, her ermine cape over her shoulders. I scurried forward boldly, ready to offend by obsequiousness, and showered her hem and her shoes with kisses.

"At once she stroked my hair, and lifted my head. 'Have you suffered enough for your stubbornness?' she asked, and as she did not take her hands away I kissed them, kissed her soft palms and her warm fingers. The sound of her laugh was beautiful to me. I glimpsed the mounds of her white breasts, and the tight girdle about her waist. I kissed her hands until she stopped me and held my face and opened my mouth with her fingers and felt of my lips and teeth and then removed the gag, saying that I must not speak. At once I nodded.

"This will be a day of tests for you, my willful young Prince," she said. And then she put me in a paroxysm of exquisite pleasure by touching my penis. She felt of its hardness. I tried to keep my hips from moving forward towards her.

"She approved. And then she ordered my punishments. She had heard of my chastisement in the garden, she said, and would my young groom, the stable boy, please punish me so for her amusement.

"I was on the round marble table in front of her at once, squatting obediently. I remember the doors were open. I saw the distant figures of Lords and Ladies moving past. I knew there were other Ladies in this very room. I could see the soft colors of their dresses and even the shimmer of their hair. But I had no thought but to please the Queen and only hoped that I might manage to remain in this difficult squatting position for her as long as she wished, no matter how cruel the paddle. The first blows felt warm and good to me. I felt my buttocks flinch and tighten and it seemed I had never experienced such full swelling pleasure, unsatisfied as it was, in my penis.

"Of course I was soon groaning from the blows, and with my efforts to conceal the sound, the Queen kissed my face and told me that though my lips must remain sealed, I should let her know how I suffered for her. I understood her at once. My buttocks were now smarting and throbbing with pain. I arched my back, my knees opening all the more, my legs stiff and aching from the strain of the squatting, and I moaned without reservation, my moans growing louder with each crack of the paddle. Understand, nothing restrained me. I was unshackled and ungagged.

"All rebelliousness was gone from me. When next the Queen ordered me paddled about the room, I was only too willing. She threw down a handful of small gold balls the size of large purple grapes, and she bid me bring each one to her, just as you were commanded to fetch the roses. The stable boy, my groom as she called him, was to achieve no more than five cracks of the paddle before I had placed one in her hand, or she should be very displeased with me. These gold balls had rolled far and wide, and you cannot imagine how I scurried to gather them. I ran from the paddle as though it were burning me. Of course I was tender and sore by this time, and broken out in plenty of hard welts, but it was to please her that I hurried.

"I brought the first one with only three blows. I was very proud. But as I put it in her hand I saw she had put on a black leather glove, the fingers of which were traced with small emeralds. She bid me turn around and part my legs and show her my anus. I obeyed at once, and immediately felt the shock of those leather sheathed fingers opening my anus.

"As I told you, I had been raped and washed out repeatedly by my crude captors in the kitchen. Yet this was a new exposure to me, to be opened thus by her, and so simply and thoughtlessly, without the violence of rape. It made me feel softened with love and weak and totally her possession. At once I realized she was forcing the gold ball which I had retrieved into my anus. And now she instructed me that I was to hold it inside me, unless I wanted her fierce displeasure.

"I had now to fetch another. The paddle came at me quickly. I hurried, brought back another gold ball, was made to turn around, and it was forced into me.

"The game went on for a long time. My buttocks were ever the more sore. It felt quite enormous to me. I'm sure you understand the feeling. I felt swollen and huge, and very naked, and each welt was stinging under the paddle, and I was growing out of breath and desperate lest I fail, as I had to scurry ever farther away from her to retrieve the gold balls. But the new sensation was this filling of me, the stuffing of my anus, which I had now to hold tightly closed not to expel the gold balls against my will. I soon felt that my anus was widened and open, and at the same time stuffed mercilessly.

"The game grew more and more frantic. I soon glimpsed others watching from the doors. I had often to hurry past the hem of another Lady in waiting.

"I worked harder and harder, was stuffed ever the more firmly by those strong leather-sheathed fingers. And though the tears were pouring down my face, and I was breathing rapidly and hoarsely, I managed to complete the game with no more than four cracks of the paddle at any round of it.

"The Queen embraced me. She kissed me on the mouth and told me I was her loyal slave and her favorite. There was a ripple of approval throughout the Court, and she let me lie against her breasts for an instant as she held me.

"Of course I was suffering. I was struggling to hold in the gold balls, and also to not let my penis rub against her gown and disgrace me.

"She now sent for a small golden chamber pot. I knew then what was expected of me. And I know I must have blushed furiously. I had to squat over it and expel the toys I had gathered, and of course I did so.

"The day was an endless round of tasks after that.

"I shan't try to tell you all of them, save I had the Queen's absolute attention and absorption, and I intended with all my heart to keep it. I still did not know for certain that I might not be sent back to the kitchen. At any moment, I might be sent back to the kitchen.

"I remember many things. We were in the garden for a long time, the Queen walking among her roses as she much enjoys, and driving me along with that rod with the leather phallus at the end of it. It seemed sometimes she almost lifted my buttocks on the rod. My knees badly needed the relief of the soft grass after the floors of the castle. And I was so sore and tender by this time that the slightest stroke to my buttocks brought pain. But she only walked me about. And then she came to a little summer house of lattices and vines, and drove me ahead of her onto the flagstones there.

"She ordered me to rise, and a Page appeared, I don't remember if it was Felix, and he manacled my hands together over my head so that my toes barely touched the ground. The Queen seated herself right in front of me. She laid the phallus rod aside and lifted yet another rod that had been chained to her girdle. It was merely a long thin strip of wood covered with leather.

" 'Now you must talk to me,' she said. 'You must address me as your Highness, and you must answer my questions very respectfully.' I felt an almost uncontrollable excitement at this. I would be allowed to speak to her. Of course I never had. In my rebelliousness I had always been gagged, and I did not know how I would feel when allowed words. I was her puppy dog, her mute slave, and now I must speak to her. She toyed with my penis; she lifted my balls on her thin leather stick and pushed them to and fro. She gave my thighs a playful smack.

" 'Did you enjoy serving the crude Lords and Ladies of the kitchen?' she asked me playfully, 'or would you rather serve your Queen?'

" 'I want to serve only you, your Highness, or as you wish.' I answered quickly. My own voice sounded strange to me. It was mine, but I had not heard it in so long, and when I voiced this subservience it was as if I had only just discovered it. Or rather I discovered it anew, and it produced an extraordinary outpouring of emotion in me. I wept, and hoped that it did not displease her.

"She rose then and stood very close to me. She touched my eyes and my lips. 'All this belongs to me,' she said, 'and this,' and she touched the nipples of my chest which the kitchen boys had never spared, and she touched my belly and my navel. 'And this,' she said, 'this too, belongs to me,' and she held my penis in her hand, her long nails scratching at the tip of it gently. It gave off a little fluid then and she withdrew her hand and held my scrotum in her hands and claimed that as well. 'Spread your legs,' she said and turned me on the chain that held me. 'And this is mine,' she said, touching my anus.

"I heard myself answer her, 'Yes, your Highness.' She then told me she had punishments worse, for me than the kitchen should I ever try to escape her again, or rebel or in any way displease her. But for the time being, she would be more than pleased with me, she was certain, and she would work me hard as was her pleasure. She said I had great strength for her sport which Prince Gerald had not, and she would test that strength to the limit.

"Each morning, she would spank me on the Bridle Path. At noon I would accompany her on her walks in the garden. In the late afternoons, I would play games of fetch for her. In the evening I should be spanked for her amusement while she took her supper. There were many positions for me to assume. She liked to see me opened wide in the squat, but there were even better attitudes in which she chose to study me. She squeezed my buttocks then and said these above all belonged to her, as it was her delight to punish these more than anything else. But to complete the day's regimen in the future, I should undress her for bed, and sleep in her chamber.

"To all this, I said 'Yes, your Highness.' I would have done anything to retain her favor. Now she said my buttocks would be subjected to the greatest tests to ascertain their limits.

"She had me unshackled, and drove me herself on the phallus rod through the garden and into the castle. We went into her chambers.

"I knew now she meant to place me over her lap and to spank me as intimately as she had done with Prince Gerald. I was in a welter of anticipation. I didn't know how I should keep my penis from discharging its craving. But she had thought of this. She inspected me and said that the cup needed draining just now so that it might fill again. It was not that I was to be rewarded. Yet she sent for a magnificent little Princess. The girl at once took my organ in her mouth, and as soon as she began to suck it, my passion exploded in her. The Queen observed all this; she stroked my face and examined my eyes, and my lips, and then bid the Princess to awaken me again quickly.

"This was its own form of torture. But I was soon enough as unsatisfied as before, and ready for the Queen to begin her test of endurance. I was placed over her lap, just as I had suspected I might be.

" 'You've been soundly spanked by Squire Felix,' she said. 'You've been well spanked by the stable boys and the cooks in the kitchen. Do you think a woman can spank as hard as a man?' I was weeping already. I cannot anatomize the emotion I felt. Perhaps you felt it when you were over her lap earlier tonight. Or when the Prince had laid you down in the same position. It is not worse than being slung over a Page's knee, or tied with your hands over your head, or even pressed flat to a bed or table. I cannot explain it. But one feels so much more helpless across the lap of the master or mistress."

Beauty nodded. It was very true. And she had felt it when laid over the Queen's lap. All her composure had left her.

"In this position alone all obedience and subjugation can be taught, I think," said Prince Alexi. "Well, so it was with me. I lay over her lap, my head dangling, my legs spread out behind me. She wanted them slightly apart, and of course I was to arch my back and keep my hands clasped in the small of my back just as you were instructed to do. I was to see that my penis did not touch the cloth of her gown, though with all my strength I wanted it to. And then she commenced her spanking. She showed me each paddle and told me its faults and virtues. Here was one that was light; it would sting; and it was fast. A heavier one, just as thin, caused more pain and must be used carefully.

"She commenced to spank quite forcefully. And as with you, she would massage my buttocks, and pinch them when she chose. But she was steady in her work. She spanked hard and long until I was soon in terrible pain, and feeling as helpless as ever I had felt in my life.

"It seemed I felt the shock of each blow disseminated through my limbs. My buttocks of course absorbed it first. They became the center of myself in their soreness and tenderness. But the pain passed through them and into me, and all I could do was quiver beneath each blow, shudder with each sound spank, and moan ever more louder but never with the slightest hint of asking for mercy.

"The Queen was quite delighted with this show of suffering. As I told you before, she had encouraged it. She often lifted my face and wiped away my tears and rewarded me with kisses. Sometimes she would have me kneel on the floor upright. She would inspect my penis and ask if it were not hers. I would say 'Yes, your Highness, all of me is yours. I am your obedient slave.' She praised this answer, and said I must not hesitate in giving her long, devoted answers.

"But she was quite determined. She picked up the paddle again quickly enough, pressed me down again on her lap, and commenced the loud and forceful spanking. I was soon moaning loudly behind my clenched teeth. I had no pride, none of that dignity you still display unless it was completely without my knowledge. Finally she said that my buttocks were now a perfect color.

"She hated having to punish me further she so admired the color she had achieved, but she must know my limits.

" 'Are you sorry you were such a disobedient little Prince?' she asked me. 'Very sorry, your Highness,' I answered through my tears. But she continued with her spanking. I could not prevent tightening my buttocks and moving as if somehow it would lessen the pain, and I could hear her laughter as though this quite delighted her.

"I was sobbing as frantically as any young Princess

when she at last finished, and forced me back on my knees, ordering me to come about and kneel facing her.

"She wiped my face, blotted my eyes, and gave me a generous kiss with a great deal of sweet flattery. I would be her valet, she said, the master of her wardrobe. I alone would dress her, and brush her hair, and otherwise attend her. I would have much to learn, but she would instruct me herself. I should be very pure.

"Of course, that night I thought I had endured the worst, the abuse of common soldiers on my way to the castle, the frightful abuse in the kitchen. I had been thoroughly humbled by a coarse stable boy, and was now her abject pleasure slave with a soul that belonged to her with all the parts of my body totally. But I was very foolish in this. Much worse was to come."

Prince Alexi paused and looked down at Beauty who lay with her head against his chest.

She struggled to conceal her feelings. She did not truly know what she felt except that the story had aroused her. She could envision each humiliation Alexi described, and though her fear was aroused, so was her passion.

"It has been much easier for me," she said meekly, but this was not what she wanted to say.

"I'm not sure that is true," said Alexi. "You see, after the rough treatment of the kitchen when I became something less than an animal to my captors, I was liberated at once into being the Queen's obedient slave. You have had no such immediate liberation," he said.

"And this is what is meant by yielding," she murmured. "And I must come to it through a different path."

"Unless . . . unless you do something to be vilely punished," said Alexi, "but that might take too much courage. And it might be unnecessary, for your dignity is being stripped away from you just a little already."

"I had no dignity tonight," Beauty protested.

"O yes, you did, you had a great deal of it," Alexi smiled. "But to continue, at this time, I had yielded only to my stable boy Lord and to the Queen. And once I was in her hands, I forgot my stable boy Lord completely. I was the Queen's property. I thought of my limbs, my buttocks, my penis, as hers. But I to truly yield, I had to experience much greater exposure and discipline . . ."

PRINCE
ALEXI'S
EDUCATION
CON-
TINUES

I WON'T tell you the details of my training with the Queen, how I learned to be her valet, my struggles with her annoyance. All this you'll learn in your training with the Prince for in his love for you he intends to make you his maidservant clearly. But these things are nothing when one is devoted to the master or mistress.

"I had to learn serenity in facing humiliations that brought others into play, and this was not easy.

"My first days with the Queen were mostly training in her bed chamber. I found myself rushing as diligently as Prince Gerald had to obey her slightest whim, and, proving very clumsy with her clothes, was often severely punished.

"But the Queen did not want me merely for these servile tasks which other slaves had been trained to perform to perfection. She wanted to study me, to break me down and make of me a toy for her complete amusement."

"A toy," Beauty whispered. She had felt like a toy in the Queen's hands exactly.

"And it amused her greatly in the first weeks to see me serve other Princes and Princesses for her pleasure. The first I had to serve was Prince Gerald. He was now nearing the end of his service, but he did not know that, and he was in a paroxysm of jealousy at my reformation. The Queen, however, had splendid ideas for rewarding him and soothing him, and at the same time developing me according to her wishes.

"Daily he was brought to her chamber and bound with his hands over his head against the wall so that he might watch me struggling with my tasks, and this was a torment to him until he realized that one of my tasks would be to give him pleasure.

"I was being driven to distraction then by the Queen's paddle, the flat of her hand, and the struggle to learn grace and accomplishment. All day I fetched, laced shoes, bound girdles, brushed hair, polished jewels, and performed any other menial task the Queen wished, my buttocks forever sore, my thighs and calves marked from the paddle, my face stained with tears as any other slave in the castle.

"And when the Queen could see that Prince Gerald's jealousy had hardened his penis to extremity, when he was all but ready to discharge his passion without the aid of any stimulant, then she set me to bathing him and satisfying him.

"I can't tell you how degrading this was to me. His body was nothing but my enemy. And yet I was to fetch a bowl of warm water, a sea sponge, and with my teeth only to hold it, bathe his genitals.

"He was positioned on a low table for this, kneeling obediently as I washed his buttocks, dipped the sponge again, bathed his scrotum and finally his penis. But the Queen wanted more than this. I must now use my tongue to cleanse him. I was horrified, and shedding tears like any Princess. But she was adamant. With my tongue I licked his penis, the balls, and then delved into the crack of his buttocks, even entering into his anus, which had a sour, almost salty taste to it.

"All the while he showed his obvious pleasure and longing.

"His buttocks were sore, of course. And it gave me great satisfaction that the Queen seldom spanked him anymore herself, but rather had it done by his groom before he was brought into her presence. So he didn't suffer for her; rather he suffered in the Slaves' Hall, ignored by those around him. Yet it was mortifying to me that my tongue stroking his welts and red marks gave him pleasure.

"Finally, the Queen ordered him to kneel up, his hands behind his back, and told me I should now fully reward him. I knew what this meant, yet I pretended I did not. She told me to take his penis in my mouth and drain it.

"I can't explain how I felt then. I felt I could not do it. And yet within seconds I had obeyed, so afraid of displeasing her as I was, and his thick penis was pushing against the back of my throat, my lips and jaws aching as I tried to suck it properly. The Queen gave me instructions, to make my strokes long, to use my tongue, and to go faster and faster. She spanked me unmercifully as I obeyed, her smacking blows in perfect rhythm with my sucking. At last his seed filled my mouth. I was commanded to swallow it.

"But the Queen was not at all pleased with my reticence. She said that I must show no disinclination towards anything."

Beauty nodded, remembering the Prince's words to

her in the Inn, that even the lowly must be served for his pleasure.

"So she sent for all those Princes who had been tortured over a day's time in the Hall of Punishments, and led me to a large adjoining parlor.

"When six young men were brought in on their knees, I begged her to be merciful the only way I could, with my moans and kisses. I can't tell you how their presence affected me. I'd been mistreated by the peasants in the kitchen; I'd humbly, greedily, obeyed a rude stable boy. But these seemed both lower and higher than those others. They were Princes of my same rank in the world, haughty, proud in their own lands, and also they were abject slaves as lowly now as I was.

"I couldn't understand my own misery. I realized then that there would be endless variations in humiliation. It was not a hierarchy of punishments I faced; it was rather endless *changes*.

"But I was too frightened of failing the Queen to think very much. Again I lost sight of the past and the future.

"As I knelt at her feet weeping silently, she ordered all of these Princes who were sore and aching and starved from the torture of the Hall of Punishments to take paddles from the chest she kept for the purpose.

"They formed a line of six to my right, each on his knees, his penis hardened as much by the sight of my suffering as by any pleasure that soon awaited them.

"I was told to kneel up with my hands behind my back. As I ran this gauntlet I would not even be allowed the easier and more concealing position on all fours. Rather I must struggle straight-backed, my knees apart, my own organ revealed, my progress slow as I sought to escape their paddles. They could see my face as well. I felt more exposed than I had when tethered in the kitchen.

"The Queen's game was simple. I would be made to run the gauntlet and the Prince whose paddle pleased her the most, that is, the one whose paddle struck me the hardest and fiercest, would then be rewarded before I again commenced the gauntlet and so on.

"I was urged by her to great speed; if I faltered, if my punishers accomplished too many blows, I should be delivered over to them for an hour of rough sport out of her sight, I was promised. This terrified me. She would not even be there. It would not be for her pleasure.

"I commenced at once. All their blows felt the same to me, loud, violent, and their laughter filled my ears as I struggled awkwardly in a position they had long ago learned to accomplish easily.

"Rest came only with each little session of satisfying the Prince who had marked me the most severely. I must return to him where he knelt. The others were free to watch and watch they did, and then given permission to offer their instructions.

"I had a half dozen masters eager to teach me contemptuously how to satisfy the one whom they supported with their arms as he shut his eyes and enjoyed the warm anxious sucking I afforded.

"Of course all of them prolonged it as best they could for fullest satisfaction, and the Queen who sat nearby, her elbow on the arm of her chair watched all this approvingly.

"Strange changes occurred in me as I performed my duties. There would be the frenzy of struggling past their paddles. My smarting buttocks, my sore knees, and above all the shame that they could so easily see my face, and my genitals.

"But as I took to sucking I found myself lost in contemplating the organ in my mouth, its size, its shape, its taste even and the sour salty taste of the fluids emptied into me. It was the rhythm of the sucking as much as anything else. The voices around me were a chorus that became noise at some point, and an odd feeling of being weak and abject came over me. It was very similar to the moments I'd experienced with my tall stable boy Lord when we had been alone in the garden, and he had made me squat on the table. I felt my excitement even on the surface of my skin then, and so it was now, sucking these various organs and being filled with their seed. I can't explain it. It became pleasurable. It became pleasurable because it was repeated and I was helpless. And it was repeated always as a respite from the paddle, the frenzy of the paddle. My buttocks would throb, but they felt warm; they were tingling, and I was tasting this delicious cock that was pumping its force into me.

"I found I *liked* having so many eyes watch me. But I did not admit this to myself all at once. I felt not *liking* so much as this weakness again, this limpness of the spirit. I was *lost* in my suffering, my struggles, my anxiousness to please.

"Well, so it would be with each new task that lay before me. I would at first resist with terror; I would cling to the Queen with my heart; then at some point in the midst of unspeakable humiliation, I would be released into some state of calm in which my punishment became sweet to me.

"I saw myself as *one* of these Princes, one of these slaves. When they instructed me in sucking the penis better I listened to them. When they paddled me I received the blow, bent my body in response to it.

"Perhaps it's impossible to explain. I was moving towards yielding.

"When finally the six Princes were sent away, all of them properly rewarded, the Queen took me into her arms and rewarded me with her kisses. As I lay on the pallet by her bed, I felt the most delicious exhaustion. It seemed even the air stirring around me gave me pleasure. I felt it against my skin, as if my nakedness were being stroked. And I fell asleep content that I had served her properly.

"But my next great test of strength came one afternoon when she, very cross with me for my ineptitude at brushing her hair, sent me to be the plaything of the Princesses.

"I could scarcely believe my ears. She herself would not even deign to witness it. She sent for Lord Gregory, and told him I was to be taken to the Special Punishment Hall and there given to the assembled Princesses. For one hour they could do with me what they liked. And then I was to be bound in the garden and have my thighs whipped with a leather thong, and left there until morning.

"This was my first great separation from the Queen. And I could not imagine myself, naked, helpless, and fit only for punishment, given over to the Princesses. I had dropped the Queen's hairbrush twice. I had spilled some wine earlier. All of this had seemed beyond my control and my finest efforts.

"When Lord Gregory gave me several hard spanks I was full of shame and fear. And as we neared the Special Punishments Hall, I felt I could not move by my own power.

"He had placed a leather collar around my neck. He pulled me along, spanking me only lightly as he said the Princesses must have the full enjoyment of me.

"Before we entered the room, he put a sign about my neck by means of a small ribbon. He showed it to me first, and I shuddered to see it announced me as clumsy, willful and bad, and in need of correction.

"He then exchanged my leather collar for another which had numerous small metal rings attached to it, each ring just large enough for a finger to be hooked in it. That way the Princesses could pull me this way or that, he said, and woe to me if I showed the slightest resistance.

"Cuffs with the same rings were put on my ankles and my wrists. I felt myself scarcely able to move as I was pulled towards the door.

"I did not know how to assess my emotions. As the door opened, I saw them all, some ten Princesses, a naked harem lounging about under the watchful eye of a groom, all girls being rewarded for good behavior by this hour of leisure. I learned later that if anyone is to be severely punished he or she is given to them, but on that day they had not expected anyone.

"They shrieked with delight, clapping their hands and immediately conferring with one another. All around me I saw their long hair, red, golden, raven hair in deep waves and thick curls, their naked breasts and bellies, and those hands pointing to me, and shielding their own shy and shameful whispers.

"They clustered about me. I crouched trying to conceal myself. But Lord Gregory lifted my head by means of the collar. I felt their hands all over me, feeling my skin, slapping my cock, and touching my balls as they squealed and laughed. Never had some of them seen a man so closely, save for their Lords who had complete power over them.

"I was trembling violently. I had not given way to tears and was most afraid that I would turn and try to escape, and receive only some worse punishment. I tried desperately to remain coldly indifferent. But their round naked breasts were maddening me. I could feel their thighs brush me, even their moist pubic hair as they crowded about examining me.

"And I was their complete slave, whom they scorned and admired. When I felt their fingers touching my balls, weighing them, stroking my penis, I was maddened.

"It was infinitely worse than my time with the Princes, because I could already hear their voices turning to mock contempt with the wish to discipline me, to return me to the Queen as obedient as they were. 'O, so you're a bad little Prince, are you?' said one of them in my ear, she a lovely raven-haired one with pierced ears adorned with gold. Her hair was tickling my neck, and when her fingers twisted the nipples of my chest, I felt myself losing my control.

"I feared I would break and try to flee. Lord Gregory meantime withdrew to the corner of the room. The grooms could aid them as they wished, he said, and he urged them to do their work well for the Queen's sake. This brought loud cries of delight. I was immediately slapped by several hard little hands. My buttocks were pulled open. I felt tiny fingers pushing into them.

"I squirmed, twisted, trying to hold still, trying not to look at them.

"And when I was pulled up and my hands were tied over my head from a ceiling chain, I was immensely relieved that I could no longer try to escape if I weakened.

"The grooms gave them what paddles they wanted. A number of them chose long leather straps which they tried first across their hands. In the Special Punishment Hall they had no need to stay on their knees and could stand around me as they liked. At once the round handle of a paddle was thrust in my anus. My legs were dragged wide apart. I was shuddering, and when the paddle handle proceeded to rape me with back and forth thrusts as roughly as any cock I'd ever received, I knew my face was red, and that my tears were threatening. Now and then in the midst of all this, I'd feel cool little lips pressed to my ear, my face pinched, my chin stroked, and then they would assault my nipples again.

" 'Beautiful little tits,' said one of the girls as she did this. She had flaxen hair, as straight as yours. 'When I've finished my work, they'll feel like breasts,' she said, and proceeded to stretch them, and stroke them.

"All the while, to my shame, my cock was hard as if it knew its mistresses even when I refused to acknowledge them. This girl with the flaxen hair laid her thighs against mine, growing fiercer as she pulled on my nipples. I felt her wet sex against me. 'You think you are too good to suffer at our hands, Prince Alexi?' she crooned. I wouldn't answer her.

"Then the paddle handle in my anus thrust harder and more roughly. My hips were pushed forward as cruelly as they had ever been by my stable boy Lord, and I was almost lifted off the floor by the thrusts. 'You think you are too good for us to punish?' she asked again. The other girls laughed and watched her as she commenced to slap my cock hard from right to left. I winced, I could not quite control myself. I wished for all the world that I were gagged, but I wasn't. She ran her fingers over my lips and my teeth to remind me of this, and commanded me to answer her respectfully.

"And when I didn't she took her paddle now, and withdrawing the instrument of rape, she proceeded, as she kept her face next to mine, her eyelashes tickling the side of my face, to spank me soundly. Of course I was already sore as we all are, always, and her blows were very hard, and they were without rhythm. She caught me off guard and when I winced and groaned, all the girls laughed appreciatively.

"My cock was slapped by others. My nipples twisted by them, but she had clearly shown her supremacy. 'You will beg me for mercy, Prince Alexi,' she said. 'I am not the Queen, you may beg me, for all the good it will do you.' They thought all that was amusing too, and she continued to spank me harder and harder. I prayed she would break the skin before my will broke, but she was too clever for that. She spread the blows. She had them lower the chain slightly, so she could spread my legs even wider.

"She held my cock now in her left hand, tightly, roughly, running her open palm over the tip to torment me, and then tightening her grip again as she spanked furiously.

"When she slapped my nipples and my cock, and lifted my balls in her hands, I felt the tears flowing, and overcome with shame I groaned unable to conceal it. It was an astonishing moment of pain and pleasure. My buttocks were raw.

"But she had only just begun. She ordered the other Princesses to lift my legs in front of me. I felt terror to feel myself hanging from the chain above me. They did not bind my ankles to my arms; they merely held them up, in place, as she brought her blows up from under, as hard as before, and then covering my balls with her left hand, paddled me from the front as hard as she could as I struggled and moaned now uncontrollably.

"Meantime the other girls were feasting their eyes on me, touching me still, and enjoying my misery immensely. They even kissed the backs of my legs, my calves, my shoulders.

"But the blows came harder and faster. She had me set down again, spread wide again, and went to work in earnest. I think she meant to break the skin if she could, but I was now broken down and wept uncontrollably.

"This was what she wanted, and as I gave in, she applauded it. 'Very good, Prince Alexi, very good, let all of that spiteful pride go, very good, you know very well you deserve it. That's better, that is exactly what I want to see,' she said almost affectionately, 'delicious tears,' as she touched them with her fingers, her paddle never stopping.

"Then she had my hands released. I was forced down on all fours. And she drove me about the room telling me that I must move in a circle. Of course she drove me faster and faster. I didn't even realize now that I was no longer restrained. That is, I did not even realize I might have broken and run. I had been defeated. And finally, it was as always when the punishment works, I could think of nothing but escaping each blow of her paddle. And how could I do that? Merely twist, squirm, try to avoid it. She was meantime very worked up with her commands, driving me faster. I rushed past the naked feet of the other Princesses. I saw them step aside for me.

"And now she told me that crawling was indeed too good for me, that I must place my arms on the ground, and my chin, and must inch along in that manner, my buttocks high in the air where she might paddle them. 'Arch your back,' she said, 'down, I want your chest pressed to the ground,' and as skillfully as any Page or mistress, she forced me along as the others praised her and marveled at her skill and stamina. I had never been in such a position. It was so ignominious I didn't want to picture it, my knees still scraping along, my back painfully arched, my buttocks thrust as high as before. And she commanding me always to move with greater speed as my buttocks grew ever more raw. They were throbbing as the blood throbbed in my ears. And my tears were now blinding me.

"And it was then that that moment came I spoke of earlier. I belonged to this girl with the flaxen hair, this impudent, clever Princess who herself was punished as shamefully as I was day in and day out but for the moment could do as she wished with me. I struggled along, glimpsing Lord Gregory's boots, the boots of the grooms, hearing the girls' laughter. I reminded myself that I must please the Queen, I must please Lord Gregory, and finally I must please my cruel flaxen-haired mistress.

"She paused for breath. She exchanged her paddle for a leather strap and proceeded to lash me.

"At first it felt weaker than the paddle, and I felt a merciful relief. But she immediately learned to swing it with such strength it walloped the welts on my buttocks. Now she let me stop so she might feel these welts. She pinched them, and in the silence I could hear my own low crying.

" 'I think he is ready, Lord Gregory,' said the Princess, and Lord Gregory said softly, he thought that I was. I thought it meant I would be returned to the Queen.

"This was very foolish of me.

"It was only that I would now be lashed swiftly into the Hall of Punishments. Of course there were a handful of Princesses chained from the ceiling, their legs tied up in front of them. Now she brought me up to the first of these.

"She told me to rise and to spread my legs very wide as I stood before her. I saw the captive Princess's pained face, her blushing cheeks, and then her naked and moist sex peering shyly from its wreath of golden pubic hair, much ready for pleasure or more pain, after days of teasing. But it hung low, at the level of my chest, I suppose, and that was just as my tormentor liked it.

"For she ordered me to bend over towards it, and to thrust my hips out behind me. 'Give me your buttocks,' she said. She stood behind me. The other girls pulled my legs wider than I myself could spread them. Again I was told to arch my back and to put my arms around the bound and doubled Princess slave hanging in front of me.

" 'Now you will pleasure her with your tongue,' said my captor, 'and see you do it well as she has suffered long, and for not even half your clumsiness.'

"I looked at the bound Princess. She was mortified, though desperately hungry for pleasure. And I pressed my face into her sweet, hungry little sex, rather eager to pleasure her. But as my tongue delved into her swollen cleft, as I licked her little clitoris, and her swollen lips, I was walloped by the belt continuously. My flaxen-haired one chose one welt after another for her work, and I was in great pain as the bound Princess finally shuddered with pleasure in spite of herself.

"Of course, there were others who had been punished enough and now must be rewarded. I did my work as best I could, finding a refuge in it.

"And then with a panic I saw there were no more to be rewarded. I was again at the hands of my captor with nothing so sweet as a bound Princess in my arms.

"And again, my chest and chin pressed to the floor, I struggled along on my knees under the wallops of her strap back to the Special Punishment Hall.

"Now all the Princesses begged Lord Gregory to make me pleasure them, but Lord Gregory silenced them at once. They had their Lords and Ladies to serve, and he would not hear one word from them more unless they wanted to be hung from the ceiling of the other Hall as they deserved.

"I was now taken away, and out into the garden. As the Queen ordered, I was taken to a large tree, and my hands were tied up high so that my feet barely touched the grass beneath them. It was growing dusk and I was left there.

"It had been excruciating, but I had obeyed, I had not run away, and there had come that moment. I was tormented now only by usual needs, my aching cock which might not be rewarded for another day or more by the Queen due to her anger.

"But the garden was quiet, full of twilight sounds. The sky was purple and the trees were thickening with shadows. In a little while, they grew skeletal, the sky was white with evening, and then darkness fell around me.

"I had resigned myself to sleep in this manner. I was too far from the trunk of the tree to rub my miserable cock against it, or I would have done this, tormented as I was, for whatever pleasure the friction could give me.

"And from habit more than training, its hardness would not die away. I remained stiff and tense as though expecting something.

"Then Lord Gregory appeared. He materialized out of the dark in his grey velvet, with the gold on the edge of his cloak gleaming. I saw the shimmer of his boots, and the dull sheen of the leather strap he carried. More punishment, I thought wearily, but I must obey. I am a slave Prince and there is nothing to be done for it. Pray I have the grace to bear it in silence and without struggling.

"But he drew close to me and commenced to talk to me. He told me I had comported myself very well and asked me if I knew the name of the Princess who had tormented me. I said 'No, my Lord,' respectfully taking some relief that I had pleased him. He is very hard to please. Harder than the Queen.

"He then told me her name was Princess Lynette, and she was new and had made a great impression on everyone. She was the personal slave of the Grand Duke Andre. 'What is this to me,' I thought, 'I serve the Queen.' But he asked me pleasantly enough if I had found her pretty. I winced. How could I help it? I could remember her breasts well enough when she pressed them to me while her paddle made me smart and groan. I could remember her dark blue eyes for the one or two instants when I had not been too ashamed to look at them. 'I don't know, my Lord. I would think she would not be here,' I said, 'were she not pretty.'

"For that impertinence, he gave me at least five rapid cracks with his belt. I was sore enough to be immediately in tears. He has often said that if he had his way, he would keep all slaves that sore always. Then their buttocks would be so tender that all he would have to do was stroke them with a feather. But as I stood there, my arms stretched painfully above me, my body pushed off balance by his blows, I was aware that he was particularly angered and fascinated by me. Why else would he come here to torment me? He had a castle of slaves to torment. It gave me some strange satisfaction.

"I was conscious of my body, its obvious muscularity, what to some eyes was surely its beauty. . . . Well, he came around and he said to me that Princess Lynette was unsurpassed in many respects and that her attributes were fired with an unusual spirit.

"I feigned boredom. I was to hang in this position all night. He was a gnat, I thought. But then he told me that he had been to the Queen and told her how well Princess Lynette had punished me, that Princess Lynette showed a flair for command and shrank from nothing. I began to grow afraid. Then he assured me the Queen had been glad to hear it.

" 'And so was her master, the Grand Duke Andre,' he added, 'and both were curious and somewhat regretful that such a display had not been witnessed by them, being wasted only on other slaves.' I waited. 'So a little amusement has been arranged,' he continued when I said nothing. 'You shall perform a little circus for her Highness. Surely you have seen the trainers of animals in circuses, who with deft strokes of their whips place their trained cats on stools, and force them through hoops, and other tricks for the amusements of the audience.'

"I felt desperate but I did not answer. 'Well, on the morrow, when your handsome buttocks have healed somewhat, such a little spectacle shall be arranged with the Princess Lynette and her strap to drive you through the performance.'

"I knew my face was scarlet with rage and indignation, or worse, it showed my frantic despair, but it was too dark for him to see it. I could see only the gleam of his eyes, and how I knew that he smiled I wasn't certain. 'And you shall perform your little tricks quickly and well,' he went on, 'for the Queen is eager to see you hop upon this stool and that, crouch on all fours, and then jump through the hoops that are just now being prepared for you. Because you are a two-legged pet with hands as well as feet, you can as well swing from a little trapeze that is being prepared for you, with Princess Lynette's paddle ever to spur you on, and entertain all of us as you show your agility.'

"It seemed unthinkable to me, performing this. It was not service after all, not the dressing and adorning of my Queen, not the fetching for her to show I accepted her power and worshiped her. Not suffering for her, receiving her blows. But rather a series of willfully executed ignominious positions. I couldn't endure the thought of it. But worst of all, I couldn't imagine myself managing to do it. I should be dreadfully humiliated when I failed in will, and was then dragged off again to the kitchen surely.

"I was beside myself with rage and fear, and this menace, this brutal Lord Gregory whom I hated so was smiling at me. He took hold of my cock and pulled me forward. Of course he had it at the root, not near the tip where it might have given me some pleasure. And as he tugged my hips so that I lost my footing, he said, 'This will be a grand spectacle. The Queen, the Grand Duke and others shall witness it. And Princess Lynette shall be very eager to impress the Court. See to it that she does not *outshine* you.' "

Beauty shook her head then and kissed Prince Alexi. She now saw what he meant when he said he had only just begun to yield.

"But Alexi," she said gently, almost as if she could save him from his fate, as if it hadn't already happened long ago, "When you were brought by the stable boy to the Queen's presence, when she made you fetch the golden balls for her in the parlor, was this not something of the same thing?" She stopped. "O, how shall I ever do these things!"

"But you can do them, all of them, that's the point of my story," he said. "Each new thing seems terrible because it is new, because it is a variation. But at the heart it is all the same ultimately. The paddle, the strap, the exposure, the bending of the will. Only they infinitely vary it.

"But you do well to mention this first session with tne Queen. It was similar. But remember I was raw and shaken from the kitchen, and thoughtless. I had regained my strength since then, and my strength had to be broken down again. Now perhaps had the little circus been constructed when I was fresh from the kitchen I would have taken to it eagerly then too. But I think not. It encompassed much greater exposure, much greater stamina, much greater surrender of self into positions and attitudes that appeared grotesque and inhuman.

"No wonder they need no real cruelty, no fire, no whips, to teach their lessons or amuse themselves," he sighed.

"But what happened? Did it come about?"

"Yes, of course, though Lord Gregory had no need of telling me beforehand except to rob me of sleep. I spent a painful restless night. I awoke many times thinking others were near, the stable boys, or the kitchen servants, that they had found me helpless and alone and meant to torment me. But no one approached me.

"During the night I heard whispers of conversation as Lords and Ladies walked under the stars. Now and then I even heard a slave driven past, crying fitfully under the inevitable smack of the leather. A torch would flicker under the trees, nothing more.

"When the morning came, I was bathed, and rubbed with oil, and all this time, my penis was not touched, save when it flagged. Then it was cleverly awakened.

"At twilight, the Slaves' Hall was full of talk of the circus. I was told by my groom, Leon, that the circle for performance had been prepared in a spacious hall near the Queen's apartments. There would be four rows of Lords and Ladies surrounding it, and they would bring their slaves, too, to see the amusement. The slaves were in a state of dread, lest they be made to perform. He said nothing more than that, but I knew what he was thinking. It was a grueling test of self-control. He combed my hair, rubbed much oil into my buttocks and thighs, even oiled my pubic hair a little and brushed it so it would be glossy.

"I was quiet. I was thinking.

"And when I was finally brought into the room, into the shadows near the wall from which I could see the illuminated circle, I understood what I had to do. There were stools of various heights and various circumferences. There were trapezes hung so and great hoops mounted perpendicular to the floor. Candles burned everywhere on high stands among the chairs of the Lords and Ladies who were already assembled.

"And the Queen, my cruel Queen sat in state, with the Grand Duke Andre beside her.

"Princess Lynette stood in the middle of the circle. So she would be allowed to stand, I mused, and I should be driven in on hands and knees. Well, I must make up my mind.

"And as I knelt there waiting I decided that resistance was impossible. Were I to try to hide my tears, were I to grow tense, my humiliation would only be more dreadful.

"I must make up my mind to do what I had to do. Princess Lynette looked exquisite. Her flaxen hair hung free down her back where it had been trimmed only enough to expose all of her buttocks. She had no more than a pink blush there from the paddle, and a blush on her thighs and calves too, which far from disfiguring her, appeared to shape her and improve her. It was infuriating. About her neck she wore a collar of gilded and worked leather that was a mere adornment. She wore boots as well, heavily gilded with high heels.

"And I of course was utterly naked. I did not even have a collar which meant I must control myself at her commands, I could not even be dragged this way and that.

"So I could see exactly what I must succeed in doing. She would put on a great show of inventiveness. She would be ready to vent her anger on me in commands of 'Hurry,' and 'Quickly' and scold and condemn for the slightest disobedience. She would therefore win the applause of the audience. And the more I struggled, the more she would shine, just as Lord Gregory had indicated.

"The only way I could triumph was through perfect obedience. I must execute all her commands to perfection. And I must not struggle either externally or inwardly. I must weep if I must weep, but I must do all she commanded, even if to think of it sent my heart to thudding in my wrists and temples.

"Finally everyone was ready. A handful of exquisite little Princesses had served the wine, swinging their pretty little hips and showing me some delightful sights as they bent over to fill the cups. And they too were to see me punished.

"All the Court, for the first time, was to see it.

"Then with a clap of her hands, the Queen ordered that her pet, Prince Alexi be brought in and that Princess Lynette 'tame' me and 'train' me before their very eyes.

"Lord Gregory gave me the usual quick smacks with the paddle.

"At once I was in the circle of light, my eyes hurt

by it for the moment, and then I saw my trainer's high-heeled boots coming nearer. In a moment of impetuousness, I rushed to her and kissed both her shoes at once. The Court gave a loud murmur of approval.

"I continued to shower her with kisses, and I thought, 'My evil Lynette, my strong, cruel Lynette, you are my Queen now.' It was as if my passion were a fluid that coursed through all my limbs, not only my swollen cock. I arched my back and spread my legs ever so slightly without even being told to do so.

"At once the spanks commenced. But clever little demon that she was, she said, 'Prince Alexi, you will show your Queen that you are a very quick-witted pet, and you shall answer all my commands with your compliance. And you shall answer all my questions, too, with perfect courtesy.'

"So I would have to speak. I felt the blood rush to my face. But she gave no time for my terror, and I said with a quick nod of the head, 'Yes, my Princess,' to a murmur of the audience's approval.

"She was strong as I have told you. She could spank much harder than the Queen, and as hard as ever the kitchen boys or the stable boys had spanked me. I knew she meant to leave me sore if nothing else, because immediately she gave me several loud cracks, and she had that knack which some of our punishers have of lifting the buttocks with the paddle as she spanked them.

" 'To that stool, there,' she commanded at once, 'at a squat with your knees wide apart and your hands behind your neck, now!' And she drove me at once to obey as I hopped up on the stool and with a great but quick effort managed to secure my balance. It was that same miserable squatting position in which my stable boy Lord had punished me. And all the Court could now see my genitals displayed if they hadn't seen them before.

" 'Turn around slowly,' she commanded, in order to show me to all eyes, 'so the Lords and Ladies can see the little pet that performs for them tonight!' and again she gave me numerous exquisite cracks of the paddle. There was a sprinkling of applause from the little crowd, and the sounds of wine being poured, and no sooner had I executed a complete turn, the slapping of her paddle ringing in my ears, than she ordered me to make a quick turn around the little stage on all fours with my chin and chest on the ground as I had done for her earlier.

"It was here I had to remind myself of my intentions. I rushed fast to obey, arching my back, my knees apart, yet moving swiftly as the heels of her boots clicked beside me and my buttocks were writhing under her blows. I did not try to hold their muscles still, but let them tense, let my hips even rise and fall as they were inclined to do, shrinking from the blows, yet receiving them. And as I moved along the white marble floor, the room a blur of faces over me, I felt this is my natural state, this is what I am, there is nothing before me or after me. I could hear the responses of the Court; they laughed at this miserable position, and there was a growing excitement to their talk. The little performance had them much engaged, jaded as they were. I was being admired for my abandon. I groaned with each crack of the paddle without even thinking to stop it. I let the groans come freely, and arched my back to even greater degree.

"And when the task was complete and I was again driven into the center of the circle, I heard applause around me.

"My cruel trainer didn't pause. She commanded me at once to hop upon another stool, and from that stool to one that was even higher. I squatted on each in turn, and when her spanks caught me my hips moved forward with them without restraint and my moans, my natural moans, were surprisingly loud to me.

" 'Yes, my Princess,' I said after each command, and my voice sounded tremulous to me, though deep, and full of suffering. 'Yes, my Princess,' I said again as she ordered me finally to stand before her, legs wide apart and slowly squat until I had achieved the height of which she approved. Then I must jump through the first hoop, hands behind my neck and somehow manage to squat again for her. 'Yes, my Princess,' I said and obeyed at once, and then through another hoop and another with the same compliance. I was agile and without the slightest shame, though my penis and balls moved ungracefully with my exertions.

"Her blows grew harder, less regular. My moans were very loud and sudden and provoked much laughter.

"And when she commanded me now to jump up and grab the bar of the trapeze in both hands, I felt the tears come purely from my stress and exhaustion. I hung from the trapeze as she paddled me, driving me back and forth, and then commanded me to twist and catch the chains above with my feet.

"This was quite impossible and as I struggled to obey, the hall echoed with laughter. Felix stepped forward and at once lifted my ankles until I was swinging as she had wished and I had to bear her spanks in this position.

"And as soon as she tired of this, I was ordered to drop to the ground, at which point she came forward with a long thin leather strap, and buckling the end of it around my penis, she now pulled me, on my knees towards her. I had never been so led or pulled before, by the very root of my cock, and my tears flowed copiously. My whole body was hot and trembling, and my hips were being tugged ahead of me so that no thought of grace could possibly exist even had I the presence of mind for it. She pulled me to the Queen's feet, and then turning, pulled me along, running on her clicking heels so that I struggled and groaned and cried behind my closed lips to keep up with her.

"I was wretched. The circle seemed endless. The strap around my penis constricted it, and my buttocks were so painfully tender now that they ached even when she was not striking them.

"But we'd soon completed the circle. I knew she had exhausted her inventiveness. She had relied upon my disobedience and reluctance, and encountering none, her show lacked any real feature save my complete obedience.

"But she had now a subtle test for me for which I was unprepared.

"She ordered me to stand up, spread my legs and then place my hands flat on the floor before her. I did so, my buttocks facing the Queen and the Grand Duke, a position which again, even in the midst of this, reminded me of my nakedness.

"She put aside her paddle, and picked her favorite toy then, the leather strap, and gave my legs a heavy strapping on both thighs and calves, letting the leather curl about me, and ordered me to move forward a few inches so that I might place my chin upon a high stool there. My hands must go behind my back, my back must be arched. I did as I was told and stood, spread-legged, bent at the waist, my face tipped up for all to see my miserable expression.

"As you can imagine my buttocks hung free in the air, and she commenced to shower them with compliments. 'Very pretty hips, Prince Alexi, very pretty buttocks, tough and round and muscular, and very pretty indeed when you squirm to escape my strap and my paddle.' She illustrated all this as I did with her strap, and I was crying softly now between my moans.

"It was then she gave a command which surprised me. 'But the Court wants to see you display your buttocks. They want to see you move them,' she said. 'Not merely to escape the punishment you so richly deserve and richly need, but to see some real show of humility.' I didn't know what she meant. She spanked me hard as if I meant to be stubborn, while I answered through my tears, 'Yes, my Princess.' 'But you do not obey!' she cried out. She had commenced what she really wanted, and as soon as she said this, I began to sob in spite of myself. What could I say to her? 'I want to see your buttocks move, Prince,' she said. 'I want to see them dance, while your feet remain still.' I heard the Queen laugh. And suddenly overcome with shame and fear, I knew the seemingly small thing she wanted of me was too much for me. I moved my hips, I moved them from side to side as she spanked me and my chest shook with another sob that I could scarce keep quiet.

" 'No, Prince, nothing so simple as that, a real dance for the Court,' she said, 'your reddened and punished buttocks must do something besides sleep under my blows!' and she placed her hands on my hips then and slowly moved them not only from side to side, but down and around and up, so that I had to bend my knees. She rotated them. It seems a small thing as I say it. But to me it was unspeakably shameful, to have to swing my hips and rotate them, to put all my strength and spirit into this seemingly vulgar display of my buttocks. And yet she meant for me to do this, she had commanded it, and I could do nothing but obey, and my tears flowed and my sobs caught in my throat, as I rotated my buttocks as she commanded. 'Bend your knees deeper, I want to see a dance,' she said with a loud wallop of her strap. 'Bend your knees and move those hips more to the side, more to the left!' her voice rose angrily. 'You resist me, Prince Alexi, you don't amuse!' she said, and rained her smacking wallops on me as I strove to obey. 'Move!' she cried out. She was triumphing. All my composure was truly lost. She knew it.

" 'So you dare reserve yourself in the presence of the Queen and her Court,' she scolded me, and then with both her hands she pulled my hips this way and that, making a greater rotation. I could endure it no longer. There was but one way to best her and that was to twist in this shameful position more wildly even than she guided me. And shaking with choked sobs, I obeyed her. There was immediate applause as I did this dance, my buttocks twisted from side to side and up and down, my knees bending deeply, my back arched, my chin resting painfully on the stool so all could see the tears coursing down my face, and my obvious destruction of spirit.

" 'Yes, Princess,' I struggled to articulate in my supplicating voice, and I obeyed with all my strength putting on such a good performance that the applause continued.

" 'That's good, Prince Alexi, very good,' she said. 'Spread your legs wider apart, wider and move your hips even more!' I obeyed at once. I was now snapping my hips, and I was overcome with the greatest shame I had known since I had been captured and brought to the castle. Not even the first stripping by the soldiers in the field, not even being thrown over the Captain's saddle, nor the raping in the kitchen compared to the degradation I knew now, because I performed all this gracelessly and obsequiously.

"Finally, she was finished with my little display. The Lords and the Ladies were talking among themselves, commenting, talking of all manner of things as they always do at such things, but the murmur was full of a certain restlessness, which meant their passions were aroused, and I did not have to look up to see they were all looking at the central circle no matter how they might have feigned boredom. Princess Lynette now ordered me to turn slowly, keeping my chin in the center of the stool, but moving my legs in a circle, all the while swinging my buttocks, so that all the Court might see this display of obedience equally.

"My own sobs were deafening to me. I struggled to obey without losing my balance. If I flagged in the slightest with the broad rotation of my buttocks, the Princess had an opportunity again to upbraid me.

"Finally, she raised her voice and announced to the Court that we had here an obedient Prince capable of even more imaginative amusements in the future. The Queen clapped her hands. The assembly could now rise and disperse, but they did so very slowly, and Princess Lynette, to continue the performance for the very last onlookers, quickly ordered me to grasp the trapeze over my head, and as she spanked me relentlessly, I was ordered to lift my chin and to march in place on my toes for her.

"Pain shot through my calves and thighs, but the worst as always was the burning and swelling of my buttocks. Yet I marched with my chin up as the hall emptied. The Queen had gone first. Finally all the Lords and Ladies were gone.

"Princess Lynette gave over her paddle and her strap to Lord Gregory.

"I stood holding the trapeze, my chest heaving, my limbs tingling. I had the pleasure of seeing Princess Lynette stripped of her boots and her collar by a Page who threw her over his shoulder, and then she was carried out, but I couldn't see her face, and did not know what she was feeling. Her buttocks were up in the air over the Page's shoulder; her pubic lips were long and thin, and her pubic hair reddish.

"I was alone, damp all over with sweat, and exhausted. Lord Gregory was standing there. And he came and lifted my chin and said, 'You are unconquerable, aren't you?' I was astonished. 'Miserable, proud, rebellious, Prince Alexi!' he said furiously. I tried to show my consternation. 'Tell me how I've displeased?' I begged, having heard Prince Gerald say that enough in the Queen's chamber.

" 'You know you take pleasure in all of it. There is nothing that is too ungraceful for you, too undignified, too difficult. You play with all of us!' he said. Again, I was astonished.

" 'Well, you will measure my cock for me now,' he said, and ordered the last Page to leave us. I still held the trapeze as commanded. The room was dark save for the luminous night sky through the windows. I heard him opening his clothes, I felt the nudge of his penis. And then he thrust it into my buttocks.

" 'Damnable little Prince,' he said, as he drove into me.

"When it was finished, Felix slung me over his shoul-

der as unceremoniously as the other Page had carried
Princess Lynette. My cock swelled against him, but I tried
to control it.

"When he set me down in the Queen's chamber,
she sat at her dresser filing her nails. 'I've missed you,'
she said. I hurried to her on my hands and knees and
kissed her slippers. She took a white silk handkerchief
and wiped my face.

" 'You please me very well,' she said. I was puzzled.
What did Lord Gregory see in me that she did not see?

"But I was too relieved to ponder this. Had she
greeted me with anger, ordered more punishments and
amusements, I would have wept with despair. As it was,
she was all beauty and softness. She ordered me to undress her and to turn down her bed. I obeyed as well as
I could. But she refused the silk dressing gown.

"And for the first time, she stood before me naked.

"I had not been told I could look up. I was crouched
at her feet. Then she said that I might look. As you can
imagine, she was unspeakably lovely. She has a firm body,
powerful somewhat, with shoulders just a little too strong
for a woman, and long legs, but her breasts were magnificent, and her sex was a gleaming nest of black hair. I
found myself breathless.

" 'My Queen,' I whispered, and after I kissed her
feet, I kissed her ankles. She did not protest. I kissed her
knees. She did not protest. I kissed her thighs, and then
impulsively I buried my face in that nest of perfumed
hair, finding it hot, so hot, and she lifted me up until I
was standing. She lifted my arms and I embraced her, and
felt for the first time, her full womanly form, and also
that no matter how strong and powerful she appeared,
she was small next to me, and yielding. I moved to kiss
her breasts, and she bid me silently do it, and I suckled
them until she was sighing. They tasted so sweet, and they
were so soft, yet plump at the same time and resistant to
my respectful fingers.

"She sank down on the bed, and I on my knees

buried my face between her legs again. But she said she wanted my cock now and that I must not 'come' until she allowed it.

"I moaned to show how difficult this would be out of love for her. But she lay back on her pillows, opening her legs, and I saw for the first time the pink lips there.

"She pulled me down. I could not quite believe it when I felt the sheath of her hot vagina. It had been so long since I had felt such satisfaction with a woman. Not since I had been taken prisoner by her soldiers had I felt it. I struggled not to consummate my passion at once, and when she commenced to move her hips I thought surely I would lose the struggle. She was so wet and hot and tight and my penis ached from punishment. All my body ached and the aching was delicious to me. Her hands caressed my buttocks. She pinched the welts. She spread my buttocks apart, and as this hot sheathing tightened on my penis, as the roughness of her pubic hair stroked me and tantalized me, she put her fingers into my anus.

" 'My Prince, my Prince, you pass all tests for me,' she whispered. Her movements grew swifter, wilder. I saw her face and breasts suffused with scarlet. 'Now.' She commanded, and I pumped my passion into her.

"I rocked with the pumping of it, my hips snapping as wildly as they had in the little circus performance. And when I was emptied and quiet, I lay covering her face and her breasts with languid and sleepy kisses.

"She sat up in bed, and ran her hands all over me. She told me I was her loveliest possession. 'But there are many cruelties in store for you,' she said. I felt myself grow hard again. She said I should be subjected to a daily discipline far worse than any she had before invented.

" 'I love you, my Queen,' I whispered. And had no thought other than serving her. Yet of course I was afraid. Though I felt powerful in all I had endured and accomplished.

" 'Tomorrow,' she said, 'I go to review my armies. I must ride before them in an open coach, as much so they can see their Queen as I can see them, and after that I must proceed through the villages nearest the castle.

" 'All the Court rides with me according to rank. And all the slaves, naked, and collared in leather, march on foot with us. You shall march at the side of my carriage for all eyes to see. I shall have the finest collar for you, and your anus shall be opened with a leather phallus. You shall wear a bit in your mouth and I shall hold the bridle. You will hold your head high before soldiers, officers, the common people. And for the pleasure of the people, I shall have you displayed in the villages in the main square long enough for all to admire before we continue the procession.'

" 'Yes, my Queen,' I answered silently. I knew it would be a terrible ordeal, and yet I was thinking of it with curiosity, and wondering when and how my feeling of helplessness and yielding would visit me. Would it come before the villagers, or the soldiers, or when I trotted along with my head held high, my anus tortured by this phallus. Each detail she had described excited me.

"I slept deeply and well. When Leon awakened me, he groomed me as carefully as he had for the little circus.

"There was a huge commotion outside the castle. It was the first time I had seen the front gates of the court-yard, the drawbridge and moat and all the soldiers assembled. The Queen's open coach stood in the courtyard, and she was already seated surrounded by her footmen and her Pages who rode on the sides, and her coachmen with their fine caps, their plumes and their gleaming spurs. A great mounted force of soldiers was ready.

"Before being led out, I was fitted with the bit by Leon, who gave my hair a last thorough combing. He wedged the leather bit well back into my mouth, wiped my lips and then told me the hardest thing would be to keep my chin raised. I must never let it drop to a normal position. The bridle, which the Queen would hold idly in her lap could of course keep my head raised, but I must never lower my head. She would feel it if I did and be in a fury.

"Then he showed me the leather phallus. It had no straps, no belts attached to it. It was as big as a man's erect cock, and I was afraid. How should I ever keep it in? From it hung a horse's tail of thin black leather thongs for a mere decoration. He told me to spread my legs. He forced it up into my anus and told me I must keep it in place, as the Queen would suffer me to be covered with nothing. The thin leather thongs hung down and stroked my thighs. They would swing like a horse's tail when I trotted along but they were short, they would conceal nothing.

"Then he oiled my pubic hair again, my cock and my balls. He rubbed some oil into my belly. I had my hands clasped behind my back and he gave me a small leather-covered bone to hold with them saying it would make it easier to keep them clasped. But my tasks were these: to keep my chin raised, to keep the phallus in place, and to keep my own penis hard and presentable to the Queen.

"Then I was led out by the little bridle into the courtyard. The bright noonday sun flashed on the spears of the Knights and the soldiers. The horses' hooves made a loud clatter on the stones.

"The Queen who was in fast conversation with the Grand Duke at her side scarcely noticed me. She threw me one quick smile. The bridle was given her. It went up over the door of the coach and kept my head quite turned up.

" 'Keep your eyes down at all times, respectfully,' Leon said.

"And soon the carriage moved out of the gates and over the drawbridge.

"Well, you can imagine what that day was like. You were brought here naked through the villages of your own Kingdom. You know what it is like to be gazed at by all, soldiers, Knights, commoners.

"It was small consolation to me that other naked slaves would follow. I was alone by the Queen's coach, and I thought only of pleasing her, and of appearing as she wanted me to appear to others. I held my head up, I contracted my buttocks to hold in the painful phallus. And soon, as we passed before hundreds upon hundreds of soldiers, I thought again, 'I am her servant, her slave, and this is my life. I have no other.'

"Perhaps the most excruciating part of the day for me was the villages. You have been through the villages. I had not. The only common people I had seen were in the kitchen.

"But this day of military parade was also the opening of the fairs in the villages. The Queen visited each of several, and after that the fair would open.

"There was a platform in the center of the square of each, and when the Queen went inside of the house of the Lord of the village to drink a cup of wine with him, I was left on display as she had told me I would be.

"But I was not to stand gracefully as I might have hoped. And the villagers knew this, though I didn't. When we reached the first village, the Queen went away, and as soon as my feet hit the platform, a great roar went up from the crowd who knew they were to see something amusing.

"I had my head down, glad of the opportunity to move the rigid muscles of my throat and shoulders. And I was quite astonished when Felix removed the phallus from my anus. Of course the crowd cheered at this. I was then made to kneel up, hands behind my neck on a turntable.

"Felix operated it with his foot. And telling me to spread my legs wide, he turned the turntable. I was perhaps more afraid in these first few moments than ever before, but never once did the fear of rising and trying to escape come to me. I was virtually helpless. Naked, a slave of the Queen, I was in the midst of hundreds of common people who would have overpowered me at once, and cheerfully for all the sport it would have given them. It was then that I realized escape was quite impossible. Any naked Prince or Princess fleeing the castle would have been apprehended by these villagers. They would have given no shelter.

"Now Felix commanded me to show to the crowd all my private parts that were in the service of the Queen, and that I was her slave, and her animal. I did not understand these words, which were spoken ceremoniously. So he told me politely enough that I must part the cheeks of my buttocks as I bent over and display for them my open anus. Of course this was a symbolic gesture. It meant I was ever to be violated. And nothing more than that which could be violated.

"But my face aflame, my hands trembling, I obeyed. A great cheer went up from the crowd. Tears slipped down my face. With a long cane, Felix lifted my balls for them to see, and pushed my penis this way and that to display its defenselessness, and all the while I had to hold my buttocks apart and display my anus. Whenever I relaxed my hands, he commanded me sharply to pull the flesh wider apart and threatened me with chastisement. 'That will infuriate her Highness.' he said, 'and amuse the crowd immensely.' Then to a loud approving cry, the phallus was shoved securely back into my anus. I was made to press my lips to the wood of the turntable. And I was led back to my position beside the Queen's coach, Felix pulling my bridle over his shoulder as I trotted with my head lifted behind him.

"By the last village I was no more used to it than at the first. But by this time Felix had assured the Queen that I displayed all conceivable humility. My beauty was unrivaled by that of any past Prince. Half the village youth of both sexes was in love with me. The Queen kissed my eyelids when I received those compliments.

"There was a grand banquet that night at the castle. You've seen such a banquet as there was one held for you at your presentation. I had not seen it before. And I had my first experience of serving wine for the Queen and for the others to whom she sent me ceremoniously as a gift now and then. When my eyes caught those of Princess Lynette I smiled at her without thinking about it.

"I felt I could do anything I was commanded to do. I had no fear of anything. And so I can say by then I had yielded. But the truest indication of my yielding was that both Leon and Lord Gregory—when they had the chance—told me I was obdurate and rebellious. They said I mocked everything. I said this was not true when I had the opportunity to answer, but I seldom had such an opportunity.

"Many other things have happened to me since then, but the lessons learned in those early months were most important.

"Princess Lynette is still here, of course. You'll come to know who she is in time, and though I can bear anything from my Queen, from Lord Gregory, and from Leon, I still find it difficult to bear Princess Lynette. But I should stake my life on it that no one knows this.

"Now, it's almost morning. I must return you to the dressing room, and also bathe you, so no one knows we've been together. But I've told you my story so that you can understand what it means to yield, and that each of us must find his or her own path to acceptance.

"There is more, however, to my story which will only reveal itself to you in time. But let it stand by you in simple ways now. If you must bear a punishment which seems too great for you, think to yourself, 'Ah, but Alexi bore this so therefore it can be borne.' "

Beauty did not mean to silence him but she could not restrain her embraces. She was as hungry for him now as she had been earlier, but it was too late.

And as he led her back to the dressing room, she wondered whether or not he could guess the true effect of his words upon her. Could he know that he had enflamed and fascinated her, and amplified for her an understanding of resignation and yielding which she had already felt?

As he bathed her, wiping away all evidence of his love, she remained still, caught in her thoughts.

What had she felt earlier this night when the Queen had said that she wanted to send her home on account of the Crown Prince's excessive devotion? Had she wanted to leave?

A horrid thought obsessed her. She saw herself asleep in that dusty chamber that had been her prison for a hundred years, she heard whispers all about her. The old witch with the spindle that had pricked Beauty's finger was laughing through her toothless gums; and lifting her hand to Beauty's breasts, she exuded some lewd sensuality.

Beauty shuddered. She winced and struggled as Alexi tightened the shackles.

"Don't be afraid. We've had the night together undiscovered," he assured her.

She stared at him as if she did not know him because she was not afraid of anyone in the castle, not of him, the Prince, the Queen. It was her mind that frightened her.

The sky was paling. Alexi embraced her. She was now bound to the wall, her long hair pressed between her back and the stones behind her. And she could not get out of that dusty chamber in her homeland, and it seemed to her she was traveling up through layers and layers of sleep, and this dressing room about her in this cruel country had lost its substantiality.

A Prince had come into her sleeping chamber. A Prince had lowered his lips to her. But it was only Alexi kissing her, wasn't it? Alexi kissing her here?

But when she opened her eyes on that ancient bed and looked at the one who now broke her spell, she saw some bland and innocent countenance! It was not her Crown Prince. It was not Alexi. It was some pristine soul liken to her own who now stood back from her in astonishment. Brave he was, yes, brave, and without complexity!

She cried out. "No!"

But Alexi's hand was over her mouth. "Beauty, what is it?"

"Don't kiss me!" she whispered.

But when she saw the pain in his face, she opened her mouth and felt his lips sealed over it. His tongue filled her. She pressed her hips against him.

"Ah, it is you, only you . . ." she whispered.

"And what did you think it was? Were you dreaming?"

"It seemed for a moment all this was a dream," she confessed. But the stone was too real, his touch too real.

"And why should it be a dream? Is it such a nightmare?"

She shook her head. "You love it, all of it, you love it," she whispered in his ear. She saw his eyes linger languidly on her and then drift away. "And it seemed a dream because all the past, the real past, has lost its luster!"

But what was she saying? That in these few days she had not once longed for her homeland, she had not once longed for what her youth had been and the sleep of a hundred years had given her no wisdom?

"I love it. I loathe it," Alexi said. "I am humiliated by it, and recreated by it. And yielding means to feel all those things at once and yet to be of one mind and one spirit."

"Yes," she sighed, as though she had falsely accused him. "Wicked pain, wicked pleasure."

And he gave her his smile of approbation. "We'll be together soon again . . ."

"Yes . . ."

". . . be sure of it. And until then, my darling, my love, belong to everyone."

THE
VILLAGE

THE NEXT few days passed as quickly for Beauty as those before them. No one discovered that she and Alexi had been together.

The following night the Prince told her she had gained his mother's approval. She would now be trained by him as his little maid, to sweep his quarters, to keep his wine cup always filled, and to perform all those duties that Alexi performed for her Highness.

And from then on Beauty would sleep in the Prince's quarters.

She found herself envied by everyone, and it was

the Prince and the Prince alone who prescribed her daily punishments.

Each morning she was given to Lady Juliana for the Bridle Path. Then Beauty would serve the wine at the noon meal and woe to her if she spilt a drop of it.

Then she would sleep in the afternoons so she might be fresh to attend the Prince in the evenings. And next Festival Night she would be entered in a race of Bridle Path slaves which he expected her to win after her daily training.

All this Beauty heard out with flushes and tears, again and again stooping to kiss the Prince's boots as he gave his orders. He seemed still troubled in his love, and while the castle slept, he frequently awakened her with rough embraces. She could scarcely think of Alexi at these times, the Prince so frightened her and scrutinized her.

And when each day dawned she was brought out in her leather horseshoe boots for Lady Juliana.

Beauty was frightened but she was ready. Lady Juliana was a vision of loveliness in her crimson riding dress, and Beauty ran fast on the soft gravel path, the sun often causing her to squint as it flashed in the overhanging trees, and she was weeping when it was finished.

Then she and Lady Juliana would be alone together in the garden. Lady Juliana carried a leather strap, but seldom did she use it, and the garden was soothing to Beauty. They would sit down on the grass, Lady Juliana's skirts a wreath of embroidered silk about her, and quite suddenly Lady Juliana might give Beauty a deep kiss that startled Beauty and weakened her. Lady Juliana stroked Beauty all over. She lavished her with kisses and compliments, and when she did beat her with the leather strap, Beauty cried softly with deep moaning breaths and a languid sense of abandon.

Very soon she was gathering little flowers in her teeth for Lady Juliana, or with great grace kissing the hem of her skirts, or even her white hands, all of these gestures delighting her mistress.

"Ah, am I becoming what Alexi wanted me to become," Beauty thought. But most of the time she did not think at all.

At meals she took great care to serve the wine gracefully.

Yet there came that moment when she spilt the wine, and must take her punishment dangling from the Page's strong grip, scampering afterwards to the Prince's boots to beg silently for forgiveness. The Prince was furious with her, and when he ordered her spanked again, she was scalded with humiliation.

That night, he whipped her mercilessly with his belt before taking her. He told her he loathed the slightest imperfection in her. And she was chained to the wall to spend the night in weeping and misery.

She dreaded new and frightening punishments. Lady Juliana hinted that Beauty was but a virgin in some respects, that she was being tried very slowly.

And Beauty feared Lord Gregory too, who was always watching her.

One morning when she stumbled on the Bridle Path, Lady Juliana threatened her with the Hall of Punishments.

Beauty fell to her hands and knees at once, kissing Lady Juliana's slippers. And though Lady Juliana relented at once with a smile and a toss of her pretty braids, Lord Gregory, nearby, showed his disapproval.

Beauty's heart was a throbbing pain in her chest as she was led away for grooming. If only she could see Alexi, she mused, and yet he had lost some of his charm for her, and why, she was not certain. Even as she lay on her bed that afternoon, she thought of the Prince, and Lady Juliana. "My Lords and Masters," she whispered to herself, and wondered why Leon had given her nothing to make her sleep when she was not tired at all and tortured by the little throb of passion between her legs as always.

But she had been resting only an hour when Lady Juliana came for her.

"I don't much approve of it myself," Lady Juliana said, as she forced Beauty out into the garden, "but his Highness must let you see those poor slaves being packed off to the village."

Again, the village. Beauty tried to conceal her curiosity. Lady Juliana thrashed her idly with the leather belt, light but stinging blows, as they moved down the path together.

Finally they reached an enclosed garden full of low limbed flowering trees, and on a stone bench Beauty saw the Prince and a handsome young Lord at his side who was talking to the Prince earnestly.

"That is Lord Stefan," Lady Juliana confided in a hushed voice, "and you must show him the utmost respect. He is the Prince's favorite cousin. Besides, he is quite miserable today. It is his precious and disobedient Prince Tristan who is the cause of it."

"Ah, and if I could only see Prince Tristan," Beauty thought. She had not forgotten Alexi's mention of him, an incomparable slave who knew the meaning of yielding. So he had caused trouble, had he? She could not help but observe that Lord Stefan was very handsome. Golden-haired and gray-eyed, his youthful face was heavy with brooding and unhappiness.

His eyes rested on Beauty only for a second as she drew near, and though he seemed to acknowledge her charms, he lapsed again into listening to the Prince, who lectured him sternly.

"You bear him too much love, it's the same with me and this Princess you see before you. You must curb your love as I must curb mine. Believe me, I understand even as I condemn you."

"O, but the village," murmured the young Lord.

"He must go and he will be the better for it!"

"O, heartless Prince," whispered Lady Juliana. She urged Beauty forward to kiss Lord Stefan's boots as she took her side beside both of them. "Poor Prince Tristan will be in the village the whole summer."

The Prince lifted Beauty's chin and bent to take a kiss from her lips, which filled Beauty with a softening torment. But she was too curious about all that was being said and dared not make the slightest movement to attract him.

"I must ask you . . ." Lord Stefan began. "Would you send Princess Beauty to the village if you felt she deserved it?"

"Of course I would," said the Prince. But he did not sound convincing. "I would do it in an instant."

"O, but you couldn't!" Lady Juliana protested.

"She doesn't deserve it, so it does not matter," the Prince insisted. "But we are talking about Prince Tristan, and Prince Tristan, for all the abuse and punishments he has endured, remains a mystery to everyone. He needs the rigors of the village just as Prince Alexi once needed the kitchen to teach him humility."

Lord Stefan was deeply troubled, and the words rigor and humility seemed to pierce him. He rose and begged the Prince to come with him and make a better judgment of it.

"They go tomorrow. The weather is already very warm and the villagers are already preparing for the auction. I've sent him to the prisoners' yard to wait there."

"Come, Beauty," the Prince said, rising. "It will be good for you to see this and come to understand it."

Beauty was intrigued and followed eagerly. But the Prince's coldness and sternness made her uneasy. She tried to remain close to Lady Juliana as they proceeded along a pathway, out of the gardens, past the kitchen and stables to a plain dirty yard in which she saw a great cart, without its horse, standing on four wheels against the walls that surrounded the castle.

There were common soldiers here, menials. She felt her nakedness as she was made to follow the brightly dressed trio. Her welts and cuts smarted anew and fearfully she looked up to see a small pen, fenced in crude sticks, in which a gaggle of naked Princes and Princesses stood with their hands bound to the backs of their necks, milling as if it were less exhausting to walk than to stand by the hour.

A common soldier dealt a blow now through the fence with a heavy leather belt that sent a squealing Princess towards the middle of the group for cover. And, catching other naked buttocks, he walloped them as well, producing a groan from a young Prince who turned to him resentfully.

It infuriated Beauty to see this lowly soldier abusing such lovely white legs and bottoms. Yet she could not keep her eyes off the slaves who backed away from the fence only to be tormented from the other side by another idle, devilish boy who struck much harder and with much more deliberation.

But now the soldiers saw the Prince and bowed at once, showing him the strictest attention.

And it seemed at that same moment the slaves saw the little group approaching. Moans and whimpers commenced from those who struggled in spite of their gags to make their plight known, and their muffled cries became a lamentation.

They seemed as beautiful as any slaves Beauty had seen, and as they writhed now, some of them dropping on their knees before the Prince, she saw here and there a lovely peach-colored sex beneath curls of pubic hair, or breasts quivering with crying. The Princes were many of them painfully erect as if they could not control it. And one of them had pressed his lips to the rough ground as the Prince and Lord Stefan, and Lady Juliana with Beauty at her side drew up to the little fence to inspect them.

The Prince's eyes were angry and cold, but Lord Stefan appeared shaken. And Beauty perceived that his gaze was fixed on one very dignified Prince who neither wailed or bowed, nor in any way begged for mercy. He was as fair, as was the young lord, his eyes very blue, and though the mean little gag distorted his mouth, his face was otherwise serene as ever she had seen Prince Alexi's. He looked down humbly enough, and Beauty tried to conceal her fascination with his exquisitely sculpted limbs and his swelling organ. He seemed in great distress, however, behind his indifferent expression.

Lord Stefan suddenly turned his back as if he could not quite contain himself.

"Don't be so sentimental. He deserves his time in the village," the Prince said coldly. And with an imperious gesture he ordered the other wailing Princes and Princesses to be silent.

The guards watched all with folded arms, smiling at the spectacle, and Beauty dared not look at them for fear their eyes would meet hers, giving further humiliation.

But the Prince ordered her to come forward and to kneel up and listen to his instruction.

"Beauty, look on these unfortunates," the Prince said with obvious disapproval. They are going to the Queen's Village, which is the largest and most prosperous in the country. It houses the families of all those who serve here; the craftsmen there make our linen, our simple furniture, supply us with wine, food, milk, and butter. There is the dairy there and the fowl are raised on the little farms, and there are all those who make up a town in any location."

Beauty stared at the captive Princes and Princesses, who though they could no longer beg with groans and cries, still bowed before the Prince who seemed indifferent to them.

"It is perhaps the loveliest village of the realm," the Prince went on, "with a stern Lord Mayor and many Inns and taverns that are the favorites of the soldiers. But it is allowed one special privilege that no other village enjoys, and that is to purchase at auction for the warm months those Princes and Princesses in need of dire punishment. Anyone in the village may purchase a slave if he or she has the gold for it."

The Village

It seemed at this some of the captives could not prevent themselves from imploring the Prince, and with a snap of his fingers he ordered the guards to go to work with their belts and long paddles, causing an immediate uproar. The miserable, desperate slaves huddled together, turning their vulnerable breasts and organs towards their tormentors, as if at all costs they must protect their sore backsides.

But the tall, yellow-haired Prince Tristan made no move to protect himself, merely allowing himself to be jostled by the others. His eyes had never left his Lord, but now slowly they turned and fixed upon Beauty.

Beauty's heart contracted. She felt a slight dizziness. She stared straight into those unreadable blue eyes while at the same time she thought, "Ah, this is the village."

"It is wretched service," Lady Juliana went on, obviously imploring the Prince. "The auction itself takes place as soon as the slaves arrive and you can well suppose that even the beggars and common louts about town are there to witness it. Why, the whole village declares a holiday. And each poor slave is carried off by his or her master not only to degradation and punishment, but miserable labor. Mind you, the crude practical people of the village do not keep even the loveliest Prince or Princess for mere pleasure."

Beauty was remembering Alexi's description of his exposure in the villages, the high wooden platform in the marketplace, the crude crowd, and their celebration of his humiliation. She felt her sex secretly ache with desire, and yet she was horrified.

"Ah, but for all its roughness and cruelty," said the Prince, now glancing at the inconsolable Lord Stefan who stood still with his back to the unfortunates, "it is a sublime punishment. Few slaves can learn from a year in the castle what they learn from the warm months in the village. And of course, they cannot be really hurt, any more than slaves here. The same strict rules apply: no cutting, no burning, no real wounding. And each week, they are herded to a slaves' hall for bathing and oiling. But when they return to the castle they are more than sweet or meek; they have been reborn with incomparable strength and beauty."

"Yes, as Prince Alexi was reborn," Beauty thought, her heart pounding. She wondered if anyone could see her perplexity and excitement. She saw the distant Prince Tristan among the others, his blue eyes calmly fixed to the back of his master, Lord Stefan.

Her mind was filled with lurid visions. And what was it Alexi had said, that such a punishment had been merciful and that if she found it too difficult to learn slowly, she might make herself ripe for some heavier punishment?

Lady Juliana was shaking her head and making little tisks. "But it is only Spring now," she said. "Why, the poor darlings will be there forever. Ah, the heat, the flies, and the labor. You cannot imagine how they are used, and the soldiers crowding the taverns and the Inns, at last able to buy for a few coins a lovely Prince or Princess that they should never possess in a lifetime."

"You make too much of it," the Prince insisted.

"But would you send your own slave!" Lord Stefan appealed to him again. "I don't want him to go!" he murmured, "and yet I condemned him and before the Queen."

"Then you have no choice, and yes, I would send my own slave, though no slave of the Queen or the Crown Prince has ever been so punished." The Prince turned his back to the slaves almost contemptuously. But Beauty continued to look, as the beautiful Prince Tristan commenced to push his way forward.

He reached the fence and though a haughty guard who was having much sport with the group flailed at him with the leather belt, he did not move nor show the slightest discomfort.

"Ah, he is appealing to you," Lady Juliana sighed, and at once Lord Stefan turned and the two young men faced each other.

The Village

Beauty watched as if in a trance as Lord Tristan knelt now slowly and gracefully and kissed the ground before his master.

"It's too late," said the Prince, "and this little sign of affection and humility counts for nothing."

Prince Tristan rose and stood with his eyes down in perfect patience. And Lord Stefan rushed forward and reaching over the fence embraced him immediately. He crushed Prince Tristan to his chest and kissed him all over his face and his hair. The captive Prince, his hands bound to the back of his neck, quietly returned the kisses.

The Prince was in a rage. Lady Juliana was laughing. The Prince pulled Lord Stefan away and said they must leave these miserable slaves now. Tomorrow they would be in the village.

Beauty lay on her bed afterwards unable to think of anything but the little group in the prison yard. Yet she saw too the narrow crooked streets of the villages she'd passed on her journey. She remembered the Inns with their painted signs over the gates, the half-timbered houses shadowing her path, and those tiny, diamond-pained windows.

She would never forget the men and women in coarse breeches and white aprons, with sleeves rolled to the elbows. How they had gaped at her, enjoyed her helplessness.

She could not sleep. And she was filled with a strange new terror.

It was dark when the Prince at last sent for her, and as soon as she reached the door of his private dining room she saw that he was with Lord Stefan.

It seemed in that moment her fate was decided. She smiled as she thought of all his boasting to Lord Stefan, and she wanted to enter quickly now, but Lord Gregory held her back at the threshold.

Beauty let her eyes mist over. She did not see the

Prince in his velvet tunic emblazoned with the coat of arms. Rather she saw those village cobblestone streets, the wives with their wicker brooms, the common lads in the tavern.

But Lord Gregory was speaking to her. "Don't you think I see the change in you!" he hissed low in her ear, so that it seemed part of her imagination.

Her eyebrows knit in a frown of annoyance and then she dropped her eyes.

"You're infected with the same poison as Prince Alexi. I see it working on you every day. You will soon make a mockery of everything."

Her pulse quickened. Lord Stefan, at the supper table, looked so forlorn. And the Prince was as proud as ever.

"What you need is a severe lesson . . ." Lord Gregory continued in his acid whisper.

"My Lord, you can't mean the village!" Beauty shuddered.

"No, I don't mean the village!" He was obviously shocked. "And don't be flippant and bold with me. You know what I mean. The Hall of Punishments."

"Ah, your domain, where you are Prince," Beauty whispered. But he did not hear her.

And the Prince, with an air of indifference, had snapped his fingers for her to enter.

She approached on her hands and knees. But she had come only a few paces into the room when she stopped.

"Go on!" Lord Gregory hissed at her angrily; the Prince had not yet noticed.

But when he turned and looked at her crossly, still she did not move, her head bowed, her eyes fixed on him. And when she saw the anger and outrage in his face, she turned suddenly and ran on her hands and knees past Lord Gregory and into the passage.

"Stop her, stop her!" the Prince cried out before he could prevent himself. And when Beauty saw Lord Gregory's boots beside her, she rose to her full height and ran faster. He caught her by the hair and she screamed as she felt herself pulled back and thrown over his shoulder.

She beat on his back with her fists, kicking, as he held her knees tight, and she wept hysterically.

She could hear the Prince's angry voice, but she could not make out the words, and when let down again at his feet, she ran again so that two Pages came pounding after her

She struggled as she was gagged and bound, and she did not know where she was being taken. It was dark and they were descending stairs, and she knew an appalling moment of regret and panic.

They would hang her in the Hall of Punishments and if she could not endure even that, how would she endure the village?

But a strange calm came over her even before her captors had reached the Slaves' Hall, and when she was thrust in a dark cell to lie on the cold stone floor with her bonds cutting into her flesh, she knew a quiet exhilaration.

Yet she continued to weep, her sex pulsing it seemed with her sobs and there was only silence around her.

It was almost morning when she was roused. Lord Gregory snapped his fingers as the Pages undid her fetters and lifted her to her feet on legs that were weak and unsteady. She felt the wallop of Lord Gregory's belt.

"Spoilt, disgraceful Princess!" he hissed between his teeth, but she was drowsy, softened with desire and dreaming of the village. She gave a little cry as she felt his angry blows, but she realized with wonder that the Pages were gagging her again and binding her hands to the back of her neck roughly. She was going to the village!

"O Beauty, Beauty," came Lady Juliana's voice crying beside her. "Why did you become afraid, why did you try to run, you had been so good and strong, my darling."

"Spoilt, arrogant one," Lord Gregory cursed her again

as she was driven towards the open doorway. She could see the morning sky over the treetops. "You did it deliberately!" Lord Gregory whispered in her ear as he whipped her onto the garden path. "Well, you shall rue the day, and how bitterly you will weep and there will be no one there to hear you."

Beauty struggled to keep from smiling. But could they have seen a smile behind the cruel leather bit in her teeth? It did not matter. She was running fast, with her knees lifted, around the side of the castle as Lord Gregory pointed the way, his blows quick and smarting, and Lady Juliana wept as she ran along, too. "O, Beauty, I can't bear it."

The stars were not yet faded away, yet the air was already warm and caressing. They crossed the empty prison yard, entering the courtyard between the great doors, and the lowered drawbridge of the castle.

And there stood the huge cart of slaves, already tethered to the heavy white mares who would pull it down to the village.

For one moment Beauty knew terror. But a delicious abandon took hold of her.

The slaves wailed as they huddled together behind the low railing, and the driver had already taken his place while the cart was surrounded by mounted soldiers.

"One more," Lord Gregory called to the Captain of the Guard, and Beauty heard the cries of the slaves grow louder.

She was lifted by heavy hands, her legs dangling in the air.

"All right, little Princess," the Captain laughed as he set her down in the cart, and Beauty felt its rough wood beneath her feet as she struggled to keep her balance. For one instant, she glanced back and saw the tear-stained face of Lady Juliana. "Why, she is actually suffering," Beauty thought in amazement.

And high above she suddenly saw the Prince and Lord Stefan in the only torchlit window of the dark castle.

It seemed the Prince saw her look up; and the slaves about her, seeing the window as well, set up a chorus of vain pleading. The Prince turned away miserably just as Lord Stefan had turned his back on the captives earlier.

Beauty felt the cart move. The great wheels creaked and the horses' hooves rang on the cobblestones. All about her the frantic slaves tumbled against one another. She looked before her and almost at once saw the calm blue eyes of Prince Tristan.

He struggled towards her as she moved towards him, though around them the slaves flinched and squirmed to avoid the spirited thrashing from the guards who rode along beside them. Beauty felt the deep cut of a strap on her calf, but Prince Tristan was now pressed against her.

Her breasts were sealed to his warm chest and her cheek rested against his shoulder. His thick rigid organ passed between her wet thighs and stroked her sex roughly. Struggling not to fall, she mounted the organ and felt it slip inside her. She thought of the village, the auction soon to begin, all the terrors that awaited her. And when she thought of her dear defeated Prince and her poor, grieving Lady Juliana she was again smiling.

But Prince Tristan filled her mind as he struggled, it seemed, with his whole body to pierce her and enfold her.

Even among the cries of the others, she heard his whisper behind his gag: "Beauty, are you frightened?"

"No!" she shook her head. She pressed her tortured mouth to his, and as he lifted her with his thrusts, she felt his heart pounding against her.

Sequel to follow:

The Village
including
The story of Prince Tristan